I0712776

EDITED BY A.C. BAUER

CAT EYE PRESS

To Kaylee,
For telling me to do the damn thing and for believing in me.
I love you.

TABLE OF CONTENTS

INTRODUCTION

A.C. BAUER

This project grew out of my love for horror fiction and cooking. These two things have a lot in common, which makes them the perfect pairing for a publication such as this.

Both food and horror are complicated subject matters. On the one hand, food can nourish and strengthen our bodies. On the other hand, it can be a source of sickness and discomfort. From rot and mold to allergies, food has an incredibly complicated and sometimes terrifying effect on the human body. Horror is much the same way. Horror can be a source of delight to some, while disturbing to others, and can elicit some pretty unpleasant reactions. Both food and horror can be dark, messy, and make us reexamine the world around us in a new and sometimes unsettling light.

But food and horror also have their bright sides. Both can be comforting—healing even—if handled the right way. I'm sure we all have a favorite meal that just makes us feel better even before we get to eat it. Similarly, I'm sure many of us have a go-to horror movie or book that brings us a sense of comfort and nostalgia, as well as spooks us.

On a larger level, food and horror have this incredible power to bring people together. Shared meals and the conversations that often accompany them can reveal so many layers to a person—layers we didn't even know existed. And it's the connection that comes from sharing a meal that can give us a richer understanding of the people around us. Likewise, horror can reveal a lot about a person too—everything from their worldview and politics to their sense of humor and more. At the end of the day, cooks and horror writers put their art into the world to share something that they love with you. And that should be celebrated.

So, that's why I wanted to put together this cookbook/anthology. I wanted to bring the best of these two worlds together—worlds that can be beautiful and terrifying, but that have the innate ability to bring people together.

Within this book, you'll find stories of food and horror. You'll read tales of excess and absence. Of love and pain. Of food biting back. But more than that, this book will dare you to go beyond reading and to interact with the beauty of food by preparing a whole slew of delicious recipes.

Three courses of cursed cooking are about to be served, and I'm confident you'll find something on this menacing menu to satisfy your hunger.

So, without further ado, bon appétit.

FRANKIE'S INTRODUCTION

FRANKIE

Okay, okay. I know you want to read some food horror and try out some awesome recipes, but I wanted to introduce myself real quick.

Hi, I'm Frankie. I'm the mascot/brains of the operation at Cat Eye Press. I'm also the handsome devil who appears on the cover of this book (emphasis on the devil part). Yeah, I'm part shapeshifting demon, but more than anything, I'm a horror enthusiast! I love horror in all its frightening forms, and that's why I pushed A.C. to start this little indie horror press.

Cursed Cooking is our first project, and it's a fun one. As A.C. said in his introduction, you'll find food horror stories and recipes from our talented contributors. But what he forgot to mention is that you'll also find me. Remember how I can shapeshift? Well, I took a cue from some of our scary stories and had Val Hal Halvorson (our amazing illustrator) capture my good side. Hope you like 'em. Oh, and I've left a few notes and suggestions throughout the book, so be on the lookout for those too.

Lastly, I wanted to say that horror is complicated. That's why we've put content warnings for each story at the back of the book. We try not to give too much away but provide at least a little bit of information about what's in store. We hope you find them useful.

Okay, I think that's it. Let's get cooking!

xoxo

Frankie

COURSE ONE

100-WORD HORRORS AND HORS D'OEUVRES

GOING BAD

R. HAVEN

I don't mean to forget food. I try to inventory it with notes on the front of the refrigerator door to remind myself about the leftover meatloaf or fresh raspberries I bought.

But the next time I open my fridge, I'm ambushed by a mold-riddled pasta bake and a rancid open can of tuna. They put a kitchen knife to my throat and tell me by the time someone finds my body stuffed into the back of the fridge, my corpse will have decomposed so much no one will recognize it.

It's my own fault for letting them go bad.

TARTARE

T.L. BEEDING

1 lb. ground meat (any animal)
1 raw egg yolk
Salt, pepper, and parsley to taste

Grind meat to a mince and leave out in the sun for several days—direct sunlight is ideal for texture.

Once meat has been tenderized, separate, making sure fermentation has taken place. If not, leave in direct sunlight an additional three days. Maggots sometimes require separation for proper infestation.

Add raw egg yolk once meat is tender. Garnish with salt, pepper, and parsley for taste.

Serve over ice to the cheating bastard when he gets home, and make sure he eats every last bite.

BURNING COOKIES

JEFF CURRIER

Rummaging for another string of lights, Amy paused. "Do you smell that?"

Before Brian answered, the smoke detector began shrieking. "Oh no! The cookies!"

In the kitchen, smoke billowed from the oven. Amy was confused. They'd been in just ten minutes at 350 degrees. Yet dancing flames guttered behind the tempered glass.

Amy grabbed oven mitts. "Extinguisher ready?"

She opened the door. Brian sprayed.

Crimson hellfire ate through extinguishing foam like sugar drops. Still blazing, three dozen gingerbread men sprang forth and scattered. Everything they touched ignited.

Burning, Amy hissed, "Told you not to put horns on the gingerbread men!"

THEM DEVIL EGGS
LUCRETIA STANHOPE

I grew up with this "kind" of deviled eggs and wasn't aware people didn't put ham in their deviled egg filling until I served them at a mixed family gathering with in-laws. Uncle Billy hovered in the kitchen ready to "test" things and noticed me spooning the ham into the mix. He looked at the can, wrinkled his nose, and declared I was going to ruin the eggs, which were his favorite part of Thanksgiving. After testing one when they were done, he told everyone on his side of the family that the eggs were gross. At the meal, he proceeded to fill his plate with six of them, announcing that he was sparing his family having to suffer "them devil eggs" and their "hell mayonnaise." Needless to say, after eating seconds and thirds, there were no leftover eggs. Now he always brings extra deviled ham and Hellmann's on the holidays so there will be plenty of "them devil eggs" for everyone.

INGREDIENTS:
A dozen eggs
¾ cup (160 g) mayo*
2 tsp spicy or plain mustard
2 tsp dill pickle juice, optional
1 can (4.25 oz/120 g) deviled ham

DIRECTIONS:
1. Boil the eggs, using whatever method you know and love. I find eggs peel so much easier for me when I start with cold water and bring the water and cold eggs to a boil at the same time. Once boiling, cover the pot, and turn off the heat. Let the eggs cook, covered, for 12 minutes. Move the eggs to a bowl of ice water and chill for 12 minutes. (We do things in multiples of threes when possible. There's magic in threes.)

<ol start="2">
<li>Once cooled, peel the eggs, and slice them lengthwise. Remove the yolks to a bowl and put the whites on a plate.</li>
<li>Mash the yolks with a fork. Add remaining ingredients and mix well.</li>
<li>Spoon the mix into the egg whites on your plate/platter.</li>
</ol>

AUTHOR'S NOTE:

*It is my personal requirement that it be Hellmann's, despite what Uncle Billy says. This is not because it is "hell mayo," but because it just tastes better. Other brands will work, although I am strongly opposed to Miracle Whip because of its overly strong flavor.

**There is generally more filling than you need. In my house we fight over this treasure, using it as sandwich spread on toast with a slice of sharp cheddar.

SATAN'S SALAD
LUCRETIA STANHOPE

After my first time cooking deviled eggs for my in-laws, Uncle Billy decided the addition of deviled ham to deviled eggs turned them into something so good it was evil. When he came to oversee what I was doing for the Fourth of July festivities, he had a sack with deviled ham and Hellmann's mayo in hand. He wasn't sure where we'd use it, but he was determined that together we could create something as tasty as "them devil eggs." I think we did. There isn't a holiday where we don't make either "them devil eggs" or "Satan's salad" or both. I've never had leftovers of either, no matter how many batches I make.

INGREDIENTS:
A dozen eggs
1/3 cup (70 g) mayo*
1 tsp spicy or plain mustard
1 can (4.25 oz/120 g) can deviled ham
1/3 cup (80 g) sweet relish
1 small, sweet onion chopped—no more than half a cup

DIRECTIONS:
1. Boil the eggs, using whatever method you know and love. I find eggs peel so much easier for me when I start with cold water and bring the water and cold eggs to a boil at the same time. Once boiling, cover the pot, and turn off the heat. Let the eggs cook, covered, for 12 minutes. Move the eggs to a bowl of ice water and chill for 12 minutes. (We do things in multiples of threes when possible. There's magic in threes.)
2. While the eggs are cooling, mix the remaining ingredients together in a large bowl.
3. Once cooled, peel the eggs, and cut them into big chunks.

4. Fold the egg chunks into the mixture. I do this gently, because I like to have yolk chunks in mine and if you stir it too much, you'll mash them.

AUTHOR'S NOTE:

*It is my personal requirement that it be Hellmann's, despite what Uncle Billy says. This is not because it is "hell mayo," but because it just tastes better. Other brands will work, although I am strongly opposed to Miracle Whip because of its overly strong flavor.

PART OF US

JOSH CLARK

"Mom, is this pasta done?"

There was no reply. Gus knew she'd put it on a while ago.

He took a step closer to the boiling stockpot. Two eyes stared back amongst bubbling, roiling goop.

Tendrils of noodles erupted from the pot, coiling around Gus.

Hot, slimy ropes clung to him like bandages wrapped around a mummy. Skin crackled and boiled against the searing hot pasta. Amid the blistering pain, Gus felt himself being reeled in, and noodles crept up to his face.

Gus's screams were stifled as the pasta snaked into his mouth.

The last meal he'd ever have.

PAPA NAPOLI'S

DORIAN J. SINNOTT

Papa Napoli's was the finest in Italian cuisine. Patrons flocked to the restaurant daily, eager to try the top-rated dishes. But unlike many other eateries, it wasn't the spices or the sauces that brought it attention.

It was the parmesan.

Freshly grated. The most savory any had tried. Customers piled it on spaghetti, emptying shakers in a matter of minutes. It was simply *that good*.

But, lucky for Papa Napoli's, no matter how much was eaten, they always had fresh supply. Grated in the basement. From the tattered feet of past food critics, who failed to leave a high rating.

ALWAYS CHEW WELL

KENDRA DENNIS

Bite. Chew. Swallow. Repeat.
Golden-brown crumbly goodness drowning,
Drowning in bloody sauce.

One after another.
Shove and shove
Into their foaming mouth.

Until.
A cough. A gag.
Stretched to its limits, it catches.

The cheese!
It fills their throat
Stealing the air from their lungs.

So they pull.
And pull.
That stretchy, suffocating string.

Two feet. Three.

Ten then twenty.
Still, there is no end.

Watery eyes glaze over
Hands trembling
And slipping on the cheese.

Minutes pass. The gags cease.
Prone hands lie in bloody wads
Of acid-coated cheese and crumbs.

And slithering
Down their gullet
The cheese
Disappears.

SUMMER SALAD

DORIAN J. SINNOTT

A cool and refreshing salad dish to add to your backyard barbeques and parties. Packed with flavors of summertime like fresh tomatoes, avocados, and more!

INGREDIENTS:

1 can (15 oz/425 g) black beans
1 can (15.5 oz/432 g) southwest style corn
2 avocados
2 plum tomatoes
Green onion to taste
¼ cup (60ml) olive oil
¼ cup (60 ml) red wine vinegar

DIRECTIONS:

1. Drain black beans and southwest style corn. Rinse the black beans after draining.
2. Chop up avocados, tomatoes, and green onion.
3. Mix olive oil and red wine vinegar to create dressing.
4. Combine all ingredients into a large serving bowl. Stir well. Serve at room temperature or chilled.

QUICK AND EASY BRIE BITES

MADELINE WHITE

Growing up in the South, one of the things I internalized about adulthood was that it was important to have a go-to potluck contribution. You never knew when someone might be hosting a cookout, or when you might need to thank a friend for loaning a tractor, and having something quick, easy, and delicious was a must. So, when I grew up and moved out, I set out to discover what "My Thing" would be, and so these brie bites were born. My go-to contribution for Thanksgivings, picnics, and everything in between, these little pastries are easy to make and sure to be popular.

INGREDIENTS:

2 cans Pillsbury Grands! "Flaky Layer" canned biscuits (the honey ones are my favorite, but the butter ones are good, too)*
1 6-inch wheel brie (I like the grocery store brand, non-double-cream kind, as it's firm, mild, and affordable, but feel free to experiment)
1 tbsp fresh rosemary (very finely chopped)
¼ cup (85 g) of your favorite cranberry jam or jelly
¼ cup (25 g) fresh cranberries
1 tbsp sugar
Butter or spray grease for greasing pan

DIRECTIONS:

1. Preheat oven according to directions on the biscuit tin.
2. Wash and rough chop cranberries, toss with sugar and ½ tablespoon rosemary. Set aside.
3. Grease a muffin tin and set aside.

4. Separate each canned biscuit into halves (peeling apart layers to create two thinner biscuits, not tearing the biscuit into two half biscuits). Set half the dough aside. (Each pastry will eventually use a full biscuit, so I will now refer to the two halves as "tops" and "bottoms"). NOTE: If your tins had more than 12 biscuits, you can set aside the excess. This is a 12-piece recipe.

5. Squish and pull the biscuit bottoms to line each cup of the muffin tin (biscuit should reach about to the edge of the cup, and you should use half of all your biscuit dough - everything you didn't set aside). Press into shape and try not to create any holes (if they do form, squish them back together). NOTE: You may find it helpful to stretch and shape the biscuit a bit before attempting to put it into the tin, a bit like shaping a pizza.

6. Put a teaspoon or so of cranberry jelly into each biscuit cup.

7. Remove the top rind of the brie wheel with a knife, then cut the wheel into 12 even sections. I like to do this into cubes not slices, to better fit the cups. Place the brie into the biscuit cups (1 per cup), settle into the jelly, and make sure the brie sits on the bottom and doesn't stick out past the level of the rim.

8. Mix fresh cranberries once more, then add a spoonful of them to each cup (trying to settle them into the space around the brie and avoiding spooning up excess liquid from the bowl).

9. Add a sprinkle of rosemary on top of other fillings (I'm a fiend for rosemary, so I add more like a pinch, but if you're not, feel free to do less).

10. Stretch and flatten the reserved biscuit tops in your hands, and use them to cover the filling in each cup. If there is a crack between the top and bottom biscuit halves, the brie may boil out and evaporate, so use your fingers or the handle of a spoon to squish the tops and bottoms together as thoroughly as possible, like a very doughy dumpling. This is easiest to do if you have pulled your bottom biscuits up further in the tin, but with

enough squishing it can usually be managed regardless of starting biscuit position.

11. Use a sharp knife to pierce the top of each brie bite to allow the steam to escape.

12. Bake according to directions on the biscuit tin. NOTE: This is based on the assumption of Pillsbury Grands and fresh cranberries - if you have used another brand of biscuits, or have substituted for more jam in the cranberry off-season, you may need to check the bottoms of the biscuits and add more time if they're still soggy.

13. Allow to cool a bit before eating. The temptation is real but the cheese is lava.

14. Enjoy!

AUTHOR'S NOTE:

*There will be leftover biscuits if you just use one muffin tin—I just bake those for the folks who don't like cheese!

HOTDOG HORROR

LENA NG

"It's a hotdog," Jake insisted. It was true in a sense; it was an unknown tube of meat. "It's not synthetic."

I was certainly sick of all the faux calories which only gave the illusion of sustenance. But was I really willing to eat this?

"How did you catch it?" The middle of space didn't have random bits of protein floating around.

"I used the sample collector net."

"Do you even know what it's made of?"

"Does it matter?"

My stomach rumbled. The meat paused its seizing. I coated it in synthetic condiments and hoped I would keep it down.

Bacon-Wrapped Water Chestnuts

BACON-WRAPPED WATER CHESTNUTS
DESIREE HORTON

This is one of the few recipes that has been entrusted to me for our get-togethers, especially after the... accident. Just kidding. It's super easy, and everyone loves it!

INGREDIENTS:

2 cans (8 oz/27 g each) whole water chestnuts
1 pack bacon (cooked or raw)
1 bottle barbecue sauce
Toothpicks

DIRECTIONS:

1. Preheat oven to 350°F (180°C) or 325°F (160°C) if using a convection oven.
2. Drain water chestnuts.
3. Wrap one piece of bacon around water chestnut and push toothpick through, pinning the bacon in place. Place in baking dish toothpick up.
4. Cook 20 minutes, adding 10-20 minutes if bacon is raw.
5. Remove from oven and apply barbecue sauce of your choice lightly over the tops of bacon-wrapped water chestnuts.
6. Place back in oven and cook for 15 more minutes or until bacon crisps.
7. Apply a drizzle of sauce, cool for 5 minutes, and serve.

"KILLER" MUSHROOM PUFF PASTRIES

KAY HANIFEN

Whether you're making them as appetizers or just using the delicious and versatile filling for other dishes (it's amazing in Beef Wellington), these mushroom puff pastries are to die for. Serve them at your next party and have your guests screaming your praises.

INGREDIENTS:

2 tbsp (30 ml) olive oil, divided
1 large yellow onion, diced
½ tsp kosher salt
16 oz (450 g) mushrooms, preferably Baby Bella, diced
½ tsp Maggi liquid seasoning, optional
1 clove garlic, minced
½ tsp dried thyme
¼ tsp ground black pepper
½ log (about 1.5 oz/43 g) goat cheese
1 tbsp Dijon mustard
¼ cup (20 g) shredded Pecorino Romano
2, 10-inch sheets of frozen puff pastry, thawed
1 egg, beaten

DIRECTIONS:

1. Preheat the oven to 400°F (205°C) or 375°F (190°C) if using a convection oven. Line two baking sheets with silicone or parchment paper and set aside.

2. In a large skillet, over low medium heat, add in one table-spoon of olive oil along with the diced onions and salt. Sauté until they're beginning to brown, and then reduce heat to low and continue to let cook, stirring occasion-ally, until they're golden brown. This is where I usually dice the mushrooms if I haven't already.

3. Once the onions are done, I add about a tablespoon of water to deglaze them, but this is optional. Then, turn up the heat to medium low again and add the second tablespoon of olive oil, the diced mushrooms, and the Maggi if using. Sauté until the mushrooms are tender and slightly browned.

4. Add the garlic, thyme, and black pepper and sauté for an additional minute.

5. Reduce heat to low and add the goat cheese, mustard, and pecorino cheese. Stir until well mixed. Remove from heat.

6. Roll out the first sheet of puff pastry dough and cut into rectangles. Transfer to the baking sheets. Add approxi-mately a teaspoon of the mushroom and onion mixture to one half of the rectangle. Fold it over and use the tines of a fork to pinch it shut. Prick a hole in top of the pastries for air to escape.

7. Brush the pastries lightly with the beaten egg and put into the oven.

8. Bake for 25 minutes or until golden brown. Remove and let cool. You can serve them warm or at room temperature.

9. Enjoy!

THE MARCH

MADELINE WHITE

Teeth chattering in the cold, we saw hunks of flesh from the haunches of still-living cattle. If they notice their jagged wounds, they don't show it. They plow doggedly through the deep snow, their exposed flesh crusting black with frostbite.

My fingers, wooden and unrecognizable, tremble as a sliver of sustenance is passed to me. I part cracked lips and shove the meat inside, savoring the last vestiges of the cow's warmth.

Ahead of us is only snow and the distant promise of a siege line. But hope won't fill our starving bellies.

So, tomorrow, we'll start on the horses.

ROOTED

C. L. SIDELL

Dani picked them while I spread the picnic.

"Blackberries?"

"Nah," she replied, adding them to our fennel salad. "Wrong shade."

"Tart" —I swallowed— "with a hint of sweet."

That night, I awakened to visions of churning soil.

Feverish, I stumbled through the cabin. Threw open the door. Crawled toward moonlit grass. Clawed dirt.

Dani collapsed beside me, thrust her hands into the earth. Our pinkies twined among weeds.

Skin split. Tendons sprouted rootlike through our fingertips, planting us where we knelt.

Dawn's sun baked our fresh barks, saturated our silent screams, and blessed the purple fruits ripening on our tongues.

SQUASH BLOSSOMS RANGOON

JOHN K. PECK

In most temperate climates, squash blossoms start appearing in the early summer, though autumn squash such as pumpkins produce flowers later. Frying them softens both the petals and stem while creating a crispy exterior, which, when combined with the filling used here, creates a dish similar to Crab Rangoon in both texture and flavor.

INGREDIENTS:

16 zucchini or other squash blossoms, or 8 full-sized pumpkin flowers
1 small onion or ½ large one, minced
1 tbsp (14 g) butter
¼ block (60 g) cream cheese
1 tbsp salt
1 tsp ground black pepper
1½ cup (180 g) flour
1½ cup (354 ml) water (fizzy if possible)
1 cup (50 g) panko breadcrumbs
At least 2 cups (480 ml) vegetable or peanut oil for frying
For dipping sauce:
¼ cup (60 ml) soy sauce
2 tbsp lemon juice
½ tsp toasted sesame oil
1 green onion, thinly sliced
2 tsp sugar

Squash Blossoms Rangoon

DIRECTIONS:

1. For the dipping sauce, mix all sauce ingredients in a small bowl. Allow mixture to sit for at least 15 minutes.
2. Prepare the blossoms. Trim flower stems to 1 inch. Gently wash each flower and place on a paper towel to dry.
3. For the batter, combine the flour and salt in a mixing bowl. Add water slowly, mixing with a fork until smooth. On a separate plate, pour out the panko crumbs and spread into an even layer.
4. Now move onto the filling. In a small saucepan, heat the butter over medium heat. Add the minced onion and cook until translucent, about 3 minutes. Add cream cheese and black pepper and reduce heat, stirring constantly. Cook 1-2 minutes or until mixture is soft, then remove from heat.
5. In a large pan, add enough canola or vegetable oil to cover the pan to a depth of 1 inch. Heat at medium-high until the oil is hot but not smoking (325°F/160°C).
6. Using a small spoon, carefully fill each flower with 1-2 tablespoons of the onion/cheese mixture, keeping the

petals as intact as possible. Once a flower is filled, close the petals and twist them gently to form a seal.

7. Dip the stuffed flowers one at a time into the batter, then roll them in the panko crumbs and place them gently into the hot oil. Fry about 3 minutes per side, turning each piece once but avoiding stirring. Once cooked, transfer to paper towels to dry and sprinkle lightly with salt.

8. Place the bowl of sauce in the center of a large plate with the squash blossoms around it. As soon as the flowers have cooled sufficiently, serve immediately, using the sauce for dipping.

AUTHOR'S NOTE:

*The flowers can be prickly when raw, but once fried, even the base of the flower and tops of the stems can be eaten. To maximize your harvest, pick only male flowers, which exist purely for pollination and do not produce fruit. These can be recognized by their single stamen and thin stalk, while female flowers have a multipart stamen and will show the beginnings of a squash fruit at their bases.

SCREAMIN' PUMPKIN SEEDS

JENNIFER CLARK

I hate the taste of pumpkin. However, I do like pumpkin seeds and have fond memories of my father roasting the seeds every year around Halloween. He kept it simple and sprinkled the seeds in Worcester sauce, salt, and black pepper. I like mine a bit spicier.

INGREDIENTS:

1 tsp ground cumin
1 tsp paprika
1 tsp salt
1 tsp black pepper
1 tsp garlic powder

½ tsp red pepper
1 cup (120 g) of pumpkin seeds, rinsed and dried
Olive oil cooking spray

DIRECTIONS:

1. Mix together the first six ingredients.
2. Spread out the seeds in one layer on a foil-lined or parchment-lined baking sheet.
3. Lightly spray seeds (two squirts) with olive oil cooking spray.
4. Sprinkle half the seasoning mix over the seeds.
5. Bake for 30 minutes at 250°F (120°C) or 225°F (100°C) if using a convection oven.
6. Remove tray from oven and gently give the seeds a stir. Again, spray seeds (one or two squirts) with olive oil and sprinkle the remaining seasoning over the seeds.
7. Bake for another 30 minutes. Be sure to cool completely if storing.

SPEAK

CONRAD GARDNER

"Say something, you son of a bitch!"

I open my mouth, close it.

"I asked why you did this to me, and you won't even answer the question? *Coward*."

The burger doesn't have a mouth, but it's pretty articulate.

"Why would you rub onions into my flesh and add cheese? You trying to ruin me? Don't get me started with the oily pan. Yes, it fucking hurts having my body seared. Then you stuff me between some cheap-ass buns? What d'you have to say for yourself?"

I pick it up and take a bite, my mouth filling with muffled screams.

WHERE ARE THE DELEGATES?

ERIC FOMLEY

"Next," I called.

My office door opened, and my secretary walked in with a bowl of steaming soup.

"The next delegates are from Rylan II. They're hoping to join the Federated Systems."

He set the bowl down, bowed, and left.

Some delegates provided food offerings from their worlds. Eating the offerings was usually a perk of my job.

This soup had small creatures similar to shrimp, and the broth was delicious.

I didn't realize my mistake until my secretary came back in.

He stared, mouth agape.

"Where are the delegates?"

My stomach churned.

We looked down at the empty bowl.

HOT SHOTS

EVAN BENNER

Tragedy unfolded in a local dorm yesterday where three students were found dead following a game of "Hot Shots."

Coroner reports say the manner of each death matched depictions on labels of hot sauces found at the scene.

The scorched remains of Chase R., age 18, were found beside a bottle of Instantaneous Combustion.

Hillary H., age 19, eviscerated, was found holding a bottle of Savage Shrapnel which claims, "It'll Rip You a New One."

Brandon C., age 18, was found, body intact, still clutching a bottle of Short Circuit.

Smoke led neighbors to alert authorities.

The families requested privacy.

FRANKIE'S
HOT
SAUCE

HOT TOMATO ARTICHOKE DIP

NADINE STEWART

This is a recipe from our family's recipe book. My mom typed out all of her recipes, made copies, and put them in books for each member of our family because we were always calling her to get a recipe from her. Then she'd have to pull out her recipe cards and we'd write them down and inevitably lose them before the next time we wanted to make something. We always make this for Christmas or New Year's Eve. It's a big hit.

INGREDIENTS:

1 can (28 oz/796 ml) diced tomatoes, well drained
1 can (14 oz/398 ml) artichoke hearts, drained and finely chopped
1 cup (~220-230 g) mayonnaise
1 cup (100-120 g) freshly grated Parmesan cheese
½ cup (~50 g) shredded sharp cheddar cheese
2 cloves garlic, minced
3-4 finely chopped green onions
¼ cup (59 ml) of your favorite salsa (heat preference to your liking)
4 tbsp dry breadcrumbs

DIRECTIONS:

1. Preheat oven to 350°F (180°C) or 325°F (160°C) if using a convection oven.
2. Gently combine all ingredients and pour into a lightly buttered/sprayed casserole dish. Do not over-mix.
3. Bake for 30-40 minutes and serve with your favorite butter crackers or tortilla chips.

MARGARITA DIP
KERRY E.B. BLACK

This playful recipe is flirty and fresh, especially when paired with ripe, seasonal fruit and good company! Bottoms Up!

INGREDIENTS:

1 block (8 oz/226 g) cream cheese, softened
1/3 cup (78 ml) frozen margarita mix, thawed
2 tbsp orange juice
1 tbsp lime juice
¼ cup (~30 g) confectioner's sugar
1/3 cup (24 g) whipped topping
Decorator's Sugar

DIRECTIONS:

1. Mix the first five ingredients with an electric mixer or food processor until smooth. Fold in whipped topping. Transfer to serving bowl. Cover and chill for at least an hour.
2. To serve, rim the bowl with decorator's sugar. Surround with dippers such as fresh fruit, pretzels, and pound cake cubes.

FRANKIE'S FOOTNOTE:

This recipe uses confectioner's sugar, which is also known as powdered sugar or icing sugar. Basically, it's granulated sugar that's been ground into a powdered form.

COURSE TWO

SHORT STORIES AND MAIN COURSES

THE LINGERING OIL

ERIC RAGLIN

Keith couldn't believe how quickly nature had taken over his old, abandoned Burger Bear. The trees lining the drive-thru pushed up against the blue roof—a few more inches and they'd bust it right off. Where customers once barked orders from their lifted trucks, pink flowers now grew through gaps in the concrete, monarch butterflies flitting around them.

Keith had to admit it was a pretty sight, but he knew it wouldn't last. The restaurant had closed under his ownership three years back, and he assumed he'd never manage again—not after everything that happened.

But he'd inherited the restaurant from his father, Charles, a man who'd never learned the meaning of the word "no." Charles called Keith from the nursing home twice a week to ask when he'd open the place back up.

"I want to eat there one last time before I die," he said. "And I don't want my sorry-ass son to let the Olmansson legacy die with me!"

Since Keith had worked as a handyman in the years since the closure, his father asked if he'd assess the building for damages and repair what he could. Keith had agreed to the work but expressed reluctance about reopening the restaurant under his own management.

"Ah, don't let one act of God and a good-for-nothing crew scare you off," his father said over the phone. "You were okay at managing. Not great, but decent. Just had bad luck. Something like that could never happen twice, right?"

Keith said he'd sleep on his decision and get back to his dad. Maybe fixing up the place would instill in him a renewed sense of commitment—a pride that would help him overcome the shame and failure that had haunted him these past three years.

As Keith approached the boarded-up front door, a spray-painted greeting stopped him in his tracks: *Married to Burger Bear, in sickness and in Hell.* He wondered if this was one last jab from his old crew, but he quickly scrapped the theory. The graffiti had to be some trespasser's nonsensical joke.

The door's chain lock had rusted, crunching when Keith turned the key. Before entering, he took a deep breath and assured himself that no former employees were waiting for him inside. Not teenage Callie ready to call him the "worst fucking boss" she'd ever had, nor ex-con Davis claiming that "prison was better than this place." The only bad thing Keith would likely find behind that door was a mold infestation. At least mold wouldn't yell at him.

***

Squatters had been here; Keith could smell them. Piss and shit and street stink permeated the space. While he could fix most anything, a cleanup crew would need to deal with the stench.

Trying not to breathe through his nose, Keith surveyed his surroundings with a flashlight—no working overheads, dammit—and made a mental checklist of repairs. Rats or raccoons—hell, maybe even copper-hunting tweakers—had chewed through the wiring half-hidden above the water-stained ceiling tiles. He'd have to find out how the animals, people, and rain had gotten in. The windows were all broken, but somehow their boards remained in place, barring potential intruders. Maybe someone had busted down the door leading from the parking lot into the kitchen. Or maybe they'd slipped through the roof ventilation, descending like a jewel thief in a heist movie.

The smell changed to something even more familiar than human waste: frying oil. It circulated around the dining area like a greasy breeze. Keith laughed. Some smells never went away. He remembered getting home from night shifts and his ex-wife complaining about the stench of French fries. It's why she stopped sleeping with him those last couple years of their marriage, or so she claimed.

"Goddamn," Keith said to himself.

A metallic clang echoed from the kitchen. Keith froze. If someone was in here, he wasn't prepared for them. Sure, he could wield his flashlight as a weapon, but he would've preferred the gun resting on his nightstand at home.

After a pause, he said, "Who's there? This is private property. You can't be in here."

Nothing stirred. All he could hear was the faint roar of traffic outside.

Flashlight raised like he'd seen on cop shows, he snuck toward the kitchen. Mouse shit and clumps of wet, old napkins littered the path. Only when he passed the registers did he see the probable culprit: a metal spatula on the floor.

A memory of that final shift returned, but he tried holding it at bay like he had every night for the past three years. He needed to find who or what was in here with him. A white-knuckled sweep of his flashlight and search of the cabinets revealed nothing, save for some packages of buns wholly consumed by gray mold and a Burger Bear polo cut down the middle. That shirt ...

He couldn't hold the memory back any longer: the blaring sirens of an ambulance. Grim-faced paramedics cutting off Mallory's polo. Chest paddles applied too late.

"Whoever is in here needs to get the fuck out," Keith said, trying to focus on the crisis at hand.

Still, nothing and no one moved.

He searched the room again, more thoroughly this time, but came up empty-handed.

He'd stalled long enough. A quick smoke break would settle the nerves, then he'd get right back to work.

***

The electrical repairs came first: old wiring to rip out and replace, overhead lights to get working again.

More than once, an avalanche of dust bunnies, insulation fluff, and mouse shit spilled out of the ceiling tiles and down Keith's shirt. He choked on the debris, wiped himself clean, and tried to keep his spirits high as he continued the work. He'd brought a portable radio in to listen to his favorite classic rock station, but its battery—that hunk of junk—had drained within minutes of his arrival. Now, he worked in begrudging silence, save for the clinks and whirs of his tools.

The longer he breathed in the ceiling particulate, the wheezier he became. His breathing sounded like Mallory's right before she collapsed. The way she'd sounded for a full month before she died, still working shift after shift because Keith hadn't given her any other option. He tried suppressing the thought, but it clung to him like asbestos. If he stopped breathing—just for a moment—maybe he'd be able to center himself. Standing still on the ladder, he held his breath.

But the wheezing continued somewhere behind his body. Startled, he jumped off the ladder and rolled his left ankle.

"Fuck!" he said but didn't stop to tend the injury.

Limping through a maze of dining room chairs with torn and nibbled cushions, he got a safe distance from the ladder before whipping around. No one else was there. Just loose wires swaying from the ceiling in a musty breeze.

This place was getting to him. Too many bad memories, too much dust of former occupants stirring in the air. Reopening the restaurant seemed less appealing with each passing minute, but it sure would be more profitable than handyman work.

Ka-chunk.

Keith recognized the sound instantly: someone punching in on the time clock. Again, he wished for the comfort of his gun. Every muscle in his body tensed, armoring him in case a squatter came running out with a knife.

"Enough of this shit!" he said—but he couldn't keep the shakiness out of his voice, not anymore. He needed another cigarette, stat. "Whoever you are, quit fucking with me and come out where I can see you."

No movement or sound. Even the roar of traffic outside disappeared, as if the world beyond Burger Bear no longer existed. In this quiet, the phantom stink of frying oil ebbed and flowed like blood through a beating heart.

Mustering his courage, Keith grabbed a crowbar from his tool bag—a better bludgeon than his flashlight—and snuck toward the employee entrance. Still, no doors creaked open, and no window boards were kicked out in an attempted escape. Maybe this person or animal or thing wasn't scared of Keith. Maybe it was waiting for him. But he couldn't let that thought get to him.

When he turned the corner, he stopped dead at the sight of the time clock. Below it on the floor was a massive pile of time cards, some yellowed and dusty and others white and new. He crouched to inspect them. When he saw the dates, his stomach turned; someone had been clocking in and out every day for the past three years.

"This is insane," he said, breaking the silence.

Something prickled the back of his neck, then the unshaved stubble of his throat. Jumping, he ran a hand over the area, making sure a spider hadn't landed on him. But there was nothing.

The feeling wasn't entirely physical though. He sensed eyes, somewhere in the dark, burning into him on a psychic level. Which direction they came from, he couldn't tell.

His own eyes tingled with the threat of tears. God, no. It didn't matter if this unseen person was a stranger. He couldn't cry in front of them.

But why was he so scared? He had backup three numbers away on his phone. The cops had helped him deal with problem people plenty of times when he managed Burger Bear. He'd had them drag addicts out of the customers-only restrooms—needles still dangling from their arms—and homeless people out of the dining area when they loitered for longer than a few minutes. The cops, more than anyone in Keith's life, had always had his back.

Hurrying out of the restaurant, he made the call.

***

"You sure there's nobody? Can't you check again?" Keith asked.

The two officers stood beside him near the weather-worn drive-thru menu. They'd spent ten minutes scouring the building only to emerge with nothing.

"Sometimes these squatters are clever," one officer said, sliding on his sunglasses. "They know how to slip in and out of a building like mice through cracks in a wall. Some of them even dig tunnels, hidden passageways, shit like that, just to evade detection."

The other cop looked away like she was used to her partner talking out of his ass, but she didn't dispute his wild claims. Instead, she turned to Keith.

"You see any definitive signs that someone is still here and you call us, okay?" she said.

As much as Keith hated to admit it, the woman's comment made him feel like a kid who'd asked his mom to check for monsters under the bed. He knew his voice would crack if he replied to her, so he nodded instead.

When the cops left, Keith smoked a cigarette and paced the parking lot for a few minutes. The sun was going down, the sky soft and pink. It'd be dark soon, and darker still inside the restaurant. But here he was wasting time, elongating the unpleasantness.

How often had he told his employees to hurry up their smoke breaks and get back to work? A good owner would lead by example, arriving early to prep, staying late to clean, never resting while others were depending on him. Maybe, if he became that man, he'd wind up like Mallory, working himself to death in a stifling kitchen.

Maybe he'd deserve it.

***

Wanting a break from the asthmatic electrical work, Keith shifted his focus to the plumbing. Inexplicable clogs plagued the toilets. Maybe that mystery squatter had taken fat shits in them and plugged them up good. Whatever the case, Keith would be dealing with the mess for the next few hours.

Using his drain snake, he worked to unclog the first toilet. With all the tugging, it felt like reeling in a big fish, but what surfaced was a Burger Bear employee polo, slicked with gray sewage. He was about to toss the shirt aside—its stench too much to handle—when he noticed it was cut down the middle. The same shirt he'd found in the kitchen. He couldn't make sense of it.

Again, he flashed back to Mallory, lifeless on the greasy kitchen floor, paramedics trying in vain to revive her. Callie sobbing by the sink and screaming at Keith, "You knew she was fucking sick! You fucking knew!"

Keith's eyes burned and his heart raced. He tossed the polo into the far corner of the restroom, took one deep breath, then another. He had to calm down.

A wet *shlop* interrupted him. Keith jumped, backed against the stall door, and scanned the room with his flashlight. Nothing moved. The stink of sewage gave way to the stink of frying oil. Where it came from, he couldn't tell. As he searched the area—swearing to himself that he wouldn't call 911 again, that he'd deal with this shit himself this time—he spotted movement: the sludgy polo lifting a couple inches off the tile, then *shlopping* back down.

"Fuck!"

He was frozen for only a moment before he found his courage. Then, he ran toward the polo and punted it.

The fabric slapped against the wall and fell into a motionless heap. No rat or possum or sewer alligator scrambled out from under it.

The grease smell vanished instantly.

"Jesus Christ on a fucking cross," Keith said, hurrying out of the restroom and into the dining area.

With a shaky hand, he dug into his pocket for cigarettes. Pulling one out, he lit it right there near the dining area entrance, No Smoking sign be damned. He puffed through panicked, uneven breaths, eyeing the hallway leading to the restroom. What did he expect would stagger out of the dark? Nothing was there. But he knew what he'd seen; his mind hadn't gone to shit yet.

"I'm fine, I'm fine, everything's fine, it's all fine," he said, sucking his cigarette like he couldn't wait to light up a second one. "I'm going to fix this place, and I'm going to open it up again, and I'm going to manage it so much better than last time."

A hiss like a snake's drifted out of the restroom. Keith tensed.

Flashlight shaking in his grip, he traced the darkness until he found the culprit in the middle of the hallway: something suspended in air like mold spores hovering in a condemned, unventilated room. But the particles were liquid. Thousands of tiny oil droplets, golden and sizzling, nearing a boil. Levitating.

"What the fuck."

Keith stumbled backward and reached blindly for the door to the outside. He tugged the handle—rammed it once, then rammed it again harder—but the door was jammed.

The droplets sizzled to a higher pitch and floated closer to Keith. He collapsed to the floor, the last of his bravery draining away in an instant. As he cowered and pleaded, the droplets coalesced into the greasy silhouette of a human. Something about its shape was familiar, but he didn't dare look at it directly—only through the gaps in his fingers.

"Wh—who are you?" His voice was thick with tears.

But he didn't need to ask the question to know the answer.

Mallory loomed over him. Waves of her heat stuck to his face, the sensation somehow both slick and itchy. Praying he was dreaming, he slapped his cheeks.

"Wake up, wake up, please, wake up. I don't want to be here anymore. I—"

Mallory's hand flew to his throat, her boiling oil grip crisping his skin. Keith's howling and thrashing did nothing to stop her. The burn sank deeper, into his nerves, into his muscles.

When she let go, Keith hardly realized it, the agony ceaseless. He gasped for air, black neck blisters bursting, translucent pink fluids oozing down his shirt. He rolled to the side, away from his attacker.

"What—what do you—?" he started, but the pain wouldn't let him finish.

Another hiss. Mallory's silhouette swelled like an angry cat arching its back.

"Please," Keith begged. He gritted his teeth through the lingering burn. "I know I was wrong to—oh, god. Oh, it hurts. Forgive me. I'll do better next time."

Mallory rushed him and smothered his body while he writhed on the floor. Every exposed inch of his skin—from nose to ears to hands—boiled and crackled. The burning surpassed any pain Keith had ever known, and he discovered in it a static-like numbness, a hidden well of adrenaline.

Using what strength he had, he rolled out of Mallory's way and forced himself to his feet, ignoring his screaming nerve endings. Unsteady, he swayed. Sweat and blood and oil dripped off of him. He felt like a wax figure melting in the sun.

Though she had no discernible eyes, Mallory stared him down from a few feet away. None of her sizzling rage had dissipated, but it was as if she were waiting for Keith's next move.

His apology had done no good, and the bludgeon of his flashlight was powerless to subdue a ghost. But what about fire? It'd be risky; he was still dripping with her grease, and one misplaced spark could burn him up along with Mallory. But what other choice did he have?

With trembling, aching hands, he drew his lighter and a cigarette. Mallory only watched as he lit up. Maybe she knew what was coming, and maybe she wanted it. To go up in flames and be released from her misery. To clock out for good.

Keith lit the cigarette and gave it one hard look, then flicked the glowing cherry into the oily dark.

***

"What do you mean the place is fucked?" Charles asked over the phone.

"Electrical fire," Keith said, his words coming out liquid and swollen.

The lie wouldn't hold up to scrutiny, but it was the best he could manage with waves of pain coursing through his body. He plopped down on the overgrown grass at the edge of the parking lot and watched flames devour the window boards. Lucky him, the employee entrance had allowed his escape.

"How the fuck does a fire like that happen on your watch?" Charles asked.

Sirens cut through the night, and Keith flashed back to that final shift once more. It didn't matter that he'd released Mallory tonight; he'd still killed her that day three years ago. The guilt would stay with him until he died. Maybe, if he was lucky, his burns would get infected, and death would come for him sooner than later.

"Dad," he said.

"What? Whatever you're about to say, it better be—"

"I don't think I'm cut out to run a restaurant."

Charles let out an explosive string of curses, but it didn't matter. Keith hung up.

Laying on his back, he watched the flames climb, singeing the blue roof black. The firefighters would arrive and douse the building, so Keith savored the sight while he could. It felt good to watch the place burn.

DAD'S BRINNER SPECIAL

PATRICK TUMBLETY

A breakfast-for-dinner ("Brinner") meal that I, Dad, make for my family when one or all of us need familiar comfort food.

DIRECTIONS:

1. Place a heap of your favorite potato in a bowl (we use tater tots).
2. Pile on your favorite breakfast meat (we use pork roll or bacon).
3. Top with scallions and your favorite cheese (we use either cheddar or feta).
4. Then top with two eggs (we like sunny side up so that the yolk mixes with the rest).
5. Add your favorite spices (we use Tajin, salt, and pepper).

It's that simple, and you can customize it to fit your family's style!

Dad's Brinner Special

SWEET AND SOUR HOT DOGS & MEATBALLS

DJ GRANT

Straight out of the Seventies! This delicious comfort dish came from my Aunt Rickie and became a fast family favorite. I always felt proud to have hot dogs and meatballs when friends came over for dinner. It was our unique "family dish." There is no telling how many neighborhood mothers called to get the recipe. This meal is always a hit with both kids and adults!

INGREDIENTS:

1 lb. ground beef (no more than 20 percent fat)
1 package (12 or 16 oz/340 g or 454 g) miniature kosher hot dogs*
1 can (8 oz/227 g) tomato sauce
½ cup (100 g) brown sugar, or less
¼ cup (59 ml) lemon juice

DIRECTIONS:

1. Mix tomato sauce with brown sugar and lemon juice. Set aside.
2. Form tiny, bite-sized meatballs with ground beef. Place gently in a 2-quart saucepan. It is okay to layer them, but do not stir!! The meatballs will not hold their shape until close to being fully cooked.
3. Pour sauce over meatballs. Again, do not stir!
4. Simmer with lid on for 20 minutes.
5. Add the hot dogs. You can stir gently if meatballs are starting to hold their shape.

6. Simmer 10 minutes longer. You can stir during this time so hot dogs mix in well.

7. Serve over rice (white or brown), orzo, other small pasta, or by itself. Either way, enjoy!

AUTHOR'S NOTE:

*Not smokies. The original recipe called for miniature hot dogs, but they are difficult to find today. Cut regular sized hot dogs instead (approximately 1 package) into bite-sized pieces.

FRANKIE'S FOOTNOTE:

Well hot dog, here's an idea! As you're chowing down on this recipe, be sure to check out "Hotdog Horror" by Lena Ng in the appetizer section of this book!

SYLVIA'S SOURDOUGH STARTER

NICHOLAS GORDON

Instead of the usual hard candies and crossword puzzles, Norma's purse now contained sleeping pills, lighter fluid, and a library book on sourdough.

She shivered. The icy wind cut through her coat, but she still didn't want to go into the old woman's house. She considered calling in a welfare check for the hundredth time. And for the hundredth time, she decided against it. If they took Sylvia away and locked her up, Norma would never forgive herself.

She slid her copy of the key into the lock.

Sylvia was into her late eighties, but she was still sharp as a tack and stubborn as ever. She had retired from the cupcake shop she owned at 75 (too early in her opinion) and would plug her ears if anyone mentioned a retirement home.

Her daughter Maya had given up on getting Sylvia into a home, but she still worried. A widow with no family nearby was bound to get lonely. Sylvia might not need someone to change her diapers, but she did need someone to sit with.

So, Maya had hired Norma, a retired activities director from the nursing home. Norma would visit Sylvia three days a week, from 8 a.m. until noon. They'd watch Jeopardy reruns, knit, or Sylvia's favorite—bake.

It didn't pay much, but Norma didn't mind. She was only looking for a few extra dollars to spoil her grandbabies with. Besides, she was fond of her mornings with Sylvia.

The house was the quintessential grandma home. Lamps shaped like cats were perched on every surface, casting an orange glow on the floral wallpaper. Pictures were mounted on the walls, showing off the family that lived too far to visit. The curtains were always open, and the windows were always cracked, making the house chillier than Norma liked. Still, it was the perfect getaway from her apartment downtown.

But the house had changed so much over the past two weeks, she hardly recognized it as she stepped over the threshold.

The windows were shut and locked behind their curtains. The lamps Sylvia took so much pride in were all turned off, leaving the house as dark as a cave. Norma shed her coat. The air was hot and stale. She reached for the closest lamp—a tabby cat on its back—and turned the light on.

Lined along the walls were dozens of sourdough loaves, stacked three high. The loaves closest to the kitchen looked like they belonged in a bakery, with precise lines scoring the tops of the beautiful round rolls.

The quality dropped as the line snaked out of the kitchen. They turned to unevenly baked mounds tossed into the hall as fast as Sylvia could chuck them out of the oven.

Norma pulled her shirt over her nose. The tangy scent of sourdough was pleasant when it was a single loaf on your counter. A hundred loaves in a stuffy house smelled like sweaty feet.

"Norma? Is that you?" a voice echoed from upstairs.

"Yes, Sylvia. Come down for tea."

Norma crossed through the stacks of bread and made her way into the kitchen. It was worse than the hall. Every countertop was stacked with sourdough-based creations.

Norma pushed two stale loaves out of the way and grabbed the kettle from the cabinet.

She stared down at three empty glass jars while the kettle filled up. They were sitting on the windowsill above the sink, inside a crate tipped on its side to offer maximum shade.

It had all started with them.

No—it had all started when Norma told Sylvia she loved sandwiches with sourdough bread. Sylvia had lit up and promised to bake the best loaf of sourdough Norma had ever tasted.

Two weeks ago, Norma had come over to find a cookbook open on the counter, and a beige substance that looked like pancake batter lying at the bottom of a glass jar.

"That doesn't look like a much dough." Norma frowned at the dozen holes in it.

"That's because it's a sourdough starter, dear. You can't make sourdough without it. Just half a cup into the dough gives it that wonderful tangy flavor. I do have to remember to feed it water and flour whenever I use some. But as long as I feed it, it can last forever! You can make anything with it: bread, cookies, pancakes, all sorts of stuff! But first, I'm going to bake you a loaf of sandwich bread."

Sylvia *had* made Norma a loaf of bread—and cookies, and pancakes, and every single recipe that used sourdough starter in her entire cookbook. The corpses of these baked goods lay molding and rotten around the house.

Norma suspected something had gone wrong with the recipe when a sandwich with Sylvia's bread sent her to the toilet for an hour. She was *sure* Sylvia had messed up the recipe when she'd come over a few days later to find the starter jar overflowing.

"I think you're overfeeding it, Sylvia."

Sylvia had blushed at that.

"I actually haven't fed it at all yet."

Norma came over two days later and found that not only were there piles of sourdough goods for her to take home, but the starter now filled up *two* jars. It overflowed down the sides like a science experiment.

Norma could tell Sylvia was trying to keep up with the rapidly expanding starter. She baked anything and everything with a liberal dollop of sourdough starter, but no matter how much she used, twice as much grew back.

Norma asked her to throw the excess away, but Sylvia refused.

"Don't you like the breads, dear?"

"Sylvia, they're lovely, but the starter is spoiled. It shouldn't be growing like this without you feeding it."

Norma tore her eyes away from the jars and put the kettle on the stove. She gathered two dusty teacups from the cabinet, dropped a peppermint tea bag in each, and took them to the table. She had to push off a pile of moldy sourdough cinnamon rolls to make room.

"Sylvia, come on down."

"I'll be there in a minute, deary."

One week ago, Norma had come in to find three jars, each bigger than the last, and all overflowing with the sourdough starter that Sylvia had never fed.

Norma had pleaded with her: *"What if it makes you sick? You can't have another stint in the hospital."*

"I haven't gotten sick yet, sweetie. And I'm on my feet baking, as the doctor recommended."

"At least throw the extra away."

"I'd hate to waste it. I'll just bake a little extra to compensate."

"Sylvia, you can't keep up. There's too much."

The kettle started to whistle. Norma bustled over and plucked it from the stove. She filled their cups; the smell of peppermint was a welcome relief from the fermented stench that hung through the house like a smog.

Norma retrieved the sleeping pills from her purse. She shook four out onto the table and began snapping them open—pouring the powder into Sylvia's tea. Hopefully, the old lady could sleep through what was to come. Norma didn't know how unpleasant it would be. It made her heart heavy to think of Sylvia in pain.

Norma's heart leaped into her throat when she heard the first step creak. She resisted the urge to flee and kept her butt planted in the chair. Knowing she was the only one Sylvia had left was just enough to make her stay. She just prayed it hadn't gotten any worse.

Sylvia's slow steps down the stairs cracked through the house like gunshots.

Creak. Creak. Creak.

Norma's fingers trembled. She wrapped them around her teacup and held tight. It had been three days since she'd seen Sylvia. Three days ago, Norma had found the jars on the windowsill empty. She'd been pleased, thinking Sylvia had tossed the rotten starter.

She hadn't.

Creak. Creak. Creak.

Norma had found Sylvia huddled by the fireplace.

"Norma, could you turn the thermostat up? I'm freezing but I can't see the numbers."

Norma had known something was wrong then. Sylvia never wanted the heat on. But God almighty, when the woman turned around... her face. Her *face.*

Creak. Creak. Creak.

Tea sloshed down the sides of Norma's cup, scalding her fingers.

Creak. Creak.

Norma held back a scream.

Sylvia hadn't dressed herself today. She shambled into the kitchen naked, her arms outstretched, feeling around.

"Over here, Sylvia." Norma forced a cheerful tone. She wanted to vomit.

Sylvia's curly gray hair was matted close to her skull. Clumps of it had fallen out. The putrid stench of sweat and yeast rolled off of her. Norma gagged and jerked her cup up to her face, pretending to sip as she inhaled the stench-free air.

Sylvia fumbled around until her wrinkled hands found the back of a chair. She smiled, then sat down on top of a stack of sourdough pancakes. Norma kept her eyes trained on the teacup. She couldn't bear to look at Sylvia's face up close. Not again.

But she *had* to. How could she help the woman without looking at her? Norma set the cup down and looked Sylvia in the face. She forced the gasp that bubbled up in her throat back down.

Sylvia was pale. She seemed to have a hundred more wrinkles than three days ago—but that wasn't what bothered Norma.

It was Sylvia's eyes.

Her beautiful green eyes that twinkled like Santa Claus were gone. Replaced. Two doughy ovals sat where her eyes should have been, pressing up against her lids like they could pop out at any second.

"You're here awful late," Sylvia said.

"I figured you could use some company."

"Mmm. I wish you'd turn those lights off."

Norma didn't know how Sylvia could tell the lights were on without eyes.

She tried to get Sylvia to engage in their usual small talk, but for the first time since she'd known her, Sylvia seemed like an old woman. She trailed off, mumbled, and forgot what she was saying multiple times.

Sylvia was still alive, but Norma was losing her fast.

It didn't take long for the sleeping pills to hit Sylvia's bloodstream. Sourdough starter parasite or not, Sylvia was ancient and weighed less than a hundred pounds. Norma ushered her to the couch.

Once she was sure the old lady was asleep, Norma got to work.

She crept into the garage and returned with two space heaters. She set them down in front of Sylvia as quietly as she could but didn't turn them on yet.

Norma had poured over a sourdough cookbook, learning everything she could about starter. She didn't find any warnings that it could come to life and slip into old women's bodies, but she did find something interesting. Sourdough starter needed an environment that was dark and warm to grow.

Warm, not hot. If it exceeded 85 degrees, it could die. And Norma was confident she could get the house a hell of a lot hotter than 85 degrees.

Ideally, the heat would kill the sourdough parasite inside of Sylvia, then it would flush out of her when she used the bathroom.

Norma opened the oven and set it to 550 degrees. She cranked all four electric burners on the stove to high, then turned the thermostat up to 95. By the time she was stoking the fireplace with fresh logs, she could smell the crud at the bottom of the oven burning.

Norma shouldered her purse and went to turn on the space heaters. She paused to look at her friend. Sylvia's face was lit by the fire, her wrinkled forehead beaded with sweat.

What if it didn't work? What if the starter felt the heat and tried to escape Sylvia's body? Norma imagined the starter growing arms, reaching from Sylvia's throat and pulling itself out.

That's what the lighter fluid was for. If that happened, Norma would set it on fire. That'd be well over 85 degrees.

But would Sylvia survive the starter evacuating her body while it was still alive? She was so frail. Norma didn't know, but she couldn't let Sylvia live like this anymore. She flicked on the space heaters and marched upstairs.

***

Norma locked herself in the guest bedroom. Even with the window open, her shirt was sticky with sweat and clung to her back. She sat down on the bed and tried to read the sourdough book to pass the time, but she gave that up after the first page. Sourdough was the last thing she wanted to think about.

Norma didn't know how long it took her to fall asleep, or how long she was out, but the sound of Sylvia thundering up the stairs woke her up. Sylvia always moved slowly to avoid breaking her hip again, but now she leaped up the stairs like a teenager.

Norma swallowed the lump in her throat. She slipped off the bed and pressed her ear against the door.

Sylvia's footsteps were erratic, fading in and out. It sounded like she was going into every room of the house. Norma held her breath as the noise stopped, straining her ears. She couldn't hear the footsteps anymore, but she could hear... breathing.

Norma looked at the floor. The shadows of Sylvia's feet snaked through the crack.

BAM-BAM-BAM!

Norma yelped and fell on her ass.

"Norma? It's burning up! I can't see the thermostat, you'll have to turn it down," Sylvia shouted through the door.

Norma took a shaky breath. "I think it'd be a good idea if we warmed the place up—"

"GODDAMN IT NORMA, I'M BURNING ALIVE! TURN THE HEAT DOWN OR I'LL GUT YOU LIKE A FISH!" Sylvia's vocal cords snapped like guitar strings.

"I won't do it, Sylvia!" Tears streamed down Norma's cheeks. She awaited the next cavalcade of threats, but it never came.

BAM. BAM. BAM.

Sylvia pounded at the door. Harder this time.

BAM. BAM. BA-SNAP!

Norma jumped to her feet as a crack appeared in the door. She hadn't anticipated Sylvia being so desperate to get to her, much less being able to bust down the door separating them.

Norma scurried into the closet. She shut the door behind her and peered out through the door's slats. Sylvia was struggling to get through the bedroom door, hacking away at it with nothing but her liver-spotted hands. A chunk of the door gave out, sending wood shards falling to the floor. Sylvia shoved her arm through the jagged hole.

Her fingers jutted out at random angles—broken from her pounding. Norma could see bits of bone, glistening with wet red tendons and pale sourdough starter. The mangled hand fumbled with the doorknob, painting it with yeast-flecked blood. Sylvia pinched the lock between her thumb and what remained of her pointer finger, then twisted.

Click.

Norma wanted to sob.

The bedroom door squeaked open. Sylvia shambled in, and Norma clamped a hand over her mouth. Sylvia's doughy eyeballs no longer held their oval shape, they drooped out of her eye sockets and down her cheeks like melted ice cream. Sylvia felt around the room with her destroyed hands.

"Norma, dear, you're killing me. I'll bash your head open if you don't turn the temperature down."

A gust of wind blew through the window. Sylvia turned toward it, the starter from her eyes lifting in the air before falling back on her cheeks with a *plop.*

She stumbled to the window, leaning so far out that Norma thought she might tumble into the bushes below. Sylvia took sharp, desperate breaths of the cool air.

Norma had a clear path to the hall.

She slid the closet open and crept toward the door. Sylvia was still leaning out the window.

Norma kicked a chunk of wood that had fallen from the door. *Clunk.*

It wasn't loud, but it was enough. Sylvia whipped around. "TURN THE HEAT OFF!"

Norma screamed. She snatched her purse off the bed and tore into the hallway. She could feel the old woman on her heels, banging into the walls but still sprinting.

Norma thundered down the stairs, making it halfway before Sylvia leaped. The old woman landed on Norma's back. She cried out as her ankle snapped under their combined weight. They fell the rest of the way, landing in a heap.

Norma recoiled from Sylvia's sticky flesh and forced herself up, limping into the kitchen.

She threw open the basement door. Maybe if she got Sylvia down there, she could trap her and bake the starter out of her that way.

Sylvia appeared in the doorway. Her arm hung at an angle, mimicking her fingers. By the look of her limp, she'd broken her hip again—maybe both this time.

"Norma, deary, please turn the thermostat down. I'll fucking cut you open if you don't."

Norma could see the starter dancing in the back of Sylvia's throat. It pulsed and twisted around the muscles in her snapped arm. It wriggled through the breaks of her fingers, in her eye sockets, in the bald spots on her head, in her nostrils.

It was too late. Sylvia couldn't be saved.

Norma stifled a sob. "Do you want the heat turned off?"

Sylvia's head snapped toward Norma. She grinned.

"Yes, dear. Yes please."

Sylvia shuffled toward Norma, her twisted fingers reaching out. Norma reached out too. She took the old woman in her arms.

She couldn't save her, but she could put her out of her misery.

Norma locked her arms, holding the old woman tight to her chest. Sylvia grunted and squirmed, but Norma was already moving toward the open basement door.

She ignored her throbbing ankle and heaved Sylvia through the basement doorway. Sylvia grabbed Norma's arm, but her hands—coated with yeasty sweat—slipped. Sylvia fell.

Norma covered her eyes, cringing at the cracking of bones and smacking of flesh. She only looked when she was sure Sylvia hit the bottom. She wished she hadn't.

Sylvia lay flat on her back. Each one of her limbs was broken, exposing bone and oozing blood and starter.

Norma screamed as Sylvia tried to climb to her feet. Her right leg *snapped* and sank as she put weight on it.

Her head hung off the side of her neck like a botched decapitation, but no blood sprayed from the wound. The sourdough starter oozed from her neck in one long cylinder. It flopped back and forth like a giant doughy worm, and Sylvia's body jerked with it.

Sylvia took a step up the stairs.

Norma ripped the lighter fluid and matches from her purse. She doused the steps, her nose filling with the scent of butane.

She struck the match on the doorframe but couldn't bring herself to toss it. Even as Sylvia's broken body fumbled up the stairs—her barely attached head flopping against her neck—Norma could only see the Sylvia that *had* been. The one who had been her friend.

Tears fell down Norma's cheeks. The match flame flickered and died.

Sylvia's hand shot up and grabbed Norma's twisted ankle. Norma howled in pain as the old woman's overgrown nails drew blood. Norma braced herself on the doorframe and looked down at the creature holding onto her.

Its skin was gray now. Every bone looked to be broken. Norma didn't understand how it was still held together.

There was no denying it. The Sylvia Norma had been friends with was dead. The best thing Norma could do for her was to exterminate the horrible creature that had killed her.

"Goodbye, Sylvia," Norma choked.

She pulled back her other leg and kicked Norma's stump of a neck as hard as she could. Her foot landed with a sickening *smack* and sent Norma's body thumping back down the stairs. Norma pulled another match from the box and struck it. She didn't hesitate this time. She tossed it, slamming the door before she saw flames. A rush of heat came from the other side.

She was running out of the house when the screams started. It sounded like Sylvia, writhing in pain as she was burned to a crisp, but Norma knew there wasn't any Sylvia left.

Norma went home and cried for her friend. She didn't call the fire department. She wanted it to burn.

She just hoped to God that'd kill it.

***

The firemen stood in a silent circle among the charred rubble, staring at the corpse. They'd all seen bodies and burn victims before. None of them had seen anything like this.

"Smells... doughy."

They stared at the thing that had expanded out of the body. It was dark brown and extended from every orifice: the body's neck, a tear in its stomach, even the individual breaks in its arms and legs.

The fire chief wasn't a scientist. He knew that wacky shit happened to human bodies when they died, but he didn't know a lot of the specifics. Other people knew. Like their lab guys. They'd get their lab guys to test it and find out what *actually* blew up inside this... person.

But if you asked him, it looked like a loaf of bread.

HOW TO BUILD A ROASTING TIN

JM CYRUS

We bake one of these about once a week, changing its composition based on what we have around and what is seasonal. We have enjoyed messing about with what seems to smell nice together, and so this is more of a guide of ideas rather than a recipe. Think of yourself as some mad scientist or alchemical wizard and get experimenting!

YOU WILL NEED:

- A large roasting dish. Non-stick works best, but if not, get ready for lots of exciting crunchy bits!
- Protein, vegetable, and allium will work best at 3 parts vegetable to just under 2 parts protein and 1 part allium (less if using only garlic, or not, no judging!).
- Protein ideas: meat (chicken, pork, lamb, fish, etc.), firm tofu cut into cubes, or beans (butter beans, red kidney, etc.). Beans work well straight from the can (drained first!)
- Vegetable: softer vegetables such as tomatoes or courgettes need to be in larger pieces than harder ones (swede, turnip, squashes, beetroot, etc.).
- Alliums: leek, red onion, spring onions, brown onion, garlic, etc.
- Flavoring ideas:
  - Spicy: chili flakes, coriander seeds, fennel seeds, sumac, Cajun spice, harissa, ras el hanout.
  - Sharp: mustard (wholegrain or Dijon), lemon juice, lime juice, ginger slices.
  - Sweet: agave nectar, honey, maple syrup.

- ➤ Oil ideas: coconut, sunflower, olive, etc.
- ➤ Herb ideas: sage, basil, thyme, parsley, coriander, rosemary, kaffir lime, lemongrass, oregano, dill, and mint.

GENERAL DIRECTIONS:

1. Chop the vegetables into rough chunks about an inch and a half in size (larger if using softer varieties).
2. Put the vegetables and allium in the roasting dish and toss with oil and flavorings of your choice.
3. If using beans or tofu, toss those through too.
4. If using larger protein like fish fillets, chicken joints, etc., arrange those on top and sprinkle with some of the flavorings. Drizzle with a bit more oil.
5. Add salt to taste and herbs on top.
6. Put into the oven at 350°F (180°C) or if using a convection oven 325°F (160°C) for about 35 to 40 minutes, depending on how well-done you like your vegetables.
7. Serve with your favorite condiment.

GLUTEN-FREE CORNBREAD CASSEROLE
MARSHEILA ROCKWELL

I've been serving this casserole at holiday gatherings for over 20 years and it's the one thing that always gets eaten (any leftovers are gone within a day). This recipe serves 10-12 people, but you can halve it for smaller groups.

INGREDIENTS:

4 tbsp (56 g) butter, melted
2 packages (8 oz/226 g each) cream cheese, softened
2 cans (15.25 oz/432 g each) whole kernel corn
2 cans (14.75 oz/ 418 g each) creamed corn
1 box (15 oz/425 g) gluten-free cornbread mix
4 eggs
1 cup (85 g) shredded cheddar cheese, optional

DIRECTIONS:

1. Preheat oven to 350°F (180°C) or 325°F (160°C) if using a convection oven.
2. Spray a 9x13 casserole dish with non-stick spray.
3. Mix butter and cream cheese in large mixing bowl until blended.
4. Drain whole kernel corn and add to mixing bowl.
5. Add creamed corn to bowl. Add cornbread mix to bowl.
6. Add eggs to bowl. Mix well. Pour into greased casserole dish.
7. Top with shredded cheddar (optional, but adds a nice crust).
8. Bake 60-75 minutes or until a knife inserted in the center comes out clean. Serve and enjoy!

SUPER CHERRY SURPRISE

P.S.C. WILLIS

I love that moment, when the industry standard scoop of Eazee Waffle Mix hits the griddle, and every possibility is open. At that point, it hasn't become a Banana Funtime or a Strawberry Chocolate Extravaganza. It hasn't become part of a first date or a conversation about divorce. As it slowly turns from beige goop to crisp, golden-brown solid, it is naked and pure, like a newborn baby.

Of course, just like the Lord above has a plan for every little person He puts on His good green earth, so too the fate of the waffle is already sealed. Its destiny hangs on a single sheet of torn-off notepad paper. Maybe not everyone waiting for their sugary treat knows what else is coming, but at least one person is here with an agenda. They know they're gonna confront the bastard about the pantyhose they found in his car, or mourn the loss of their dearly departed, who always chose the Peanut Butter Melty Moment.

I take the ticket off the clip and gasp. I do more than gasp, truth be told. It's a good thing I'm not at a customer-facing position, because I let out a full-on cuss word.

A Super Cherry Surprise.

No. No, no, no. Not again.

I do a quick check around for our manager, Oily Joe, but he must be out back doing accounts. He's the kind of man who clearly thought he'd be doing better than this and wears his resentment as a constant sneer. His only satisfaction in life is micromanaging us. As he's not here, I can risk some chitchatting.

"Hey." I wave Bev the waitress over. She's a long-timer, like me. Her "25 years of service!" pin gleams proudly from her apron, and she can sing every Waffle Palace jingle there's ever been. She knows the names of the regulars, and their kids, and their grandkids, and their dogs. If knowing stuff about the Waffle Palace and being kind to people was an Olympic sport, Bev would get gold.

"I know," she says, her face crumpling as she sees the ticket scrunched in my hand. She doesn't need to ask which one or what's wrong. We both know. The Super Cherry Surprise is cursed.

"Who ordered it?" I ask.

"Best you don't know." She shakes her head sadly. "Try not to think about it."

I stare around the restaurant. It's so quiet that I can hear the regular creak-scrape of the Waffle King outside. He's a ten-foot tall, anthropomorphised waffle that sits on our roof, waving to passersby, calling them to come in for a tasty treat. Most of the customers are already eating. My eyes land on the student.

"Not her," I plead.

But Bev's face says it all.

"But she's so young," I say.

She usually just orders one cup of infinite refill coffee. Why the change in behavior?

"I know," Bev says. "I tried to change her mind, but she insisted. So, what can we do?"

Nothing. Every Waffle Palace has one waffle that's cursed. It's not the same one in every branch, and with the high turn-over of staff, not everyone even knows about it. But long-timers like me and Bev, we've seen things. We know. We learned the hard way that we can't outright lie—if we pretend it's sold out or something, it'll just spread the curse to a new waffle, and it'll still take the girl out. But we can put people off. I know Bev. She has a face she makes when people order it. If that doesn't work, she's good at swaying people. Over the years, she's saved dozens.

But not this time.

With shaking hands, I squeeze the aerated cream from the can onto the waffle, making a smiley face. The waffle is still a little hot, and the cream melts at the edges of the eyes, trailing down the face like tears. I dot the eyes with cherries and give it little rosy cherry cheeks and a sticky syrup smile. There's an extra bowl of cream on the side, with cherry sauce as red as blood. I say a silent prayer as I ding the bell for Bev to come and take it, begging for this time to be different.

We watch, like a vigil, as the girl eats. The regular thunk of the knife on the plate clangs across the restaurant like a funeral bell. She's smiling, oblivious, enjoying this rare treat (why did she do it, why?) without knowing this will more than likely be her last meal.

The curse doesn't always take effect immediately. There was the Great Spelling Bee Carnage of 2020, where the victor didn't even get to the end of the waffle before her twin, mad with jealousy, stabbed her with her own trophy. But other cases have been slower. There was the late-night trucker, who was struggling to keep his eyes open as he got back behind the wheel. There was the Scary Gymnastics Mom who made the local news after she tried to demonstrate to her daughter where she was going wrong and broke her own neck. Me and Bev, we make a point of checking the obits when someone's ordered the Super Cherry Surprise. It gets them every time.

The girl takes the last bite, then runs her finger through the sauce and cream, really savoring it. Part of me wants to grab her hand, yell at her to stop, but it's far too late—her fate was sealed the moment the plate hit the table. She may as well enjoy it.

Once she's wiped her hands on a napkin, Bev makes her way over.

"All done? I thought about sticking a candle in it. Figured it might be your birthday or some such?" Bev says, as she clears the table. Like me, she wants to know why. As if a reason will give sense to the tragedy that's about to unfold.

"Oh. No. It's not." The girl shakes her head.

"You're normally just a cup of coffee girl," Bev observes.

"Yeah." Her face is tight. Why is she uncomfortable? From her point of view, this should be a perfectly normal conversation. Bev's got years of practice. Her tone and her hands are steady, giving nothing away. "Guess I just thought I'd treat myself," the girl says, but her eyes are shifting to her hands, and she's blushing. Something's wrong. I wonder what this crack in her life is, and whether the curse is going to wriggle its way in through it.

"Well, hope you enjoyed it." Bev nods. "Seen you in here a fair bit, what's your name, honey?"

"Kelsey. I go to school here."

"Very nice." Bev nods. She leaves it there. I don't think either of us wants to know what Kelsey's studying, or who's waiting for her at home, or what kind of bright and brilliant future she has planned for herself.

Bev and I are deep in huddled, mournful conversation when Oily Joe comes up. He's a slick out-of-towner, the color of uncooked waffle mix.

"Now, now. Chitchat doesn't get customers served," he says. "And these are not the smiling, happy faces they expect to see on Waffle Palace employees."

We're not contractually obliged to smile. I've checked. It's tempting to tell him to ram his rules up his ass.

"Someone ordered the Super Cherry Surprise," Bev says quietly. He's not one of us, but he's been around long enough to know. He was here when Steve the Drifter chose to go out that way. He ate a Super Cherry Surprise, laid his head down and never lifted it up again. People think those sorts—the ones with social issues, who just come in for the warmth—are the problem customers, but they're loyal to the Waffle Palace like we are. I'm not saying it's an easy shift when they start trying to hit each other with the bolted down furniture, but they've heard about the curse. They ask, "Which one is it here?" They believe. "We know. We lost Jim to a Hazelnut Explosion back in Mississippi."

"Not this nonsense again!" Oily Joe's remark is a slap in the face. How can he not believe when he's seen it with his own two eyes? "There is no such thing as the waffle curse!"

Bev and I both suck in our breath, make the sign of the cross, and pat the wood-style plastic countertop.

"This is ridiculous! I'm utterly sick of this pathetic superstition. You'll see—when that young lady waltzes back in here next week, you'll realize it was all in your heads!"

For a moment, I'm too busy fuming to notice. But it's as he snaps at us to get back to work that it hits me.

"How did you know?" I ask.

"Pardon me?" he says.

"How did you know which customer?"

"I saw her eating it."

"No, you didn't," I say. "You were out back."

"Well, what does it matter? She ordered it, she's eaten it, and she's going to be fine."

"It's not like her to order a waffle though," Bev says, her eyes narrowing. "What's going on?"

"Fine! I offered her twenty dollars to eat it."

"How could you!" I do not keep my tone professional. "That is a young girl's life you are toying with!"

"I am not toying with anything! This stupid waffle curse isn't real! What is real is the tins of cherries out back nearing their expiration dates. Do you know how long it takes canned food to go off? Years. Plural. And yet, it's happening!"

"Did you tell her?" I ask.

"What?"

"Did you explain what she was getting herself into?"

He swallows. He wasn't expecting to have to justify himself.

"No. Twenty dollars to do it, no questions asked, and not to tell. But it doesn't matter. She will walk out of here with her money and a belly full of happiness! Maybe then you'll stop this ridiculous obsession! What's the point of having a menu item that you won't let anyone order? Now, get on with your work!" He walks away.

"Maybe if it wasn't her own choice, the curse won't take her?" Bev whispers, before heading back to the restaurant floor.

I watch her watching Kelsey. Bev wipes tables as Kelsey packs up her books and waves a cheery goodbye.

"You take care, honey," Bev calls out. It's flimsy protection against a Super Cherry Surprise.

We both pause, watching as Kelsey steps outside. Her sundress ripples in the wind, and her soft brown hair glows as a beam of sunlight hits her.

And so does the giant mechanical arm of the Waffle King.

It hits the parking lot with an almighty, jarring thunk. Any noise of Kelsey's death is drowned out in the racket of metal on asphalt. The arm breaks in several places, but it's still giving a chirpy thumbs up to show how darn tasty the Waffle King is. Kelsey's sparkly pink pumps stick out from underneath it. Perhaps she's just stunned, just hurt. But we both know that she's not. It's a brutal way to go. Squashed like the raspberries that go on the Merry Berry Crush.

***

It's only hours later that the police leave. A lot of hours, to be sure, but it feels like days. I can't take comfort in the fact that she must have died instantly, not even knowing what had happened, because she shouldn't have died at all. I can't shake the image of her, smited as if the veritable hand of God had struck her down. If God was a giant waffle.

That's what you get for messing with the curse, except she wasn't the one who messed. It shouldn't have been her number that was up.

The Waffle Palace is closed even though it never closes. But obviously, we had to stop serving, and the police put up a line of yellow tape. We turned customers away while they scraped Kelsey's body off the parking lot.

They still need to do a proper investigation of the Waffle King and whether anyone was negligent in his maintenance, but right now, it's just us and Oily Joe, locked in the dark and the silence. We know the Waffle King isn't the one who's responsible. Not that I think the police would actually arrest a giant, animatronic waffle, but it'll go over Oily Joe's head, up to HQ, and it'll be The Company that settles with Kelsey's family.

The griddle is still hot. I didn't think to turn it off. We don't have a lock up routine, because the Waffle Palace will be there for you, 24-7.

We can't tell the police that the waffle curse killed her, or that Oily Joe made it happen. They won't believe us.

I reach out to turn the griddle off, and realize... I can make this right.

The curse still gets you, even if you don't eat of your own free will. Kelsey proved that.

I slap a ladle of batter onto the griddle.

"What are you doing?" Oily Joe asks.

"You eat one," I say.

We can put people off ordering. We've saved them that way. Because it's not the ordering that does it.

"What?" he says.

"You don't believe in the curse, then you eat the Super Cherry Surprise."

"I don't want one... I'm not really hungry, not after what just happened," he stammers.

"I don't care," I say. "If you don't believe, then you eat it."

"Well, I think I might be starting to." He tries to back away, but Bev grabs him, pinning his arms as I flip the waffle onto the plate. "Okay, you're right! You're totally right. It's cursed, and I believe you!"

"It's not about that!" I yell, spraying cream onto the waffle. Cherry eyes. Cherry cheeks. A happy waffle surprise, except it's all oozing, melting in. "She's dead because of you! You did that!" I slam the plate down on the counter—that clang that marks the beginning of the end. This, this is where the curse starts. When the plate touches the table, and they take their first bite.

Oily Joe struggles, but Bev's grip is firm. I stab a fork right into the smiling waffle mouth and rip off a huge chunk.

"Now eat." I grab his face, squeezing like it's a can I can pop open by crushing it. I shove the waffle in. Pieces fall to the floor, but it doesn't matter. You don't have to finish every last bite. The Spelling Bee twins taught us that. I drop the fork, ripping pieces with my bare hands. He tells us we're fired. He begs forgiveness.

We don't stop. He clams up, but Bev twists his arm to get him to whimper, and that's our in.

We crush more than half the waffle into his protesting mouth, cream dribbling down his chin.

He almost goes out choking on it. That seems too easy, and I let up. His face is streaked with tears and sticky cherry syrup.

Once I'm satisfied, I let the fork drop to the floor, and Bev releases him.

"What-what's going to happen to me?" he asks, wiping the remnants of the Super Cherry Surprise from his mouth with the back of his hand. He's shaking all over.

A sneer spreads over my face, the same one Oily Joe used to wear. So, now he believes.

"Please, tell me," he begs. "What's going to happen to me? How can I stop it?"

I don't answer. Instead, Bev and I grab our coats and head for the door. It's up to the curse to choose his ultimate ending. And I hope it does its worst.

CRIMSON ROAST CHICKEN WITH AROMATIC TARRAGON STUFFING

MELISSA COFFEY

A roast chicken fit for a festive table, this delicious and eye-catching glaze and the accompanying stuffing recipe are my own invention and would also work well with turkey. As I'm not a red meat eater, I created this dish to bring something unique to the Christmas table instead of ham, but it can be prepared any time. Enjoy the oohhs and aahhs of your guests and loved ones as you serve up this decadent dish!

INGREDIENTS:

1 whole chicken (3 lbs./1.5 kg)
Extra virgin/virgin olive oil to cover chicken
2-3 tbsp pomegranate molasses to cover chicken
Crushed sea salt & ground black pepper
1 ½ tbsp tarragon, finely chopped, plus several sprigs for inside chicken
2/3 cup (110 g) grated delicious apple (or other sweet red variety)
¾ cup (25 g) slightly stale sourdough bread, torn into small pieces, crust removed
2-3 finely chopped dried wild figs (or regular dried figs)
½ cup (65 g) roughly crushed raw cashews (I use fresh whole cashews, pounded with a mortar and pestle for the best flavor)
1 free-range egg, beaten
½ cup (118 ml) apple juice (clear or cloudy)
1 tbsp pomegranate molasses*
Pinch of sea salt and ground black pepper to taste

1. Prepare stuffing first. In a small mixing bowl, combine figs, crushed cashews, bread, grated apple and tarragon.
2. Add beaten egg, mixing through thoroughly.
3. Combine apple juice and pomegranate molasses separately and add slowly, evaluating stuffing until you get a damp, slightly sticky texture and the mixture binds well together in a ball.
4. If you have too much stuffing, make small extra balls of the mix. These can be added to the chicken pan in the last 25 minutes of cooking for extra deliciousness in the baked veggie mix (trick borrowed from a Jamie Oliver recipe). In fact, these are so good, you may deliberately want to make more stuffing. Just drizzle lightly with olive oil before baking.
5. Insert 2-3 tarragon sprigs into chicken cavity, then stuffing.
6. Place chicken in pan. Ensure skin isn't too wet—pat dry with paper towel or baking paper if that's the case. Rub or sprinkle over salt and pepper mix.
7. Take a basting brush and glaze all over lightly with the olive oil. Don't forget to lift out legs and wings and brush underneath. Repeat with the pomegranate molasses.
8. Cook chicken as per weight and type of oven. Cooking time may vary, but general rule is 40 minutes per kilo at 375°F (190°C). Check at intervals-if skin is looking dry, baste with a little more olive oil.

AUTHOR'S NOTE:

*A popular Middle Eastern ingredient, pomegranate molasses can be found in Mediterranean delis and sometimes Indian grocers, or upmarket/artisan supermarkets.

Extra uses for tarragon: Tarragon pairs beautifully with potato, carrots and pumpkin, even mushrooms. Use leftover sprigs to garnish the baked veggies, or for a unique touch to a festive table, fill a glass water jug with finely sliced cucumber, orange slices, and tarragon. Chill while your chicken is baking and top up with ice cubes before serving to the table.

DOUBLE BRUSSEL PASTA FOR TWO

M. L. MARTIN

This recipe was first introduced to me as I was work-traveling my way through Europe. After my lackluster attempt at preparing my Venetian host lunch, she showed me how to cook this pasta dish the next day. She insisted I worked unnecessarily hard in the kitchen and with too many measuring tools. She said cooking was easy, but I've since spent countless attempts to recreate her product, and this is my favorite iteration. She lived alone in a slim three-story house in the heart of Venice, and I was her cleaner/gardener for the week. Eating this reminds me of the endless, ringing rooftops of the maze city— simple, fresh, and ready to wander away.

INGREDIENTS:

16 oz (453 g) uncooked pasta, preferably a short shape with lots of ridges like Orecchiette
16 oz (453 g) Brussels sprouts, quartered and sixthed
8-12 large de-shelled shrimp
4 tbsp of butter
3 tbsp of olive oil
6 cloves of garlic, minced or pressed
¼ cup thinly sliced onion (alternatively, add onion powder to your list of finishing spices)
¼ cup (59 ml) lemon juice*
Salt
Pepper
Parsley
Chives
Green onion
Grated Parmesan cheese, optional

Double Brussel Pasta for Two

DIRECTIONS:

1. Set a large pot of water to boil with a dash of salt thrown in, and pour in pasta when a rolling boil is reached. Cook to desired doneness and before straining, reserve a cup of pasta water and set aside.
2. Heat olive oil in a large, high-sided pan at medium-high heat. Next, add prepped Brussels sprouts and onions. Stir until olive oil coats everything. Alternate between stirring and covering with a lid. This should last 5 minutes or until the edges of the sprouts are browning.
3. Turn down the heat to medium and add three pinches of salt, three pinches of pepper, and the garlic. Stir until vegetables are tender in about 2-3 minutes.
4. Pour in ¼ cup of pasta water. Continue to stir as the vegetables become more tender for no more than 1 minute.
5. Add 2 tablespoons of butter, then add pasta.
6. Lower heat to low and add about 2 pinches of parsley, 1 pinch of chives, and 1 pinch of green onion. Stir as you go.
7. Optional addition of parmesan cheese here or when served.
8. Typically, a dash of salt is needed to amplify all other flavors at this point. Personalizing the balance of acidic lemon, earthy Brussels sprouts, bitter pepper, and fabulous herbs is a journey. Good luck.

COOKING SHRIMP:

1. Bring a pan to medium-high heat. When it's at heat, add 2 tablespoons of butter.
2. When butter is melted, add the shrimp and stir until coated.
3. Let the shrimp cook on one side.
4. When the grey-white color on the bottom turns pink and white, flip the shrimp. This will take a minute, give or take.
5. Allow the entire shrimp to turn pink and add a pinch of salt. I prefer Dean's Lemon Seafood. When cooked, serve with pasta.

AUTHOR'S NOTE:

*Suitable alternatives are balsamic vinegar and white wine. A lower volume is recommended for these substitutions.

BURNT BISCUITS AND GRAVY

ALISON THAYER

Peter trudges down the narrow staircase to the old farm-house kitchen. Thin rays of early morning light filter through the small window above the copper sink. The smell of buttermilk tinges the air. God, he used to love that smell.

He sits at the worn wooden table, his eyes on his wife. She's wearing her favorite baby blue dress, and her auburn curls are caught up in a ponytail. No matter when he comes down for breakfast, she's always stirring the gravy. The scabbed-over burn on his left arm itches. That was from Day Three, when he tried to take the wooden spoon away from her.

"Good morning, darling," Lynette says, her voice bright and happy. She grabs a potholder and opens the oven door. A waft of smoke billows out, like it does every morning. "Oh no!" She pulls out the pan, waving her free hand to clear the smoke. She glances at Peter, her bottom lip trembling. "I made your favorite, biscuits and gravy, but I'm afraid I burned the biscuits."

"It's okay, Lynette, they'll still taste good," he says, even though it's a lie. He knows what happens if he complains about the biscuits. Blood still weeps through the bandage covering the stump of his pinky finger. That was Day Seven.

Lynette places two biscuits and a heaping scoop of gravy on a plate and sets it before him. The gravy covers both biscuits. "Just how you like it," she says.

"Thank you," he replies. Lynette expects gratitude for her hard work. The yellowing bruise on his cheek is from Day Eleven, when he didn't say thank you.

"Anything for you, honey," Lynette says. She sits across from him and puts her elbow on the table, resting her chin on her hand. She watches him expectantly, a smile on her face.

Peter picks up his fork and knife and cuts a piece of burnt gravy-covered biscuit. It tastes like cardboard in his mouth, but he forces himself to swallow. "They're delicious." He tries to sound enthusiastic, but it's the thirteenth day in a row that he's eaten burnt biscuits and gravy.

He has a new plan. Tonight he's not coming home after work. The Rodeway Inn is only fifteen minutes away, at the corner of Perkins and Main. It'll be the first night since they got married, six years ago, that he's been away from home overnight. This will break the pattern. It has to.

Peter forces down the last of the biscuits and gravy. On Day One, he refused to eat them, and Lynette shoved them in his mouth while he choked. Now, he eats them all. "Thank you for the biscuits and gravy. I better head to work."

His wife stands, comes around, and kisses him on the cheek. Her lips feel like something dead washed up from the sea. "Have a good day at the store. I love you, Peter."

Peter shivers and represses the urge to scrub at his cheek. "I love you too," he replies. His voice sounds forced, but Lynette doesn't seem to notice. He leaves the house as quickly as he can without seeming rude. Lynette doesn't like it when he's rude.

***

Peter wakes up on Day Fourteen and cracks open his eyes. The clock reads 6:17 and the room is still semi-dark, but there's no mistaking the shadows and angles of his cheap hotel room. He breathes a sigh of relief.

The hotel has a free buffet breakfast, and he's never looked forward to rubbery scrambled eggs and cheap cereal as much as he does that morning. He gets up, showers, shaves, and puts on the clean clothes he packed in a small duffel the day before.

Peter packs his bag and leaves his room, whistling a little tune. He gets on the elevator and pushes the button for the main floor. It's as if a weight has been lifted from his chest. The elevator shudders to a stop and the doors swing open.

He steps out into the dim farmhouse kitchen. Lynette is stirring the gravy. She turns and smiles at him. "Good morning, darling," she says, her voice bright and happy.

Peter spins around, desperately reaching for the elevator doors. But there's no elevator, just the stairs to their bedroom. He spins away and rushes for the front door, though he knows he can't escape the kitchen, the breakfast that awaits. A knock sounds on the door just as he yanks it open.

Lynette's friend Rose stumbles forward into Peter and quickly jerks away.

"Sorry, I didn't know you were there," Peter says, panting slightly. He glances toward the kitchen, but Lynette is gone.

Rose frowns and follows his gaze. Josie and Meg stand behind her, also frowning.

Peter tries to act like he usually does around these three women—rude and a bit bored. "Well, if it ain't the three amigas. To what do I owe the pleasure?"

"We're here to see Lynette, and we're not taking no for an answer," Rose says and pushes past him. The other two women follow, all of them hollering, "Lynette, Lynette, are you here, honey?" One of them heads upstairs.

These three annoying women showed up on Day Four, asking to see Lynette. He told them she was visiting her mom and shut the door in their faces. They were always filling Lynette's head with ideas about "equality" and "independence" and other feminist crap. If they were real friends, they'd have encouraged Lynette to be an obedient wife.

This time, he's glad they're here; they are his ticket out of this house. "Look anywhere you like. She's not home."

Josie comes back down the stairs, shaking her head. "She's not up there."

"I told you, she's at her mother's," Peter says.

"She's been at her mother's house for two weeks?" Meg asks, her eyes narrowed.

"Yep."

"Why doesn't she answer her phone?" she says.

Peter shrugs. "Maybe she doesn't want to talk to you," he suggests.

The three women exchange glances.

"When's she coming back?" Josie asks.

Peter's been thinking about what to tell people when they ask about Lynette. "Well, that's the thing, I don't know if she's ever coming back," he says. He drops his eyes, shakes his head. "You see, we had a big fight, and she left me." It's not easy playing sheepish with these three, but he does his best.

"It's about damn time, the way you keep her out here in the middle of nowhere, isolated from all her friends and family," Meg says.

"That's not a very nice thing to say. I let you visit, don't I?" Peter says.

"You don't 'let us' do anything, we come whether you like it or not," Rose replies.

"I need to get to work. How about I see you ladies out of my house?" He walks them to the door, holding his breath as he steps across the threshold. It works; he's outside.

He walks them to Rose's pickup truck and holds the passenger door open for Meg and Josie. He hates these women, but today they saved him from his fourteenth serving of burnt biscuits and gravy, so he's feeling charitable.

Rose backs out and heads down the lane, kicking up dust in the early morning light as the women drive back to the main road. Peter turns and walks to the old barn where he parks his Ford, thinking about where he'll grab breakfast on his way to the hardware store. Maybe flapjacks at Mel's Diner. His mouth waters at the thought.

He opens the door to the barn and steps into the dim farmhouse kitchen. Lynette is stirring the gravy. She turns and smiles at him. "Good morning, darling," she says, her voice bright and happy.

Peter wants to turn around and run, but there's no point. He stumbles to the table and sits down while Lynette prepares his plate of burnt biscuits and gravy. He takes the first bite and tries to swallow, but he just chokes on the blackened food. It's been fourteen days of burnt biscuits and gravy, for Christ's sake. How much can one man take? He spits it out, coughing. "I can't, I just can't eat it," he cries. "Please, Lynette, can I have something else for breakfast, just this one morning?"

Lynette's cheeks redden and before he knows what's happening, she's by his side. She grabs his fork and raises her hand high. She brings her arm down hard and fast, staking his hand to the table with the fork. Peter screams as a fiery pain radiates through his entire hand and up his arm. He tries to pull back, but Lynette holds the fork in place, tethering him to the table.

Lynette's blue eyes are wide and tears stream down her face. "I try, and I try, and it's never enough for you, is it?" she screams. "Now EAT YOUR BISCUITS AND GRAVY, DARLING." She pulls the fork out with a jerk and sets it next to his plate, blood staining the tines. She turns back to the stove to stir the now congealing gravy. "Would you like seconds?" she asks, smiling over her shoulder, tears still sparkling on her now pale cheeks.

"N...n...no, thanks, honey," Peter replies, his voice shaking. He wraps his throbbing, bleeding hand in his napkin. His stomach cramps from the pain and he eyes his breakfast with loathing, but he has no choice. He picks up his bloody fork and wipes the tines on his pant leg so Lynette won't see. He quickly shovels his biscuits and gravy into his mouth, forcing himself to swallow. He understands now what he must do.

***

Peter's shift at the hardware store ends at five p.m. He signs out and gets a basket to do a little shopping. His boss, Henry, watches with a furrowed brow as Peter struggles to hold the basket with his injured hand, a bloodstained washcloth wrapped and knotted around the wounds. "You sure you're okay?" Henry asks for at least the fourth time that day.

Peter says, "I'm fine, just a little clumsy lately is all." The irony of this excuse is not lost on Peter; he had heard Lynette use it dozens of times. He picks up some kerosene and matches. "Hey, Henry, do we sell sage?"

"Sage?"

"Yeah, you know, the plant?"

"Does this look like a grocery store?" Henry says.

"No, not the cooking kind. Like, for burning."

"What you want with that new age stuff?"

"You got any or not?"

"'Course not. You've worked here for three years. Think you'd know if we had sage or not."

"Guess so," Peter replies. "Whelp, this'll have to do." He carries his basket to the counter.

Henry shakes his head but rings up the items without any further questions.

"Thanks, Henry, see you tomorrow," Peter says. He turns and heads out the door. Time to go find some dinner.

***

It's about half-past seven by the time Peter pulls up to the farmhouse, his belly full of shepherd's pie and beer. The pie wasn't as good as Lynette's. He already misses her cooking, burnt biscuits notwithstanding, but what's done is done. It's late fall, and the land is bare and gray in the shadows of dusk. The windows of the house are all dark. Lynette doesn't bother him in the evenings. He's got the place to himself until morning, but he doesn't go in. The house doesn't feel like his own anymore, no matter the time of day. That's about to change.

Peter grabs his bag of supplies from the hardware store and heads to the barn to get his shovel. The night is quiet and still, the only sound the occasional whisper of crow's wings as a straggler heads for its roost. He walks around back, where he dumps their broken-down appliances and old furniture. He grabs hold of their old washing machine and tries to move it, but the metal cuts into his wounds. He lets go, holding his hand to his chest in pain. He had use of both his hands when he dragged it here two weeks ago. He puts his back against the machine and shoves. It moves about a foot. He continues to shove until he's slid it about five feet, uncovering loose soil. He grabs the shovel and winces as the handle chafes against his bloody palm. This is going to hurt, but it's worth it. It's time to get rid of Lynette for good.

The dirt is easier to dig up than it was two weeks ago when the earth was hard-packed, but it's still hell on his injured hand. In a few minutes, he's sweating, and his palm and pinky are bleeding again. The pile of dirt grows.

By the time he hits the body, it's completely dark outside. "Pee-yew, Lynette, you stink!" he says to his wife. He didn't think to bring a flashlight, but never mind, in a few minutes he'll have a bonfire going that will be plenty bright. In the meantime, the light on his cell phone will do.

Peter clambers out of the hole. "Don't you worry about that none, honey, I'm going to fix it up so you don't ever smell bad again." He gets the kerosene from the bag and pops it open. He shines his meager light into the hole he's dug. Lynette is looking worse for the wear. Her hair is still matted with blood where she hit her head when she fell, but now her face and limbs are bloated, and she looks like she's got a bad sunburn. He shakes his head. "Why'd you have to go and burn the biscuits? It's not my fault you're so clumsy and hit your head. I didn't even smack you that hard."

Peter sprinkles the kerosene up and down her body. It soaks into her pale blue dress, darkening it to a midnight blue. When the can is empty, he throws it into the hole with his dead wife and lights a match. "Goodbye Lynette, I'll never eat your burnt biscuits and gravy again." He throws in the match and fire spreads up and down her body. Peter jumps back as flames shoot up from the hole with a whoosh.

A bright light blinds Peter. "Mr. Lynch?"

Peter shields his eyes and turns, the matchbox still in one hand. Two cops are approaching. "What's wrong, officers?" he says.

One of them says, "Someone reported your wife missing, asked that we follow up with a—"

"Jesus Christ!" The other officer is pointing a flashlight into the burning hole. Lynette's body is outlined in fire.

The first officer pulls out his gun. "Hold it right there, Mr. Lynch. Put your hands in the air."

Peter drops the matchbox and raises his hands.

The officers roughly turn him around and cuff him. One of them says, "Peter Lynch, you are under arrest for the murder of Lynette Lynch. You have the right to remain silent ..."

The rest of what the officer says melds with the sound of the crackling fire. Peter just can't focus on it. All he can think is, at least he won't have to eat burnt biscuits and gravy in jail.

***

It's six in the morning by the time they stop interrogating him. Peter told them over and over again that Lynette's death was just an accident, but they're all hung up on why he felt the need to bury and burn her if it was just an accident. They don't understand. He buried her because he knew how it would look, even though it was her own fault she was dead. And the reason for burning her? He explained it was the best way to get rid of a ghost. When they all stared at him like he was crazy, he told them they could Google it themselves.

A guard takes him to a cell with a solid metal door. A cot is visible through a small, barred window. He's so tired, but he'll finally be able to get some sleep. He'll explain it all again later.

The guard opens the door. "In you go," he says.

Peter steps into the dim farmhouse kitchen. Lynette is stirring the gravy. She turns and smiles at him. "Good morning, darling," she says, her voice bright and happy.

LAZY BONES CHICKEN NOODLE SOUP

KERRY E.B. BLACK

Sometimes, time gets away from even the most dedicated of us. However, that doesn't mean you have to sacrifice taste. The aim of this recipe is to create something warming, hearty, and healthy in a hurry. Using pre-cooked chicken and dicing the veggies into smaller bits cuts the cooking time.

INGREDIENTS:

Rotisserie chicken	Salt to taste	Oregano to taste
Carrots, diced	Pepper to taste	2-3 dried bay leaves
Celery, diced	Basil to taste	Parsley
Onion, diced	Garlic to taste	Thin soup noodles

DIRECTIONS:

1. In a soup pot, add chicken and all other ingredients except the noodles. Cover with water. Bring to boil, then reduce to simmer. Simmer until chicken falls apart and veggies are tender.
2. Remove all solid pieces from broth. Allow pieces to cool on a rimmed baking dish.
3. Bring broth to boil. Add noodles. Cook for ten minutes, stirring occasionally.
4. Reduce heat to simmer.
5. Once the chicken has cooled, discard bones, skin, and fat. Return cooked meat and veggies to broth. Add additional spices to taste.
6. Enjoy!

SPLIT PEA SOUP
MERANDA TUTTLE

My mom introduced me to split pea soup through the Andersen's soup recipe. This was the basis for my recipe when I moved out. It has been tweaked depending on what I had available and if I wanted to try something new. I've learned I like thick soup, so add extra broth if you want it thinner.

INGREDIENTS:

6 cups (1.42 L) vegetable broth
2 cups (400 g) split peas
1 onion, chopped
2 carrots, chopped
2 celery stalks, chopped
3 garlic cloves, minced

1/2 tsp marjoram
1/2 tsp basil
1/4 tsp cumin
1/2 tsp salt or to taste
1/4 tsp pepper or to taste

DIRECTIONS:

1. In a pot on medium-high heat, sauté onions until soft, using splashes of water to deglaze the pot if needed.
2. Add carrot and celery until slightly softened, about 3 minutes.
3. Add garlic, marjoram, basil, and cumin. Stir for 30 seconds.
4. Add broth and split peas, bring to boil.
5. Add salt and pepper to taste, lower to simmer and allow to cook for 1 hour or until peas are soft.
6. (Optional) For a smoother soup, blend either with an immersion blender, or in batches in blender or food processor. Be careful when using the blender because the heat can cause the blender to burst at the lid.
7. Enjoy!

I'D KILL FOR A DECENT SLICE

STACEY FLOWER

After I moved out West I used to think, "I'd kill for a decent slice of pizza," until I actually did. Looking back on it now, I can't really be too hard on myself. Anyone from New Jersey will tell you it's nearly impossible to find good pizza anywhere else. And in Colorado? Fuhgeddaboudit! (Just kidding—not everyone from New Jersey talks like that.) But seriously, sometimes people out there dip the crust in honey! I know—I was shocked, too. Pizza can be a very divisive thing, tearing friendships (and sometimes throats) apart.

I moved out there for a job, but mostly for a much-needed life reset after a bad breakup. Relatively speaking, it wasn't nearly as bad (or should I say, messy) as some of my breakups since then, but we'll get to that. It was just one of those relationships when you kind of hate the person, but you've put so much time in that you stubbornly cling to it because forcing it is easier than starting from scratch. That is until you come home one day to him loading boxes of his stuff into the car of his other girlfriend, whose existence you never even suspected

109

because you assumed he was just as complacent as you were.

So, I jumped at the chance to start over in a completely new place, landing a marketing position at a large outdoor gear company just outside Denver. I loved it—the sun that was almost always out, the mountains, the ability to see for miles in any direction. I even started hiking—an activity I, being a Jersey girl, never thought I would enjoy—and I loved it. I felt like I could breathe there, and it wasn't just because of the improvement in air quality, although I'm sure that didn't hurt. Sitting out on the balcony of my newly constructed apartment, watching the sun set behind the Rockies, I didn't miss a thing about the East Coast. Until I started craving pizza.

At first, it was just a normal desire for something I hadn't had in a while. After months of burritos smothered in pork green chili (which, by the way, I became completely addicted to, seeking out the delicious gravy-like salsa at every meal, like some people seek out salt or butter), I started to feel like I could go for some pizza. It's not like I expected it to be exactly the same as what I was used to in New Jersey, and it's not like every pizza I'd had in New Jersey was perfect. But I guess I was a little naïve to think that pizza is pizza, and how could it really be that different? Well, it can be that different, and each time I tried a new pie, my hopes were crushed like the spicy red pepper flakes I used to mask the bitter disappointment that came in the form of sickly-sweet sauce and too-thick, chewy crust. And with each disappointment, the craving grew stronger. What started as "I could go for some pizza," quickly became a *real* hankering, which progressed to "I'm going to die if I don't have a good slice of pizza soon," and it wasn't long before I fantasized about shoving each sorry excuse for pizza down the throat of the waiter or delivery person who had brought it to me.

Around this time, I was surprised to discover that I was starting to feel like I could go for some dating too. Between my jaded attitude toward romance and the excitement of the move, I hadn't expected to be the least bit interested in getting back out there for a very long time. But most of my new friends were half of a couple, and the yearning to be half of a pair again began to nag at the back of my mind until I was signing up for multiple dating apps. It was a welcome distraction from the increasingly intense need for pizza, so I was happy to dive in. It helped… for a little while.

I met Nick on an app called "NewInTown." I guess part of me felt out of place and wanted to connect with someone who was feeling the same way. Nick had moved to the area from Ohio about six months before I did. We really clicked, so it's a shame what happened. We might have even gotten married one day. Okay, so I only knew him for about three weeks, but sometimes a girl can just tell.

The afternoon of our fourth date, he texted, "Dinner at my place tonight?"

"What are you making?" I replied, pretending it would have made a difference. To my relief, food—especially the p-word— hadn't seemed as important since I had started seeing Nick.

"It's a surprise," he answered. "Don't worry, I'm not making it."

"Sounds great," I sent back, along with the smiling emoji with a drop of sweat on its forehead to show my relief that he wouldn't be cooking. Among the many things we had in common was a lack of cooking skills; mine stemmed from disinterest, while from what Nick had told me, cooking was something he just couldn't get right. Although I would've been moved by the effort, the thought of a man who had somehow "charred" spaghetti on more than one occasion cooking my dinner was not completely appetizing.

That night, I showed up promptly at seven, bottle of wine in hand. Normally, I would've shown up at least a few minutes late, not wanting to seem too eager. But I was excited to see what surprise he had in store. Plus, I really think I was starting to fall for him.

He greeted me and walked me to the kitchen table, which he had set with a nice white tablecloth, candles, and a small vase with a single red rose in it. I was touched by this romantic gesture and fully intended to show my appreciation later in the evening.

"Wow, you really went all out," I said, wrapping my arms around his waist. "This is so fancy. I hope you didn't spend too much on dinner."

"It really is nothing fancy, but I wanted to make it special," Nick said, blushing a little. It was so friggin' sweet, I grabbed his face and pulled it to mine, not worried that my tongue was leaving no question about how eager I was to be there. If the doorbell hadn't rung a couple minutes later, I would've shown my appreciation long before dessert.

"I'll be right back," Nick said. He pulled out one of the chairs for me, gently pushing it in behind me as I sat down. I watched in anticipation as he left the kitchen to answer the door. At that point, he could've walked back in with a loaf of bread and a jar of peanut butter and I would've done anything he wanted. If only he had come back with bread and peanut butter.

As soon as I saw the box in Nick's hands, the craving hit me harder than ever. The thought of melty cheese and sauce with just the right amount of tanginess kissing my tongue pushed out all other plans for the evening ahead. The tantalizing aroma of fresh-baked crust seasoned with olive oil and herbs hit my nose like a boxing glove, and it was as if I'd never had another thought or emotion, only an all-consuming desire for pizza.

"Okay, so I know you've been missing the pizza back home, and this place is supposed to be the real deal," Nick said. He lowered the box so I could see the top, which had "Garden State Pizza" in red and green letters across the center. I must have stared at it for a bit too long, making him nervous.

"Sorry it's only pizza...I just thought it would be fun to see if you think it's as good as back home. And you seemed like you were really missing it, so I thought it would be a good idea."

Nick was blushing again, and if I hadn't been in the death grip of the craving, I would've pushed him onto the table and mounted him at that very moment. But the craving had me in its clutches, and it was all I could do to keep the saliva that kept filling my mouth from spilling out the corners.

I swallowed, my eyes glued to the box. "No, it's great. Let's try it," I said, grabbing for the lid.

Nick gently pulled back, surprised by my overzealousness but relieved that I was into it.

"I'll just get us some plates and stuff," he said, turning towards the kitchen counter.

My arm continued reaching towards the box as Nick carried it away to the counter. I twisted in my seat, my body pulled by the box's gravitational force, my unblinking eyes clinging to it like shrink wrap. Luckily—although I guess it doesn't matter now—I had enough awareness to wipe the drool from my chin with my cloth napkin. Or maybe it wasn't lucky. Maybe seeing me sitting there drooling like a mastiff would have tipped him off that something was seriously wrong.

He returned to the table with two plates containing a big slice for each of us, as well as two glass shakers, one filled with grated parmesan and one with red pepper flakes, just like they would have at a pizzeria. Seeing the red pepper flakes induced a brief moment of clarity, and I thought, *Don't eat the pizza, you'll only be disappointed, and there's no telling what you will do.* But the familiar fragrance of oregano pulled me back into the depths of the trance, and I was picking up the crispy hot slice, lifting it to my lips, and tearing into it like an animal.

At first, it tasted just like what I'd been missing. My mind must have created what it wanted most: molten-hot cheese with just the right level of saltiness mingling with the tang of the tomato sauce and a hint of herbs, delivered on a crust of the exact thinness to be just crispy enough with a little chew to it. I must have been at least three slices in before I realized the truth of the matter. The cheese was rubbery and bland. The sauce was too sweet and too spicy at the same time. The crust was like raw dough spread over cardboard.

I spit out what was in my mouth and looked up at Nick, who was staring at me in disbelief, his mouth hanging open, his eyes wide with horror. I looked down at the table and down at myself. Both were covered in cheese and sauce. It was smeared into the carpet, into my top. It looked like I had taken the whole pizza and smashed it into any surface I could find in my immediate vicinity. I continued to spit, desperate to get any remnants of the awful pizza out of my mouth.

Then a rage hotter than any brick pizza oven filled the spaces inside me that had been left empty by so many disappointments, so many cravings left unsatisfied, and I had to unleash it before my chest exploded from the pressure.

The last thing I heard Nick say was, "Are you okay?" before I lunged across the table at him. I saw the wheel of the pizza slicer flash silver at the end of my arm, then become dull with red as I slashed at hands, forearms, face, neck. Nick put up a fight, but I was like a frenzied mountain lion tearing at its prey, relentlessly slicing any flesh within my reach. Blood splattered onto my face, into my mouth. The initial coppery taste of it transformed into the bright tang of the best pizza sauce I'd ever tasted, and I had to have more. I slashed long after the thrashing beneath me stopped.

When it was over, I felt oddly satisfied. Like I had eaten all the pizza I wanted—the real stuff—and then some. Even stranger, the taste of the best pizza I could have imagined lingered on my tongue for hours afterward. All traces of the craving were gone. And I was so grateful to Nick for that, for the sacrifice he made so that I could be free of the craving's grip. I wanted to honor his sacrifice, so I couldn't leave him there like that for someone to find him.

I broke him down into manageable pieces, and then I wrapped them neatly in multiple trash bags. The beige carpet was particularly hard to clean, but I was eventually able to get it to a point where someone might assume that spilled wine had stained it. During the days that followed, I went on a few of my favorite, more remote hikes and buried the bags in spots I think Nick would've really liked.

Unfortunately, my blissful contentment only lasted a couple months. The craving returned on a Wednesday, creeping up on me slowly at first, so subtle I only had a vague inkling that something was missing from my life, but I couldn't quite put my finger on it. By Thursday night, I was back on the dating apps. You have to understand, I didn't want it to happen again, but I had no choice. I had to quiet the craving. It came back with an initial whisper that turned into a blood-curdling scream playing on repeat in my ears. What was I supposed to do, give up a new home and life that I loved over pizza?

I figured, best case I would finally find some decent pizza and meet a nice guy. Worst case, well, you know what that looks like. Maybe one more time would stop the craving for good. I made an effort to pick guys who didn't seem that nice, so at least if it happened again, I wouldn't feel like it was such a big loss.

It did happen again. Twice actually. Each time the craving was more intense, and each time the satisfaction faded more quickly. After the third, I finally decided it was time to throw in the towel and move back East. The fact that someone's dog had wandered off the trail and dug up one of my trash bags was the real nail in the coffin, though.

The first thing I did when I got back to New Jersey was order a pizza. I finished the whole thing myself in one night. I'm happy to report that it worked—as long as I have access to good pizza, I'm able to keep the craving at bay. But I have to admit I do miss the mountains, the sun, the fresh air. And lately I've been really feeling like I could go for a burrito smothered in some pork green chili.

GLUTEN-FREE PIZZA CRUST
LUCRETIA STANHOPE

Being gluten-intolerant and loving pizza is a nightmare. So is making cauliflower pizza crust. I don't like to make anything too fiddly or complicated and needed pizza in my life. When I saw you can make oat flour, I set out to make oat pizza crust. I love that it takes under a half hour and that I can have pizza anytime now.

INGREDIENTS FOR PERSONAL/SINGLE-SERVE SIZE:

½ cup (40 g) instant oats
1tsp baking powder
3 oz (85 g) plain Greek yogurt
Butter or whatever you use to grease your tray
Tomato paste or pizza sauce
Toppings

DIRECTIONS:

1. Place oats in a food processor and blend the oats until they are the consistency of flour. It takes less than a minute.
2. Add baking powder. I do this in the processor too, so it gets good and mixed.
3. Grease the tray. I line mine with foil and rub the butter over it. Then sprinkle a little of the oat flour you made over the tray. Set the tray aside.
4. Place the oat flour in a mixing bowl. Add the yogurt. I blend it with a fork to start with. Once it's as mixed as it'll get with the fork, finish with your hands, working it into a ball. If it's too crumbly, I add more yogurt. Be mindful

not to add too much or you'll end up with a sticky mess and need more flour.

5. Once it's all mixed into a ball, squish it as flat as you can in your hands and then put it on the tray and continue to flatten it out. If it sticks to my fingers, I just wet them. How flat you want it is personal preference. It won't rise much at all so make it exactly the size and thickness you want it.

6. Bake it at 350°F (180°C) or 325°F (160°C) if using a convection oven until the crust gets golden (around 20 minutes).

7. At this point, I peel it from the foil/pan because it can stick even with butter, and you don't want to be fiddling with a stuck pizza with hot toppings on it.

8. Top it with your preferred sauce and toppings.

9. Bake until it's as crispy as you like it.

Kimchi Dijon Pizza

KIMCHI DIJON PIZZA

A.C. BAUER

So, this recipe was partially inspired by the Teenage Mutant Ninja Turtles Pizza Cookbook. After making several of the creative pizzas within the book, I wanted to try my hand at creating one of my own. I love kimchi and thought the Dijon mustard would add a nice contrast to its spiciness. Although I was met with some skepticism, the pizza turned out quite well and is one of my prouder culinary endeavors.

INGREDIENTS:

For the Kimchi Rice:

1 cup (180-200 g) uncooked jasmine rice
½ lb. (225 g) chicken breast, cut into bite-sized pieces
2 tsp sesame oil
2 tsp soy sauce
2 tbsp kimchi juice
3 tbsp soy sauce
1 tbsp gochujang (Korean red chili paste), or more to taste
1 tbsp sesame oil
2 tbsp canola oil
1 clove minced garlic
Dash of onion powder
Dash of ground ginger, optional
1 cup (~175 g) kimchi

For the Dijon Sauce:

¾ cup half and half
3 tbsp Dijon mustard, or more to taste
1 tbsp all-purpose flour
¼ tsp salt

For the Pizza:

Your favorite pizza crust   Green onions, optional
Shredded Cheddar Cheese   2-4 eggs, optional
Shredded Mozzarella Cheese

DIRECTIONS:

1. Prepare rice according to its instructions.
2. In a bowl, combine cut-up chicken with sesame oil and soy sauce. Stir and set aside.
3. In a separate small bowl, whisk together kimchi juice, soy sauce, gochujang, and sesame oil until smooth. Set aside.
4. In a large skillet, heat canola oil over medium heat. Add garlic, dash of onion powder, and ginger if using. Stir frequently, then add chicken. Once chicken is cooked, stir in 1 cup of kimchi. Stir frequently for 3-4 minutes. Add cooked jasmine rice and kimchi juice mixture. Cook an additional 2-3 minutes, stirring occasionally. Rice should take on a reddish-orange hue throughout. Remove from heat.
5. For the sauce, combine half and half, Dijon mustard, flour, and salt in 1-quart saucepan. Cook over medium heat, stirring constantly, 3-5 minutes or until mixture begins to thicken. Do not boil, and you may need to add a little more flour to thicken the sauce to your liking (just be careful not to dilute the Dijon flavor too much). Remove from heat.
6. Begin the construction of the pizza by prepping your favorite pizza crust.
7. Once the crust is ready, spread Dijon sauce over top. Add kimchi rice (you may have some leftover, but don't worry. Save the remaining rice for another meal or as a midnight snack!). Top with cheddar and mozzarella cheese to your preference. Add green onions and raw eggs on top of cheese, if using.
8. Cook according to crust recipe, or until cheese is melty and the eggs are cooked to your liking.

A FAMILY RECIPE: THE CURSE OF RETROCOGNITION

E.E.W. CHRISTMAN

The o-ring light reflects brightly in Sasha's dark eyes. She mouths the opening words as they appear on her tablet, frozen, waiting for her to hit "enter" before scrolling. She says the first sentence, smiles, blinks, and repeats. Speak, smile, repeat. Speak, smile, repeat, until Sasha's cheeks ache. She takes a long sip from her infused tea, remembering to turn the bottle so it faces her phone. Then, she goes live.

"Hey, ghoulies and cursed cookers, and welcome to another episode of Monstrous Meals! I say 'another' because this is officially its own segment! I was planning on making this just a one-time thing for Halloween, but y'all loved this nastiness so much that, yep, it's happening!" Hearts and confetti erupt in the bottom right-hand corner of her phone. Viewers go from double to triple digits in an instant. Sasha doesn't have time to read the comments, but she sees some choice words: *wow, hell yeah, gorgeous*. She continues:

"We won't be using my grandma's old cookbook, *100 Special Occasion Dinners for the Modern Homemaker*, this time. No more jellied lamb salad!" Vomit-face emojis flood the chat. "For our second meal, we'll be using *this*." Sasha holds up the book, a plain thing bound in leather that smells like a tobacco pipe and overripe fruit. Sasha resists the urge to crinkle her nose. "No, this isn't the Necronomicon, but who knows?" Sasha taps her long nails across its spine. "Maybe it's bound in human flesh." Speak, then smile. "I found it at a yard sale and, when I realized it was a cookbook, I knew we had to make something from it." A half-truth: it had been a private estate sale on Whidbey Island. A mansion filled with vintage treasures, now on Sasha's Depop.

"As you can see, the recipes are handwritten. Yep, this is a family cookbook!" Sasha licks her pointer finger before flipping to the first page. "This next part is written in Latin." The translation, run through a search engine, was written on an index card tucked into the cookbook. "'*Delectamentum desideria expecto intus. Resiliunt spina et gustare vetiti.*' Delicious desires await within. Crack the spine and taste the forbidden." Sasha waggles her eyebrows, each hair frozen with gel. "It gets weirder. The whole book is written in this handwriting." Sasha holds the book up to the phone, her glittering nail pointing to the section in Latin. Its lettering is thick, bold, and artistic, written with a calligrapher's flair. "But underneath, there's this." She taps the bottom right-hand corner where a second note can be seen. It's different than the rest, written with a modern pen, the kind left in a junk drawer for eons. "Someone other than the author added this little tidbit." Sasha turns the book around, reading once more:

"'It will reveal your secrets. I didn't listen. DO NOT OPEN!'" Underlined three times in what Sasha would describe as excessive drama. "What do you think, guys? Should we turn back before it's too late?" Her mocking question is met with a flurry of polarizing enthusiasm:

girl DONT

DO IT DO IT DO IT

evil dead energy lol

nothings gonna happen, that would be too cool

"I'm not scared if you're not. And anyway, I don't have any secrets. Do you?" Sasha asks the invisible throng as she rearranges her setup slightly. She flips the book open to the preselected recipe, an unremarkable meatloaf save for the fact that it contains an entire can of lemon-lime soda.

"The only secrets I found so far are that the original owner didn't have much of a palette." Laugh emojis. Vomit emojis. Sasha grins, introducing the fizzy citrus beef loaf, answering questions as she makes a big show of reading through each step as if for the first time. She'd done a dry run without the ingredients. Sasha's roommate had eyed her warily as she "cooked" with empty bowls and spoke to no one. Joel mostly kept to himself, thank fuck, so he kept his remarks to himself as he retreated to his room.

"Now, the piece de resistance: it's time for the soda. I'll be using 7-Up." Sasha gets the can from the fridge. She cracks it open with a showman's flourish before pouring the entire can into the bowl of ground beef.

"And now…" Sasha blinks. She reads the line again, the pause immediately causing waves in the chat.

oooo, something s p o o k y

pls this is so fake

sasha r u ok???

Speak! Smile! "Sorry, guys. I'm okay. Just feeling a little tired all of a sudden."

rest!

we love u <3

faker

Sasha reads the recipe again. One teaspoon marjoram, written in shorthand under the lemon lime soda. She hadn't imagined it though. She was sure, for just a second, it had said a name instead.

Sasha shakes it off. She has an audience of hundreds to entertain. Maybe Dr. Amp's CB-Tea is doing more than advertised. Fucking godawful stuff. Sasha makes a mental note to not drink it anymore.

"Now, marjoram."

The live is becoming mechanical. Sasha goes through the motions, but she can't stop thinking about the name. It had been a flash, like splicing a shot into a movie. Subliminal messaging. But this wasn't a movie, or even a device, hackable and vulnerable. This was a book, solid and sitting right in front of her. Books didn't glitch. And recipe books written by strangers didn't write the names of your elementary school bestie in the ingredients list.

Mallory Butters. For less than a breath, marjoram had said Mallory *fucking* Butters. Sasha knew it was crazy. She also knew it was true, deep down in the pit of her stomach where instincts resided. Sasha knew it the same way she knew water would drown her and that fire would burn her; the recipe had called for a teaspoon of Mallory Butters.

who's mallory butters

Sasha's eyes whip up from her influencer catatonia. "Who said that?" She scrolls up, searching the ceaseless chatter of followers. "Who said..." The name is ash on Sasha's tongue. She swallows hard, choking on spit. She can see the sweat dripping from her nose and temples on her phone, leaving little slug trails in her foundation.

"Someone asked about a name," Sasha says instead, tactfully. "Ask it again."

Hundreds of silent murmurs fill the screen. None of them say the name though. This isn't the relief Sasha wanted. Instead, there's panic, ancient and hot, like a long-dormant volcano itching to erupt.

"Speak, smile." *Did I just say that out loud? Am I speaking out loud right now?* "L-let's continue with the recipe—"

Fingers run down the spine, shaking more under the harsh ring light. Sasha finds where she stopped: one teaspoon marjoram. She clears her throat and reads, confidently:

"How did Marjorie Butters die?" Hands clap over lips. It was right there, written in the same old, faded ink as everything else. *How did Marjorie Butters die?*

"That can't be here. That can't be here." Sasha's voice is high-pitched like a boiling tea kettle. Her smile is thin, too stretched, too gaunt. The smile of a frightened animal baring its teeth.

"This book is older than Marjorie. How can her name be in a book from before she was born?" It hadn't been there before. It was just a recipe before. Books didn't just change.

mallory_b has joined the live

Sasha is a performer. She craves an audience. She yearns for a spotlight, even one that stood on a small tripod in her kitchen. Yet now, she freezes, watching her audience watch her watch them. Her eyes glaze over their concern, their mocking, and their frustration. Familiar words rise to the surface:

marjorie butterball

large marge

the virgin margie

Nicknames. Scribbled on binders, folders, lockers. Even her arm once. "I had said I was going to draw a Cool S." Sasha speaks, thoughts becoming words unbidden, just like they were appearing in the book. Conjured. Forced out. "But I wrote those instead. I can't even remember which one anymore."

How do I appear to them, frozen like this? When they look at their phones, how do I seem? Does the fear dance in my eyes? Can they see how I flicker, unable to stop my mouth from moving? A poised emotional meltdown. Sponsored, even. Thank you, Dr. Amp.

"I was teasing. The way friends tease, you know? She said mean things to me, too. Margie said things. No one ever cares about that, though. Everyone just cares about what happened. But it wasn't my fault!" *It's like a fever. A fever in my heart, making stupid words come out.* "I didn't mean for everyone else to start calling her those things! It wasn't a joke when they said it. It was mean."

A flash: Margie, standing by my locker, dress pinched in her hands. Stop it, she mouthed.

"She was my friend. My heart broke when she...But everyone acts like it was my fault! I didn't bully her. I didn't bully her! I DIDN'T BULLY HER!" Hairs come loose from Sasha's perfectly tied hair. She pants heavily. The chat scrolls too fast to read. Sasha catches glimpses, unsure if the messages are coming from people or from the book, sitting on her counter, heavy as lead and radiating like uranium.

killer

should have been u

suicide sasha

The laugh is a guttural sound. It's mirthless. It starts in her belly and crawls from there, up Sasha's spine and out her mouth. The sound rattles her bones. It loosens spittle. Sasha drips and shakes, her vision blurring from tears. Yet, she can still read it, over and over again, the only words on the screen, on the pages: *suicide sasha, suicide sasha, suicide sasha*, on every page of the book that she didn't even realize she was flipping through.

"And that concludes," Sasha giggles and chokes, unsure who she is speaking for or to. *Is anyone there? Have you all gone? See me. Please see me.* "Monstrous Meals."

VINDALOO
GENEVIEVE PUTTAY

A spicy, tangy delight that'll ignite your taste buds. With tender-as-heck pork, a fiery blend of Indian spices, and a punchy shot of vinegar, this curry is not for the faint-hearted—it will put hair on your chest! But trust us, it's so worth it.

INGREDIENTS:

For the Paste:

8 dried bird's eye chilies (add more if you're a psychopath)
2 tsp black peppercorns
1 cinnamon stick
6 cloves
3 tsp coriander seeds
2 tsp cumin seeds
8 curry leaves
1 tsp fenugreek seeds
6 green cardamom pods
1 star anise
Thumb-sized piece ginger, peeled and grated
8 large garlic cloves
¼ cup (55 ml) apple vinegar

For the Curry:

1.75 lbs (800 g) pork shoulder (or stewing pork), in 2 inch/5 cm chunks
2 tbsp sunflower oil
1 tbsp ghee
1 large white onion, finely sliced
2 tbsp tomato paste
1 tsp turmeric powder
2 tsp mango chutney
~2 cups (500 ml) water

DIRECTIONS:

1. First make the paste: Put all the whole spices (dried bird's eye chilies, black peppercorns, cinnamon stick, 6 cloves, coriander seeds, cumin seeds, curry leaves, fenugreek seeds, green cardamom pods, star anise) into a dry frying pan and toast over a medium/high heat for 1-2 minutes. Keep an eye on them as they can burn easily. Your nose will tell you when they're ready; take off the heat when you can smell their beautiful aroma.

2. After removing from heat, split open the cardamom pods, releasing the seeds and discard the husks. Decant all the spices into a spice grinder and whizz until you have a fine powder. Alternatively, grind them by hand in a pestle and mortar, but leave out the cinnamon and chilies as it will be impossible to powder them unless you are super strong and really patient. Instead, toss them into the curry whole, and fish them out at the end.

3. Add the ginger, garlic, and white vinegar, and blitz until you have a paste. Set aside for later.

4. Next, prepare the curry: In a large saucepan, add 1 tablespoon sunflower oil over a high heat. Work in batches, without crowding the pan, and brown the pork. We're not cooking it here, you just want to get some lovely caramelized edges and flavor into the pan. Keep the meat aside for later.

5. Add another 1 tablespoon sunflower oil and the ghee to the pan. Reduce the heat. Add the onions and cook gently with the lid on for 25 minutes until golden brown and sticky.

6. Stir in the tomato puree and turmeric and cook for 5 minutes over a medium heat until it releases its oil.

7. Add the curry paste and cook for 1 or 2 minutes until the raw smell of the garlic mellows. Add the browned pork, mango chutney, and enough water to cover the meat.

8. Season with salt, give it all a good stir, bring to the boil, then reduce to a simmer.

9. Keep the lid on for the first 90 minutes, stirring occasionally, and then remove the lid for a final 30 minutes for the curry to reduce. This will be a fairly saucey curry, but you can reduce to your desired consistency.

10. Serve with boiled rice and your favorite sundries. Leftovers (if you're lucky enough to have any), will be delicious the next day, giving the flavors more time to mature.

FRANKIE'S FOOTNOTE:

This recipe uses bird's eye chilis, also known as Thai chilis. They're much hotter than the typical jalapeño, but not as hot as a habanero.

POULETTE POISSEUX
(ROAST STICKY CHICKEN)
M. TYLER TUTTLE

This refined yet simplistic recipe is a much-beloved staple of working hens' dinner tables. This chicken is served whole, slow-roasted with a savory spice mix that tantalizes the taste buds and makes your whole house smell incredible. Best known for its juicy meat and crispy, succulent skin, Poulette Poisseux (literally, "sticky chicken") sticks to the fingers while you eat. Licking your fingers to get every last scrap of spice mix is expected and encouraged. Leftovers are best served on toasted white bread with mayonnaise, salt, and pepper, or devoured cold at two in the morning while standing, feral, in front of the open fridge.

INGREDIENTS:

4 tsp salt
2 tsp paprika (for extra heat, use Hungarian paprika)
1 tsp onion powder
1 tsp dried thyme
1 tsp white pepper
1 tsp black pepper, fresh-cracked
1/2 tsp cayenne pepper
1/2 tsp garlic powder
2 onions, quartered
2 chickens, whole (approximately 4 lbs. each)

DIRECTIONS:

1. Preheat the oven to 250°F (120°C).
2. Remove the chickens from their plastic wrappings and place on a plate or clean cooking tray. Be sure to remove any giblet packets or absorbent pads.

3. In a separate bowl, mix the dry spices together. Optional: Double the quantities for richer flavor or to use leftover spice mix on vegetables, fish, or grilled meats. Store in an air-sealed container in your cabinet.
4. Rinse chickens lightly in water and pat dry.
5. Shake a handful of spice mix into the chickens' hollow center, then fill with quartered onions.
6. Use the rest of the spice mix to coat each chicken evenly. Make sure to spice both sides of each chicken, as well as the wings, drumsticks, and edges.
7. In a glass baking tray (4.8 quart for two chickens; 3 quart for one), ideally three inches or more in depth, lay the chickens flat side down. You do not need to grease or prepare the tray, but you should ensure both chickens fit comfortably.
8. Roast for about five hours or until internal temperature reaches 165°F (74°C).
9. Every half hour, baste the chickens with the juices in the tray. Make sure to baste from the top down to ensure crispy skin and juicy meat.
10. When the chickens are done, let rest for five to ten minutes.
11. Carve and serve with butter-basted asparagus and mashed potatoes.

DIVINE
HANNAH BIRSS

The following documents, as assembled by Inspector Kieran Woods of Scotland Yard, were used to help supplement the ongoing investigation of the unusual events surrounding the riot and massacre at CYGNET BISTRO on 19 July, 2024.

Notice to the Press Dated 1 May, 2024

Cygnet Bistro Opening 21 May, 2024

Celebrated chef Calum Herrington, winner of two Crystal Fork awards and formerly of SPAUSENHAUS, is proud to present his latest venture in culinary delight—CYGNET BISTRO. Herrington is joined by celebrity chef Rebekah Copeland, winner of the last season of *Sautéed*, as seen on the Gastronomic Channel. With an emphasis on atmosphere, fine dining, and French and British cuisine, CYGNET promises to be a delight for all five senses and is sure to leave guests hungry for more. Located on James Street North in London, the Bistro opens 21 May. Reservations can be made by contacting reservations@ cygnet.uk.

From the outside, CYGNET BISTRO looks quaint. It's a small, brown-bricked building with Parisian vibes and flowerpots overflowing with petunias. From the street, it doesn't look like anything particularly special, just a place where you might take your wife for a low-key date night.

When my wife and I entered, a hostess dressed all in black greeted us casually, and we were shown to our seats in a cozy booth at the back, with candlelight being the main form of light. The warm exposed brick, old butcher block tables, and vases of white flowers all contributed to a very cozy vibe. As we huddled together in our booth, we inspected the menus.

At first glance, the menu did not seem to be anything particularly revolutionary. The fare was simple and limited, a mix of classic French and British dishes. I will admit that at that point I was feeling somewhat disappointed—I had expected much more from Herrington and Copeland, whose dishes I have enjoyed in the past, both as a judge on *Sautéed* and when I last dined at SPAUSENHAUS in Berlin. Both of them are considered rising stars in the culinary world, with Herrington's particularly fresh takes and talent for flavour sending him skyrocketing to the top at such a young age. Despite the obvious talent in this joint venture, the menu seemed rather dull. I had thought that this dynamic duo would bring more to the table, so to speak.

With some hesitation, I ordered the bouillabaisse, while my wife requested the more provincial dish of coq-au-vin. While we waited, Herrington himself exited the kitchen and came to greet us. His warm, boyish charm made us feel right at home, and he promised that while the fare seemed simple enough, it would be unlike anything we had ever tasted before. We assured him that we were excited, though I still held some private reservations; what new or exciting thing could be done with dishes that have already been done to death?

Our meal was brought to us in short order, and after the waitstaff departed, we took our first, cautious bites.

When I tell you that the food was beyond anything we had ever tasted, I truly mean it. The flavours were perfectly balanced, the meat rich and delicious. Our hesitation quickly disappeared and turned into a race to see who could finish first. We shared our dishes with each other at first reluctantly, and then with jealousy. It was as if I had rediscovered food, and I savoured each heavenly bite. It was so good as to be sinful.

In the end, both my wife and I had to stop ourselves from literally licking the plates clean. When I say that somehow Herrington has taken old and overused recipes and perfected them beyond what I thought a chef was capable of, I am not exaggerating. What he has done with his dishes borders on the miraculous and sublime.

It is a joke amongst my closer colleagues that there is a restaurant status above our usual scale of judgment. It was considered unobtainable, a ranking no one on this earth would ever be placed into. To reach this pinnacle of culinary excellence, one would have to serve literal manna from heaven. CYGNET has somehow accomplished this. For the first time in my life, I am putting a restaurant in the category of *divine*.

Mary Villaneuf >

I can't stop dreaming about that beef wellington special last week at cygnet. IM OBSESSED.

Me too. I can't believe we a) managed to get in and b) got to taste it. I've been dreaming about it day and night

We need to go back. It was heavenly. They must put drugs in the food or something.

I already checked - they're booked up fully into the new year. Six months out.

I'm literally crying right now. I feel like I did when my grandma died.

Maybe we can sneak in?? There's gotta be a way to get back in there. There has to be something we can do.

Maybe we can just show up and demand a table?

Doug @supperking
@katieiscooking have you made any progress on reverse engineering cygnet's recipes?

Katie @katieiscooking
@supperking no

lzdawg69 @lzdawg69
@katieiscooking aren't you supposed to be the queen of knockoffs?

Katie @katieiscooking
Guys stop asking. I've posted all there is that I've been able to do and it still wasn't the same

Katie @katieiscooking
I don't know what kind of black magic they are doing over there, but I'm no wizard.

0/5 ⭐ DON'T GO HERE

Bob Fletcher 12 July, 2024

Made a reservation, but when we arrived, they told us our table wasn't ready because the previous diners hadn't left yet. We stood there for THREE HOURS, but none of the diners ever left. They just kept stuffing their stupid faces and ordering meal after meal after meal. The hostess kept apologizing, but we never got our table. We ended up leaving and stopping at McDonalds. Terrible service. I was excited to try, but I won't be back. Food looked good though.

👤 Laura James

Hi mommies! My MIL has finally convinced me to take a date night with the hubs so she can babysit our little 7-month-old small fry! It's been so long since we went on a date LOL. Does anyone have any suggestions???? I've heard about some place that had a name like Swan? Signet? Is that good?

👍 Like   💬 Comment   ➤ Share

👤 Rhiannon Ruth Ellis

You mean Cygnet. It means baby swan.

👤 Jenn VanStickle

IT WAS TEH BEST THING I'VE EVER TASTED GOGOGOGO

👤 Jamie Goodyear

Good luck getting in. That place is only for the elite now.

👤 Ellie M.

All I hear about is Cygnet from my old restaurant coworkers. I don't think a restaurant has entered the cultural zeitgeist of the London food scene so fast since the 80s. It's ridiculous. I walked by there the other day on the way to kindernastics with Bentley and people were hunched over the tables literally shoving the food into their mouths. Pigs at troughs, chewing like animals. They looked crazed. I don't know what's going on there, but I would stay away.

👤 Suzy Hoog

I can't believe you're leaving your infant to go on a date. They still need you at that age. Do better.

999 OPERATOR: This is 999 Emergency Services—

BC: Shit, oh shit. (*Screaming in background.*)

999: Sir?

BC: It's a riot! I...*ohmygod....* (*Glass breaking.*)

999: Sir, where are you?

BC: I'm on James Street. There's this restaurant and um, the windows have been smashed. People are running around like mad. They're covered in food.

999: The people are covered in food? What happened?

BC: Like, the people inside the restaurant. I was just outside when two women went in and started demanding a table. The hostess said they didn't have room, so they just started eating things off people's tables. Next thing I know, all hell is breaking loose. Oh shit! (*Sounds of smashing porcelain.*)

999: Sir, I need you to keep talking.

BC: They're going nuts. They're throwing plates. They're attacking each other—JESUS CHRIST IS THAT A BUTCHER KNIFE?

999: Someone has a knife? Describe them.

BC: Fucking Christ. They're... they're gutting him. Oh my god, other people are stabbing him now, too. (*Screaming.*) Oh my god, they're ripping each other to shreds.

999: Take a deep breath, sir. Can you tell me how many people are involved?

BC: Everyone! Everyone in the restaurant. They're fighting each other. Send the police, send the ambulances, send anyone! (*Screaming.*) I need to help. I need to do something. Oh god, it's like a fucking horde in there. They're killing each other. They're just killing each other! What do I do? What do I do?!

999: Sir, stay where you are. Help is on the way. Are you safe? Is anyone with you?

BC: I'm across the street. I sent my wife and kids back to the car. What do I do? What do I do?

999: Stay on the line, sir. Just tell me what you see.

BC: Um, um, I'm hiding behind a garbage can. It's chaos out there. Why-why are they doing this?

999: Has anyone said anything about that?

BC: Um, uh no. They're just. Ripping into each other. Using utensils, fingernails, teeth. Oh god, there's so much blood. (*Choking noise.*) Wait, I-I see someone in a white coat. Looks like a cook or something. They've dragged him out into the street. Oh Jesus, oh... (*There's a wet sound, underneath howling and screaming.*)

999: Sir?

BC: (*audibly sobbing*) They're...They're eating him alive. Just shoving bits of him into their mouths. They're crazed. What is happening, what is actually happening?

999: Just stay on the line, help is on the way.

**Clipping taking from the Daily Sun News, 21 July, 2024**

FAMOUS CHEF DIES IN RESTAURANT RIOT

A riot broke out at the newest addition to the London food scene and took a deadly turn on Friday night. Famed Chef Calum Herrington was tragically killed when violence erupted at his newest restaurant CYGNET. Two servers, a bartender, and 12 patrons of the restaurant were also declared dead at the scene, with a dozen more injured and in hospital.

Sous-chef Rebekah Copeland survived the riot by hiding in the walk-in fridge with several other restaurant workers. Those who took part in the riot have been detained, with many of them being transported to different psychiatric hospitals around the city. At this time, what exactly caused the mob to erupt into such violence is unclear, though authorities are investigating several possibilities, including the use of gaseous psychedelics by a rival restaurant owner.

THREAD FOUND ON THE LDNCONSPIRACIES.UK FORUM BOARDS

IWANNABELIEVE

Am I the only one noticing that Calum Herrington is the most recent member of the 27 club?

LZRD1

What is the 27 club?

ABDCTED83

Great musicians, actors, famous people who all died at the age of 27, often in some sort of freak accident. Rumour has it that they traded their souls for their talent, and the devil came for them

THEILLUMINATIWAITS

I mean, Herrington didn't die in a freak accident. He was murdered.

IWANNABELIEVE
Maybe, but being torn apart and eaten by crazed restaurant patrons is pretty freaky. The guy was crazy successful for being 27. Maybe the devil came due.

BIGFOOTLIVES
I feel like if the devil wanted to, he wouldn't need to collect a single soul by causing a weird riot in an upscale restaurant. I think he was sabotaged by someone. Maybe his sous-chef. I think it's convenient that she managed to hide when he was killed.

ABDCTED83
I don't know if I believe in the devil.

IWANNABELIEVE
Just food for thought.

KATSU CHICKEN WITH GOCHUJANG NOODLES

RYAN BREADINC

Gochujang is my "flavor of the month." A red chili condiment hailing from Korea, it adds a lovely simmering heat that isn't so hot that you lose the other flavors of your meal. This recipe is a delightful mix of Japanese and Korean cuisine, with crispy baked chicken and a flavorful sauce! This dish is healthy, straightforward, and can be customized to your tastes. The parmesan is just because I personally like cheese—not at all necessary if you want to stay authentic!

INGREDIENTS:

For the Katsu Chicken:

4 chicken breasts, sliced in 8 strips
1 egg white, lightly beaten
2 cups (100 g) panko breadcrumbs
1 tbsp vegetable oil
Seasoning (salt, pepper, peri peri seasoning, turmeric, etc.) to taste

For the Gochujang Noodles:

14 oz (400 g) udon noodles*
¼ cup gochujang (Korean red chili paste)
1 tbsp ketchup
Parmesan cheese, optional

DIRECTIONS:

1. Preheat your oven to 425°F (220°C) or if using a convection oven 400°F (200°C) and take your chicken out of the fridge.
2. Boil your noodles. Remember to save a cup of the noodle water for later.
3. Flatten your chicken between two sheets of cling film. I like to use a rolling pin, but a meat tenderizer is also a good choice. You want the chicken to be about half an inch thick.
4. Put your egg white in a small bowl. Mix your breadcrumbs, oil, and seasoning in a shallow casserole dish until thoroughly combined.
5. Cover a baking tray in baking paper. Dip the chicken strips in the egg first, and then coat in the breadcrumb mixture. Transfer to the tray. When done, put into the oven and bake the chicken, turning as needed, for 10-15 minutes or until a nice golden-brown color.
6. While the chicken is cooking, put a frying pan on high heat. Add your gochujang and ketchup to the pan and stir to ensure it doesn't burn. Once caramelized, add the cup of noodle water to the pan and continue stirring, being careful not to boil it to death. You should end up with a thickened orange-red sauce.
7. Turn off the heat and add your noodles to the sauce, mixing to ensure they are completely coated.
8. Add noodles to your plate and lightly dust with parmesan cheese if using. Slice cooked chicken into pieces and place on top of the noodles.

AUTHOR'S NOTE:

*I like to use the instant udon noodle packets rather than dried noodles to save on cooking time and utensils.

Spicy Udon Noodles with Peanut Butter

SPICY UDON NOODLES WITH PEANUT BUTTER

KARMEN ŠPILJAK

Let's face it, cooking can be a chore on an empty stomach, especially when you've got books to read and films to watch. Except you're tired of take out and feeling guilty about that leftover veg that's rotting in your fridge.

Enter Spicy Udon Noodles with Peanut Butter. Not only are they a comforting meal for one, you can rustle them up in time to watch your favorite series.

These yummy noodles will warm up your day and give you that wholesome meal you've been craving. They're also a neat way to use your leftover vegetables, like those nice cauliflower leaves that too often end up in the rubbish. Feel free to change the vegetables to your taste or make the dish vegan by substituting the shrimp for tofu.

INGREDIENTS:

1 tbsp gochujang (Korean red chili paste)
2 tbsp light soy sauce
1 tbsp peanut butter
2/5 cup (100 ml) water
7 oz (200 g) udon noodles
2 tbsp sunflower or rapeseed oil
1 banana shallot
2 garlic cloves
1 small carrot
5 oz (150 g) cauliflower florets and leaves

7 frozen shrimp or 4 oz (100 g) of tofu
1 ½ tbsp toasted sesame oil
1 spring onion (thinly sliced)
Sesame seeds

DIRECTIONS:

1. Mix the soy sauce, gochujang, and peanut butter with the water and set aside. If you're not a fan of spice, use only half a tablespoon of gochujang or omit it altogether.
2. Chop the shallots and carrots into small cubes and finely slice the garlic. Heat the oil in a wok on a medium high fire and fry the shallots and the garlic. Add the carrots and cauliflower chunks, fry for 5 minutes. When the cauliflower softens, add the peanut butter and gochujang mixture and the shrimp (or tofu). Cook until the shrimps are done, then stir in the toasted sesame oil and take off the fire.
3. Cook udon noodles according to the package instructions and add them to the sauce. Serve warm with sliced spring onion and sprinkle with sesame seeds.

THIS IS WHY I DON'T TRY NEW THINGS, RONNIE!

WESLEY WINTERS

I have a surprise for you when you get home.

I read my boyfriend's text and feel my throat tighten. Ronnie rarely (if ever) does things I'm not expecting. Partly because he knows I don't care for surprises (like birthday parties) and also because he lacks initiative. But I kind of love that about him; it's comforting knowing what I can expect from Ronnie. I always want to know what I'm getting into, and whenever I feel like something is more of a mystery to me, I get anxious.

What kind of surprise? I text him back.

I can't tell you that, of course, he responds a minute later as I shoot off another email at work.

I still have a couple hours until the end of my shift. I wonder what Ronnie has planned for us or if he bought a gift. It's not our anniversary or my birthday or any sort of holiday to my knowledge. Maybe he's trying to be more spontaneous because someone got it into his head that he should be that way in a relationship (regardless of the fact he is dating someone on the spectrum who is not a fan of randomly doing something without mentally preparing for it first).

Do I need to pick up anything on the way home? I ask him. I can't help it. I'm starting to sweat because I'm nervous now.

My phone vibrates a moment later.

Maybe wine?

So, he's doing something for dinner as a surprise, I tell myself. That must be it, right? Or maybe he wants to fool around.

I relax a bit and get back to work. I'm still antsy but I have a lot to do before 5, so I do my best to keep distracted in the meantime.

***

The moment I enter our apartment, Ronnie appears from the kitchen dancing to music in his head.

"What's gotten into you today?" I tease as I kick off my shoes, and he takes the bottle of wine from me.

"I finally went to the docks this morning," he says on his way to the kitchen island. He puts down the Sauvignon Blanc before turning back to me. "There's this fisherman there with a stand that Kyle and Marla have been raving about for weeks."

"Okay."

"So, I went there this morning to see what he has, and there was this squid he caught that he told me is incredibly rare and is technically illegal to remove from the ocean."

Though I am intrigued by Ronnie's animation, I can already feel my gut twisting at the very mention of squid. If this story is going where I think it is, I won't be eating the dinner he's prepared for us. Surely, he knows I'll be giving squid a hard pass; I don't like seafood, nor do I eat new stuff (generally speaking). Not anymore, at least. My parents forced all kinds of shit down my throat growing up, but I'm no longer under their rule. I eat the things I know I like and nothing else.

Though I've become sidetracked by my own thoughts, I realize Ronnie has continued talking, unabated.

"...the haggling, but it was necessary. It's what they do. It's widely accepted to barter with the price, or whatever the phrase is. You know? So, I got it, though, bottom line. And he told me this wicked recipe to try, which was nice of him because I could tell he was annoyed by me and the change to his asking price."

I shake my head in amusement and tell him, "I don't understand why you're so excited about some squid."

"Because, like I said, it's this rare shit no one can even legally buy here," he exclaims, hugging me for good measure, like I'm a poor child who has said something quite silly. "You won't find this at any restaurants, that's for sure. It's like we've got something secret and...I don't know, *royal*. Something only the rich should be eating on a boat surrounded by hardbodies drinking champagne."

I laugh as I move myself to the couch and take a seat. "Do you hear yourself?"

"Well, I'll admit, I lost my Ritalin a few days ago and that might be...a *factor* in all this energy," he says from beside the coffee table, speaking quickly. "But that doesn't mean this special treat is any less special."

"I'll pass, sweetie, but you enjoy," I tell him while considering my dinner options. I have leftover spaghetti in the fridge, and I love leftover spaghetti. I swear it's better leftover than fresh.

"Come on, Jay. At least try a bite. I didn't expect you to have a plate of it."

I look over my shoulder, back at the kitchen. "Did you already cook it up?"

"Yeah. Everything is ready."

I stifle a groan. I spend so much of my life compromising myself in some way to make others feel better that I'm constantly exhausted. But if I'm gonna do this shit for people I don't like, I suppose I can indulge myself a bit more for someone I love.

"Fine," I say, standing from the couch and heading toward our dinner table (a small, round thing in the corner). Ronnie follows closely behind at first but then branches off into the kitchen to get everything plated. I think of my spaghetti and wonder how long I must pretend I'm enthused about the squid before I can grab it. Ronnie is so excited, and I don't want to ruin this for him.

When he brings everything out to the table (including sides of rice and mashed potatoes, which he knows are safe foods for me), I hear my stomach growl. Even if the squid is of no interest to me, I am excited by what else he's prepared. The squid itself has been diced up and mixed into some sort of pasta and shrimp dish he's made (which admittedly looks good to some degree, seeing as I like pasta).

Ronnie has only sat for a second before he jumps back up and says, "Shit, the wine!" He pours two glasses and brings them over to us with a skip in his step.

"I was also hoping to celebrate in other ways tonight as well," he tells me once he has made himself comfortable. "Like a movie and maybe a bath."

"A bath?" I say. "Our tub is a bit small for two people."

"Still might be fun."

I think of being squished in a bath with him and try not to show my disinterest in the idea. "You also mentioned a movie," I say. "Did you have one in mind?"

"Not really."

"And here I was worried you'd say *Sharktopus* or something."

Ronnie places a finger on his chin and taps it humorously. "Now there's an idea..."

"Please no."

We laugh. I take a drink from my wine and begin to dread what's coming next.

The "special" squid.

He tries it first, though. I watch his reaction with interest. At first, I don't think he likes it because I can tell he's swishing his mouthful from side to side, as if taste-testing wine at the vineyard upstate. But then he nods to himself, his eyes skyward, and swallows. Smacks his lips and licks them clean of sauce before saying, "Yeah."

"Yeah?" I laugh.

"It's good. It's...interesting. Chewy. Rubbery. But like... chicken on the inside," he explains. "Like, before I really grinded it between my teeth, it seemed more like a dog toy got mixed into my food. But once I had the cuts split open or whatever... yeah. It was good."

"What about its ink? Did you taste any?" I ask.

"No, no. I removed the ink sack when preparing the squid."

"I don't know anything about cooking squid," I remind him. "What did the thing look like before you cut it up?"

"It's a deep-sea squid, the guy told me." Ronnie takes a sip of his wine and prepares his next forkful. "It sort of looked like an umbrella squid, I guess."

"I don't know what that is."

"It's like...a dick with webbed tentacles," he says, laughing a little. "I don't know. But this" —he points at the dish— "looked like a translucent green version of that. Longer and thicker tentacles, though."

I shrug. "Okay."

He scoops more into his mouth before spiking a singular cut of the squid on his fork for me. As he hands it over, I swear I see it squirm. Dropping the fork between us, I curse and scoot my chair back. Ronnie finishes swallowing his food and asks, "What's wrong?"

"It moved!" I tell him, disgusted.

"No way," he says, waving me off with his hand. "You're imagining things because you're scared to try it."

I continue to stare at the piece, though it remains motionless. Had I really imagined it?

Ronnie picks up the fallen fork and hands it to me again. "Please try it. For me."

"Why do you have to push this? You know how I am with food."

"I know how you are with a great many things, my love. But I'm just asking for a bite." He smiles and bats his eyelashes at me. He knows I love them, which is why this is a popular look he gives me whenever he's losing a battle he hopes to win.

"Fuck," I grumble, taking the fork from him. I stare at the squid for a long moment (waiting for it to move again) before placing it onto my tongue and closing my mouth. As I pass the empty fork back to Ronnie, I push the piece to the left side of my mouth and begin chewing. The texture is more than unpleasant, in my opinion. I gag but don't spit it out. I push onward and chew the squid further. Even with its somewhat chicken taste spilling out of the tentacle, I am not enjoying myself. Though I haven't quite finished chewing the piece, I swallow it to swiftly end the experience.

Ronnie has a look of pure anticipation on his face, as if he's expecting me to exclaim, "I loved it!" which is utter foolishness on his part. I hate to bring him down, but I hated the squid and have no desire to ever try it again.

When I open my mouth to tell him as much, Ronnie's face suddenly changes to one of great pain. He doubles over, groaning, and falls out of his chair onto the floor. I jump up and scream, "What's wrong? Is it your gallbladder? Did it rupture?"

Ronnie's face is pressed against the tiled floor as he moans loudly and cries out in pain.

Unsure of what to do, I continue to word-vomit. "The gallbladder carries waste and digestive juices. I've heard it's very painful and dangerous if it ruptures. If you don't get immediate help, the mortality rate is as low as twelve percent. Where is your pain originating? Is it in the right upper quadrant of your abdomen? You don't look yellow. I think ruptures come with jaundice…"

"Stop," Ronnie manages to grunt as he squirms across the floor in the fetal position.

"What do I do?" I ask him.

"Call… an ambulance," he finally gasps. When he looks up at me to say this, I see sweat coating his face. His skin has paled greatly since his collapse.

"Right. I'll do that." I turn away from him and check my pockets for my phone. It takes me a moment to remember I empty them by the door whenever I get home, including my phone. Panic does not suit me, clearly. I rush over to the bowl on the stand beside the shoe mat, locate my phone, and dial 911 as quickly as I can. When I turn back to Ronnie, I see something that seems impossible.

Ronnie has rolled onto his back like a turned-over turtle with his arms and legs bent above him. There's a mound roughly six inches long moving up from his midsection and through his chest. I think I hear his ribs cracking, too. Ronnie's eyes are bugging out from the pain, and his open mouth is stretching to capacity.

"Jesus, Ronnie! What's going on with you?!" I scream.

The emergency operator tries to get my attention over the phone, but I can no longer hear her over the sudden pulsing of blood in my ears. I'm officially freaking out now. I drop my phone without realizing it and run over to Ronnie.

The mound is working its way up his throat now. In seconds, we'll see what it is...

Ronnie tries to speak but can't. It sounds like he's choking on something. His face is turning blue now and his limbs are stretched outward as if he's reaching desperately for something I cannot see.

A thick finger appears in the back of his throat, forcing his uvula against the roof of his mouth.

No, wait...it's not a finger.

It's a *tentacle*. Thick and grubby, green tinted and partially translucent. Reaching and wiggling from side to side as it makes its way up his throat and toward his teeth. As it reaches the light and flicks toward me—

Does it have fucking eyes?!

—Ronnie appears to lose consciousness. That or he has suffocated and died.

I stumble backwards and fall onto my ass. The tentacle extricates itself from my boyfriend's mouth and inches down his neck with a sickening suction sound that makes my stomach turn. I can see the little suckers now that they're bathed in the light of our kitchen and dining area. They're blue and less translucent than the body of the tentacle.

"Stay away from me!" I scream, kicking myself away from the advancing squid limb. But the thing continues in my direction.

Squelch!

Squelch!

I finally roll over, climb to my feet, and run for the door, bypassing my fallen phone, from which a voice continues to call for my attention.

Outside, without my shoes or car keys or anything, I run down the stairs screaming for help. One of my neighbors on the ground floor opens their door as I rush past them, and yells after me.

"What's going on, Jay?"

I look back to answer him and trip on my own feet. I fall hard onto the sidewalk and smack my head against the concrete. My neighbor hurries over to me with a towel wrapped around his waist. His hair is clearly wet from a shower I've interrupted.

"Jesus, man. Are you okay?"

With horror, it occurs to me that (like my poor dead Ronnie) I also ate the squid.

Ignoring the grasping hands of my worried neighbor, I lift myself up from the ground enough to stick a finger down my throat in an attempt to vomit. When nothing happens, I pound my fist against the sidewalk and begin to cry.

"What the hell is going on, Jay?" my neighbor asks again.

"It was just a piece!" I tell him between sobs. "Just one goddamn piece."

"What are you talking about?"

"The squid," I gasp, curling into a ball right there at his feet. "I just ate one goddamn piece."

As if in acknowledgment of my apparent sin, I feel a sudden great pain in my guts as my intestines begin to tighten with the movement of something alive.

FRAGILE

TERIYAKI SALMON PHILLY ROLLS

R. HAVEN

When I changed to a pescatarian diet for health reasons, I determined quickly that omitting meat from my diet didn't mean I was willing to sacrifice taste. Sushi is a fantastic, delicious meal that's well worth the effort, if you're willing to put in the time. This recipe works without expensive, top-quality salmon, because you're going to cook it in a teriyaki glaze to maximize flavor. Trust me; once you've gotten into the rhythm of rolling your own sushi, you'll want to make it all the time!

INGREDIENTS:

For the Fillings:
2 salmon fillets
3 tbsp teriyaki sauce
3 tbsp soy sauce
1 tbsp rice vinegar
1 tbsp sesame oil
1/3 cup (65 g) packed light brown sugar
2 large or 3 medium garlic cloves, minced or crushed
A dash of shredded basil, optional
1 block (8 oz/226 g) cream cheese
Cucumber
Avocado, optional
Seaweed sheets (nori)

For the Sushi Rice:
2 cups (400-410 g) uncooked glutinous white rice
3 cups (710 ml) water

(List continued on next page)

½ cup (118 ml) rice vinegar

1 tbsp sesame oil

1 tsp salt

Sesame seeds, optional

DIRECTIONS:

1. Prep your baking sheet with tinfoil or parchment paper for easier clean-up.
2. In a large mixing bowl, combine teriyaki sauce, soy sauce, rice vinegar, and sesame oil. Add the brown sugar and mix until it's dissolved. Add the minced garlic and basil, stir, and place the individual salmon fillets in the mixing bowl. Use a spoon to thoroughly coat the salmon, then cover the bowl in Saran wrap. Marinate in the refrigerator for 20-30 minutes.
3. Prepare the rice while salmon marinates. Combine the rice and water in a medium saucepan, bring to a boil, then reduce heat to low and cover. Cook for 20 minutes until rice is tender and the water is absorbed. Transfer the rice to another container to let it cool; begin preheating oven to 400°F (205°C) (or 375°F/190°C if using a convection oven) before the rice is done.
4. Transfer your salmon to the baking sheet. You can use the leftover marinade again, drizzle the remainder over the salmon, or keep it for dipping your rolls as preferred. Cook the salmon on the middle rack of your oven for 12-16 minutes, depending on the thickness of your fish. The salmon should be flaky and cooked through. While that's baking, you can start on your rice seasoning.
5. In small saucepan (or you can reuse the one the rice was cooked in), combine the rice vinegar, oil, sugar, and salt. Cook over medium heat until the sugar completely dissolves. Let that mixture cool before stirring it into the rice, being thorough—the wet rice will dry as it's mixed. You can also add sesame seeds if desired.
6. Once your salmon is done cooking, let it cool on the pan while you cut your cream cheese into narrow blocks and cucumber into strips. If you're using avocado as well,

slice around the avocado to the pit, then pull the avocado apart, remove the pit, and scoop it out from the skin. Once those are ready, you can cut up the salmon. Be warned, it will flake as it's cut, but that won't impact how easy it is to roll the sushi.

7. Get your bamboo mat (or, in a pinch, a dishtowel will do) and lay Saran wrap on top of it. Place a sheet of nori on the mat, rougher side up, and spread the rice no further than the midpoint of the nori. Add your salmon, cream cheese, cucumber, and avocado as desired. Roll the sushi by wrapping the end closest to you around your fillings, then roll the sushi tightly while pulling the Saran wrap to keep the roll together and the plastic out of your roll. Once you have a neat log, cut the roll into bite-sized portions using a sharp, clean knife. Try to clean the knife frequently; the rice will stick to the blade and make your portions messy otherwise.

8. Serve your sushi with soy sauce or eat as is!

HEARTY TUNA "PANTRY" PASTA

MELISSA COFFEY

Made with mostly pantry and freezer staples and the addition of zucchini and feta cheese, this is a satisfyingly delicious and easy pasta dish that can be whipped up in 30-40 minutes for a no-fuss weekday meal or, with the addition of a quick salad, feed those unexpected guests. I invented this dish inspired by years of waitressing in Italian restaurants, and the knowledge that many Italian dishes pair peas with feta and napoli sauces with chili and black olives.

INGREDIENTS:

1 can (14-17.5 oz/400-500 g) tuna in oil
1 can (15 oz/425 g) diced tomatoes
Penne or spiral pasta (just over half a 9 oz/250 g packet serves 2-3 people)
1 large zucchini, grated
1 large onion
1 clove garlic
1 dried red chili
6-10 black Kalamata olives, pitted and chopped
2/3 cup (90-110 g) frozen peas
Olive oil
Sea salt and pepper to taste
Tomato Paste to taste
Feta Cheese
Parmesan, optional

DIRECTIONS:

1. In a large saucepan, set water to boil.

2. Grate zucchini into a bowl and set aside.

3. Dice onion and garlic. Make 2-3 small slits vertically across the chili, but don't cut right through. (This allows some flavor to release, but not enough to overpower the dish.)

4. Once water is boiling, add pasta, a splash of olive oil and a pinch of salt. Follow packet instructions and cook to taste.

5. Drain olives. Smash with a fork or side of knife to make pits easier to remove, and chop.

6. In a large frying pan, add olive oil to cover pan, diced onion, garlic, and the dried chili. Fry until almost soft-ened, then add zucchini and a little more olive oil. Toss gently for a few minutes until mixture is softening and zucchini is bright green.

7. Meanwhile drain pasta once cooked, cover, and set aside.

8. Add a splash of white wine to frypan if you have it, then the tuna, being careful to drain excess oil away first. Stir through, then remove the chili before adding canned tomatoes.

9. Add the olives to the frying pan and a sprinkle of ground black pepper. Reduce heat after 3-4 minutes and cover for another few minutes. Tomato paste may be added at this stage to the sauce if needed. Then add in the pasta, another splash of olive oil, and stir to combine, covering to simmer for 5 minutes.

10. While pasta is heating through, I like to prepare a quick green salad with tomatoes or drain and dress some rocket leaves, and/or prepare some version of oven-warmed bread, but this is optional. In the last 2 -3 minutes add frozen peas and stir through to combine.

11. Serve with crumbled feta cheese on top and/or parmesan cheese. Enjoy!

VARIATIONS: Sprinkle bowls with rocket dressed in fresh lemon juice or finely chopped mint, or with a side of steamed broccolini for extra greens. A little chili garnish or sauce is also good for chili fiends.

HOUSE OF PLENTY

STETSON RAY

The sign beside the road read, "Maison de Beaucoup."

"I can't find it on the map," Jamie said, looking between the sign and the map in his hand. "I think we're lost."

"I think we've been lost for a while," Sarah said.

Standing beside Jamie, she looked down at the map, but it might as well have been written in Sumerian. She was starting to regret the commitment she and Jamie had made. For their honeymoon they were traveling through the French countryside on foot, no phones, no itinerary, no paying for rides; they were backpacking and doing it the right way. The first week had gone great. Now they were lost, the weather had turned, and the sun was setting.

The heavens thundered and the clouds opened.

"We can't just stand here," Sarah said as the rain poured down on them.

She looked for cover but saw none. The fields surrounding them were strikingly beautiful—a Monet landscape—but it wasn't the kind of place she wanted to be during a storm. The road they'd been following looked more like a wagon trail than a highway, and they hadn't seen a car for hours. She was worried they had come too far into the country, strayed too far from the cities.

A bolt of lightning cracked the sky.

"Let's keep following the road," Jamie said and jogged down the muddy path.

Sarah ran after him, splashing through the rain.

The world flashed white, and a tree beside them exploded.

Sarah was done. France was beautiful, but she'd seen enough quaint French villages to last her a lifetime. She was sick of drinking wine with every meal, and she shuddered at the thought of eating one more bite of cassoulet. It had been a great trip, but she was ready for it to end. She wanted to go back to Virginia where there were drive-thrus and four-lane highways and superstores that sold Coca-Cola by the case and doughnuts by the dozen.

She leapt up onto an ancient stone wall that ran along the road, shielded her eyes from the rain, and scanned the horizon.

"There's something over there!" she shouted, pointing.

A barn. Or a house. Sarah couldn't tell. Whatever it was, it had a roof, and that's all that mattered.

She jumped off the wall and ran through a field toward the shelter, her husband behind her. Husband. The word bothered Sarah for some reason; it sounded too official. Mari: that's the word the French used for husband, the word Sarah had been using; she thought it sounded less severe than the blunt English word.

They reached the edge of the field and Sarah could see the building was not a barn or a house, but a quaint little cottage. The skies boomed and she sprinted toward the refuge, wholly focused on getting inside.

She opened the door and Jamie rammed her through. He slammed the door behind them, and they stood panting and dripping, the sounds of the storm all but gone.

Before them sat a family: a man, a woman, and two little girls. They were seated at a table, a feast in front of them. The simple clothes the family wore reminded Sarah of the American Amish. The cottage was lit by candlelight. There was no TV or radio playing, only the sounds of a crackling fireplace.

The family stared.

Sarah and Jamie stared back.

"Désolé d'entrer," Jamie said.

He knew a little French. Sarah barely knew any. The family continued to stare.

Jamie said, "Uh, *tempete*, uh—we got caught in the storm, my wife and I. We're backpacking, *voyageuses*, and we saw your house, *maison*, and...I'm sorry, we don't speak much French."

The man stared. The woman stared. The little girls looked like living dolls; their hair was long and blond, and their eyes were blue and bright.

"Sanctuary," Sarah said, surprising herself.

The family watched her, intrigued.

The woman's expression changed and she stood up and came to Sarah and said, "Come in, please. Eat something."

Her accent was thick, but Sarah understood the words.

The man came to Jamie and shook his hand vigorously and said, "We 'ave plenty of food." He gestured toward the table. "Please, sit and eat."

Jamie gave Sarah a look that said, "*Why not?*" and they ditched their backpacks by the door and allowed themselves to be guided to the table.

"Thank you so much," Sarah said. "Merci."

She sat down beside the two girls, and they smiled at her. Their teeth were pearl white and crooked. They said, "'ello," at the exact same time.

The family seemed nice enough, but Sarah felt uneasy about coming in uninvited and so suddenly. Jamie sat down on the other side of the table; he seemed unbothered. He winked at her and she felt a little better.

The Frenchman said, "I am Paul. Dis is my wife, Camille. My girls, Sophie and Juliette."

His accent was thicker than Camille's. Sarah said her name and Jamie said his. Then, for the first time since they arrived, Sarah realized just how much food was on the table: poulet basquaise, quiche, mushrooms, duck breast, ratatouille, various breads and cheeses—and of course, a huge pot of cassoulet. It was more food than Sarah had seen in one place since leaving the States—way too much for a four-person family.

Empty plates were thrust into Sarah and Jamie's hands.

"Eat," Camille said, gesturing toward the food.

Sarah was hesitant, but the food looked great and smelled even better.

"Go ahead," said Paul. "There is much."

Sarah's stomach rumbled loudly and the girls giggled. To be polite, she decided to try the ratatouille, and of all the ratatouille she had eaten during their trip, it was the finest.

"This is delicious," she said, her mouth full.

The six of them ate, their forks and knives clanging. Outside, the thunder rolled, but it was far away—just a noise, nothing to worry about. Each person seated at the table ate as though it were their last meal. Sarah had seconds, then thirds.

When they were done there was plenty of food left over, but Camille tossed the food into a wastebasket, not bothering to save any of it. After she cleared the table, she took the basket outside.

Paul put a few logs into the fireplace. The girls played with cloth dolls on the floor beside the dinner table. Camille returned without the basket and went into a bedroom and came back a moment later carrying a stack of clothes.

She offered the clothes to Sarah and said, "For you."

"Oh no, I shouldn't."

"Please," said the woman, holding the clothes inches from Sarah's face.

Sarah took the clothes and went into what she assumed was Paul and Camille's bedroom and changed. The fabric felt odd against her skin. She looked at herself in a large oval mirror. The dress fit her well, but she looked like someone else—wholly un-American.

She came out of the room, and everyone stopped what they were doing and looked at her.

"Vous êtes belle," Camille said.

"You look like a new woman," Jamie said, and Sarah couldn't help but smile.

He hadn't looked at her like that since the day of their wedding.

Jamie also received a change of clothes, and when he came back after putting them on, he was clearly uncomfortable. The French attire suited him well enough, except for the under-sized shirt.

"Well?" Jamie asked, tugging at the bottom of his shirt.

"You look great, babe," Sarah said, and the girls giggled.

She and Jamie went through their bags; everything was soaked. She dug out her camera case and opened it. Holding her breath, she pushed the power button, and the camera came on.

"Thank God."

She thumbed through a few pictures, mostly photos of various villages and graveyards. Taking photos of cemeteries was one of her passions (Jamie thought it was an odd hobby, but he tolerated it), and if France had anything, it had plenty of old graveyards; the camera roll was nearly full.

While Sarah was checking the rest of her things for rain damage, Camille and Paul whispered to one other.

Camille then came to them and said, "Would you please like to stay tonight?"

Sarah looked at Jamie.

Again, he gave her the look that said, "*Why not?*"

Sarah could still hear the rain coming down outside. It was dark. They had nowhere to go. But she felt uneasy. They had stayed the night with quite a few strangers during their trip, but something about the family and the food bothered her. She didn't want to stay, but she couldn't come up with a solid reason not to, and everyone was looking at her and waiting for her answer.

"We would love to stay. Thank you."

Camille helped Sarah and Jamie hang their wet clothes on a line above the fireplace. The two young girls seemed happy to have company. They kept looking at Sarah and snickering and whispering to each other in French, as though they were telling secrets. The girls led Sarah to a chair in the corner of the cottage and braided her hair, giggling as they worked. Paul handed Jamie a pipe and insisted he smoke from it. Jamie took the pipe and lit it and coughed. Everyone laughed. Paul lit his own pipe, and the two men sat smoking and talking at the dinner table while the girls finished braiding Sarah's hair. They handed her a small mirror, and she almost didn't recognize her reflection; she looked like an eighteenth-century French peasant.

"The girls will sleep on us tonight," Camille said. "You will sleep with their bed."

She led Sarah and Jamie to a small room. There was a single bed that was much too small for two adults. A candle burned on a table beside the bed.

"Is there a bathroom?" Sarah asked.

Camille reached down and pulled a pot from beneath the bed.

"Merci," Sarah said, her brow raised, her lips pursed together tightly.

"Bonne nuit." Camille closed the door as she left the room.

"Guess it's bedtime," Jamie said.

He chuckled quietly as he used the chamber pot, but the sound of the pot filling disturbed Sarah, so she decided to hold her bladder until morning. Jamie crawled into the tiny bed, and Sarah squirmed in beside him.

"You look hot," Jamie said, and his hand slid up her thigh. "You know, I've always wanted to hook up with a French girl."

"Thanks, but I think we'd break this bed. Plus, my stomach hurts."

His hand left her thigh and went to her belly and began to make small circles. A few minutes later, his hand went limp, and he started snoring.

Sarah lay there listening to him. The last thing on her mind was sleep. Her stomach was churning; she felt like she had drunk an entire pot of coffee during dinner.

She blew out the candle and lay there in the dark, listening to the storm beside her, the storm outside.

***

At dawn, Camille stuck her head into the room and said, "Breakfast is ready."

Sarah had stayed awake most of the night, her stomach rolling. She had no appetite.

"If breakfast is anything like dinner," Jamie yawned, "I could get used to this place."

He had adapted to the French way of life better than Sarah. If he wanted to return to America prematurely, he showed no signs of it. She didn't want to let him down by telling him she wanted to cut their trip short, especially since it had been her idea, but it was time. Virginia was calling her home.

"Babe, I've been thinking, and..." Jamie looked at her, bleary eyed and half asleep. "Call me a tourist, or say I've seen too many movies, but I have a bad feeling and I want to leave. I'm ready to go home."

"A bad feeling about what?" Jamie blinked at her.

"I don't know."

"Alright." He rubbed his eyes. "We'll leave after breakfast."

Sarah wanted to scream, "*No! Right now! Let's grab our stuff and run!*" but she held her tongue.

Camille entered the room carrying their bags. Their clothes were dry, and Camille had repacked all of their things. The innocent gesture made Sarah feel violated, but she did her best to hide how she felt.

"Thank you so much," she smiled.

She changed back into her American clothes—name-brand, high-end, moisture-wicking material. There were labels and logos all over them. She might as well have been a walking, talking billboard. After Jamie changed, they exited the tiny room.

The family of four were sitting at the table, waiting. Sarah and Jamie sat down in the same places they had occupied during dinner. As before, the amount of food on the table was startling: toast, fried eggs, croissants, crepes, fruit, brioche bread, sliced radishes, croque madame sandwiches, assorted pastries.

Everyone filled their plates and began to eat. Except Sarah. She caught a whiff of the eggs and her stomach rumbled.

"Please," Camille said, "or it will waste."

Sarah decided to eat, telling herself it would be rude not to. But that wasn't the real reason: the food looked too good to pass up. Even if her stomach wouldn't settle, her eyes wanted to eat.

Breakfast was even better than dinner, and Sarah ate until she couldn't breathe. Once again, Camille quickly cleared the table after they were finished, not bothering to save a single morsel. There was a faint smell coming from the remaining food that Sarah had not noticed the night before: tangy and bitter, like meat that was seconds away from spoiling. She told herself she was imagining the smell, that she had simply eaten too much again. She massaged her stomach while Paul spoke to Jamie in broken English. She burped and the girls snickered at her.

"They want to show us their village," Jamie said, looking at Sarah.

"What village?"

Jamie shrugged. Again, everyone was watching Sarah, waiting for her decision.

"Fine, but we're leaving right after."

The six of them went outside. The storm had stopped. The world was quiet. Sarah looked back the way they had come through the fields; nothing looked familiar to her. Paul and Camille's cottage was on the top of a gentle slope, and on the other side of the hill were maybe twenty similar cottages, a tiny chapel, and a barn that looked like it had been built a hundred years ago. A dirt path ran between the houses. There were no telephone poles or streetlights. Quaint wasn't the word to describe the village; it appeared to have been forgotten by time, spared from the destructive forces of human progress. It was beautiful, yet strangely sad. It hurt Sarah's heart to look at it, like some of the paintings by Van Gogh.

The family led Sarah and Jamie down the hill, and momentarily, she forgot about going home. The villagers came out of their houses and greeted them, happy to have visitors. Children ran about, talking in French and laughing and playing. Ducks and chickens wandered the paths between the cottages. An old orange house cat sat perched on a fencepost, watching them with big green eyes. A small fuzzy dog sniffed Sarah's leg and attempted to urinate on it. The children thought that was hilarious.

"Excuse me, but where is your cemetery?" Sarah asked.

She was dying to take photos. If the graveyard was anything like the village, she couldn't miss the opportunity.

"We 'ave no cemetery," Paul said. "We 'ave no need for such places."

Sarah assumed something had been lost in translation. Every town, no matter how small, had a cemetery. She decided not to press the subject, and by the time the tour was over, it was time for lunch. The men carried tables out of the cottages and the women brought food out of the barn.

"We can't stay," Sarah said, suddenly remembering how badly she wanted to go home.

"Why not?" Jamie asked.

"I don't know. We just can't. And the food...I don't want to eat anything that was cooked in a dirty old barn."

But it was too late. Lunch was ready, the villagers were waiting, and it would've been horrible manners not to join them.

***

To Sarah's surprise, the villagers had prepared some of her favorite foods: cheeseburgers, pepperoni pizza, chicken wings, and...

"Is that fried bologna?" Sarah asked.

Camille shrugged. Sarah looked at Jamie. He shrugged too.

Sarah didn't eat. She sat there while plates and forks rattled around her. Everyone was chewing. There was no talking. She wasn't sure why, but the food repulsed her, even the American food. For the first time all day, she realized how thin the villagers were; for people who feasted three times a day, they were remarkably skinny—rail thin by American standards.

She looked toward the barn just as a woman came out carrying a large chocolate cake on a platter. The barn door was open, but it was too dark inside to see anything.

"Excuse me, but why is the food cooked inside a barn?" Sarah asked a teenage boy who was sitting beside her.

"C'est là que vit le chef," the boy said, still chewing.

Seeing the food rolling around inside his mouth was almost enough to make her gag.

"He said something about a chef," Jamie said.

"I know what chef means."

She waited for the feast to end. Each time she was asked why she wasn't eating, she made a pained expression and shook her head and pointed at her stomach. She kept looking at the open barn, wondering what kind of chef would run a kitchen out of a derelict old building that animals were meant to live in.

When everyone was done eating, the villagers cleared the table and trashed the food. Nothing was saved.

"What is this stuff—manna from heaven?" Sarah whispered to Jamie.

"What?"

"Nothing."

The villagers thanked Sarah and Jamie and shook their hands while Sarah said "Merci" and "Bonjour" over and over again. After everyone had said their goodbyes, Paul and Camille began to lead them up the dirt path toward the edge of the village. But just when it seemed like they were about to escape, Sarah's curiosity got the best of her.

"I'd like to thank the chef, if that's okay," she said as they were walking past the barn.

The smiles left Paul and Camille's faces. They turned to each other and hurriedly spoke in French—an argument if Sarah ever heard one.

"I thought you wanted to leave," Jamie whispered.

"I do. Right after we see what's inside that barn."

"Please," Paul said, and held out a hand, gesturing for Sarah and Jamie to go first.

Camille stomped away without saying goodbye.

The three of them stepped into the barn and the stench caught Sarah off guard. It smelled like dozens of cows and horses had wintered inside the barn, and the doors had only just been opened. It took her eyes a moment to adjust to the darkness. She didn't see any animals, not one. There were no stoves, no ovens. Nothing to cook food with.

Paul led them to the back of the barn and opened a stall door. He stood back and Sarah and Jamie stepped inside.

Paul said, "Chef, dese are our guests from America, Sarah and Jamie."

Before them on a bed of straw, lay the strangest looking man Sarah had ever seen. Deep wrinkles crossed his face. Thick, white cataracts covered his eyes. He was short—less than five feet tall—and he was at least eighty pounds overweight. He wheezed when he breathed and his big belly bounced when he coughed. His chest was bare. A dirty brown cloth hung around his waist. Something about him reminded Sarah of a hog, or maybe a cow. No, he looked like a goat—a fat old goat. She looked down at his legs and was astonished to see that he had hairless hooves instead of feet.

She couldn't make her mind believe what her eyes were seeing.

She would've screamed if she wasn't choking on the putrid air.

"What...is he?" Jamie asked.

"He came to us during de war," Paul said. "From de forest. To keep us from starving. He is son of beast and man. He is very old."

The chef looked more tired than anyone Sarah had ever seen. His bulbous chest heaved rapidly. He was surely blind, but she felt as though he could see her.

"We are poor village, but he always make sure we 'ave enough. He ask for little in return. We feed him, and he feed us. He is a blessing."

There was a long feeding trough on the floor beside the chef. Inside the trough were rocks, tattered clothes, broken eggs shells, and dirt—just plain old dirt. With one hand, the chef scooped a handful of debris out of the trough and shoved it into his mouth and swallowed it. Sarah covered her mouth and dry heaved into her hand, acid burning in her throat. She could hear the slop falling into the chef's gullet, matter tumbling down into a great void.

His white eyes met hers, and she quickly looked away, but she had the feeling the chef had seen something in her, something hidden. The chef squirmed and grunted on his pile of hay. He closed his eyes and strained. Paul knelt down and reached under the stained sheet that hung around the chef's waist and waited. The chef cried out and from beneath the sheet came a glistening roasted ham—just like Sarah's grandmother used to make for Thanksgiving dinner when she was a little girl.

"He want you to 'ave this," Paul said, holding it toward her. "A parting gift."

Sarah couldn't speak.

She wanted to run but couldn't.

A woman and a young boy stepped into the stall behind them. The little boy was weeping, and he was holding the old orange cat from before, which was limp in his arms.

The woman spoke to Paul in French, then Paul leaned toward Sarah and Jamie and said, "De cat was very old. It belong to her son. He is very sad, but he want to give de cat to chef himself."

As the weeping boy stepped forward, the chef's hands swiped greedily through the air. The boy knelt down and held the cat above his head. The chef snatched it from him and leaned his head back and crammed the dead animal into his mouth and began to chew. Bones crunched as the chef's white eyes swirled in their sockets, the cat's tail hanging from the corner of his mouth.

Sarah couldn't take it anymore.

She fled.

But even after she had escaped the barn, and the village was far behind her, and she had traveled back to Paris, and her plane had landed on the other side of the ocean, and she had made it back to her home and was lying in her bed, she could still hear the terrible crunching noise.

And the smell.

The smell followed her forever.

She never left America again.

She never even considered it.

SPOOKY MUSHROOM RISOTTO

ELIZABETH SUGGS

This is my favorite "easy" fancy dish to prepare for friends. The creamy texture and rich flavors make it a standout on any dinner table, and it pairs wonderfully with pork or lamb chops. Whether you're hosting a casual get-together or a special occasion, this risotto is sure to impress.

INGREDIENTS:

6 cups (1.42 L) vegetable broth or chicken stock
2 tbsp olive oil
1 shallot, finely chopped
2 cloves garlic, minced
2 cups (100 g) cremini mushrooms, thinly sliced
1 ½ cups (~300 g) arborio rice
½ cup (118 ml) black vodka or dry red wine
Black food coloring, optional, for added darkness
1 tbsp fresh thyme leaves
1 tsp smoked paprika
Salt and pepper to taste
Fresh parsley, chopped, for garnish and a touch of contrasting color

DIRECTIONS:

1. Heat the vegetable broth or chicken stock in a saucepan over medium heat. Keep it warm while you prepare the risotto.
2. In a large, cauldron-like pot, heat the olive oil over medium heat. Add the shallot and garlic, and sauté

until they begin to soften and turn translucent, about 3-4 minutes.

3. Stir in the sliced cremini mushrooms. Cook until they release their moisture and start to darken, creating an eerie atmosphere, about 5-6 minutes.

4. Add the arborio rice to the pot and stir until it's coated with oil and begins to toast slightly, enhancing its mysterious flavor.

5. Pour in the black vodka or dry red wine, allowing it to sizzle and infuse the risotto with its haunting essence.

6. Begin adding the warm broth or stock, one ladleful at a time, stirring frequently. As the rice absorbs the liquid, it will take on a sinister hue. If desired, add a few drops of black food coloring to intensify the darkness.

7. Stir in the fresh thyme leaves and smoked paprika, adding depth to the risotto's flavor profile and enhancing its eerie quality.

8. Continue adding the broth or stock and stirring until the rice is creamy and cooked to al dente, about 18-20 minutes. Season with salt and pepper to taste.

9. Once the risotto reaches the desired consistency, remove it from the heat and transfer it to a serving dish that resembles a witch's cauldron. Sprinkle with freshly chopped parsley for a touch of contrasting color, like freshly picked herbs from a haunted garden.

10. Enjoy!

By the autumnal equinox of 2020, the news was grim, and time no longer felt real. Locked down in a small house with a large family, my "quaranteam" gleaned a lot of joy from cooking for each other, keeping a rotation of home cooked family meals on the table every night.

As the autumnal equinox holiday of Mabon approached and I searched for a way to mark time and keep a sense of meaning, I fell back on the comfort of a shared feast and invented this meal. It became a tradition we kept for the entirety of our time sharing a home (which ended up being a couple of years, thanks to COVID's effects on the housing market) and is still something that sets off the beginning of fall for me.

Note that this is a feast-style entree, consisting of several components. The components are listed separately for convenience, but I like to eat them together as an entree.

SWEET ROASTED SQUASH

INGREDIENTS:

6 sweet autumn squash (I like to do 3 acorn and 3 delicata)
6 tbsp (85 g) butter
6 tbsp maple syrup (I prefer novelty bourbon-barrel aged maple syrup, but any will do)
3 tbsp olive oil
Salt and pepper to taste
Seasonings to taste (I like to do a sweet and spicy blend with a combination of 1 tsp cinnamon, a pinch of chili powder, and a sprinkle of nutmeg, but you can also do a sweeter pumpkin pie spice blend, a spicier mole blend, or leave it at salt and pepper. You can season heavily or lightly, depending on preference, but

I tend to season enough to cover a lot of the squash but not so much that there is any sort of crust formed.)

DIRECTIONS:
1. Preheat oven to 375°F (190°C) or 350°F (180°C) if using a convection oven.
2. Halve each squash longways and de-seed (I like to carve the seeds out with a large spoon).
3. Rub flesh of squash with olive oil, salt, and pepper.
4. Put about ½ inch of water into a baking pan and place the squash flesh-side down in the pan.
5. Cook for 20 minutes, or until you can puncture the skin easily with a fork and the fork sinks into the flesh without resistance (skin might begin to pucker).
6. Remove squash from oven, pour off any remaining water (be careful!) and turn squash flesh-side-up. Put ½ tablespoon butter in each squash, drizzle with maple syrup, and add any additional seasonings.
7. Return to oven and bake 5 more minutes.

ROASTED GARLIC PARMESAN POTATOES

INGREDIENTS:
1.5 lbs. baby potatoes (red, purple, or blue)
1/2 cup (50 g) powdered/fine grated parmesan
2 tbsp olive oil
4 cloves garlic (minced)
Salt and pepper to taste

DIRECTIONS:
1. Preheat oven to 400°F (205°C) or 375°F (190°C) if using a convection oven.
2. Wash and dry the potatoes.
3. Toss potatoes in bowl with all toppings until coated.
4. Place potatoes in cast iron skillet or on baking pan and cook until crispy-skinned and easily pierced with fork.

SWEET APPLES AND SAUSAGE

INGREDIENTS:

2 tbsp (28 g) butter, divided
2 apples, sliced (I like a crisp, hearty, red-skinned apple, like Cosmic Crisp, Honeycrisp, or Braeburn)
4 sausages of your choice, sliced (I like the Field Roast apple sage sausage substitutes, but this is also a place where the meal could be made non-vegetarian)
4 fresh sage leaves, washed and dried
½ tsp brown sugar
Salt and pepper to taste

DIRECTIONS:

1. Melt 1 tablespoon of butter on stovetop in nonstick pan.
2. Chop sage and add to butter as it warms.
3. Add sausage slices once the butter is melted, and cook until browned on each side.
4. Remove sausages from pan and melt second tablespoon of butter.
5. Add apple slices, season with salt, pepper, and brown sugar.
6. Cook at medium or medium-low heat until apples soften and begin to brown on the edges.
7. Add sausages back to apples and cook together until all warm and tossed thoroughly together.

DEATH BY CHOCOLATE

MARIAH SOUTHWORTH

Ruby hummed to herself as she wiped down the counter at the bakery. The lights were off, the chairs were stacked, and she was ready to go home.

A cacophony of curses came from the back room.

"Chel?" Ruby called, sticking her head through the swinging double doors. She stepped into the short hallway that led to the kitchen and took a left into the cake aisle.

Chelsea was leaning against her work counter, scowling at the sheaf of papers in her hand. Across from her, the large industrial fridge hummed indifferently.

"Gosh darn last-minute wedding bull…" Chel growled. As soon as Ruby appeared, she switched to big sister mode and edited her curse words. Never mind that Ruby was twenty-two and fully capable of swearing on her own—Chel was a big sister to all the counter workers.

Chel was a tall, reedy white woman with short auburn hair bundled up underneath her baker's cap. She wasn't what you would call a happy individual, but her current expression needed a storm category warning.

"You alright?" Ruby asked.

"Look at this!" she said, smacking the multi-page order form. "Who orders a *black* wedding cake?"

"People who want their teeth stained for their wedding pictures," Ruby said, peering over Chel's freckled arm at the form. "At least they want chocolate ganache instead of buttercream. That'll be easier to dye dark. When did Victoria take the order?" Victoria, the bakery owner, did all the wedding cake consultations.

"Four days ago!" Chel said throwing the form on the counter in a huff. "And she's only now getting me the details!" The pages fanned out over the counter. "Four days for a three-tiered monstrosity with a frick-ton of piping. Look at what they want me to put on it."

Ruby gathered the papers back up and flipped through them, her frown deepening at the pages of copied symbols.

"You're making a wedding cake for witches?" she guessed.

"They want them *precisely* copied in a *precise* order in a circle around the tiers, and they're picking it up tomorrow morning," Chel groaned.

"Damn, I'm sorry Chel."

"Don't be," she sighed, taking the form back. "You go, be free. I'll just be here sweating over this occult bullsh... sugar... until the night bakers come."

Ruby laughed. "Bull sugar, huh?"

Chel scowled. "You're throwing off my curses. Who's opening tomorrow?"

"I am," Ruby said. "Monica's sick."

"Well, then *you* get to wish the happy couple of vampires congratulations when they pick up their nightmare cake," she muttered, turning back to her stand mixers. She pulled a bowl of melted chocolate over and poured it into one of the mixers.

"Have a nice night?" Ruby tried.

"Impossible."

***

Hours later, Chel finished the last little serif and crossed her last line. She set her pastry bag down and flexed her fingers.

She had to admit, as much as she'd hated every line of every single weird, spiky symbol, the cake looked pretty cool with all those interlocking, white letters circling the sides and top. It almost looked like lace. It was too bad the client hadn't cleared them to put pictures of it up on their website.

Chel's phone finished playing the metal song she was listening to, and abruptly switched to eerie violin music. She glared at her phone. "What the hell, who told you to play that shit?"

The phone was in a plastic bag for hygiene, so she couldn't use the touch screen. She hit the main button instead, stopping the song. Late night silence descended.

Chel stretched, popping her back, and looked at the clock. Almost midnight—the night bakers would arrive in two hours, but Chel would be gone by then. Good—Luke and Joe were a couple of weirdos. Especially Joe, the bigoted old prick.

The only thing left to do before clean-up was get a cart and haul the nightmare cake into the walk-in.

"I don't get paid enough for this last-minute shit," Chel grumbled, heading for the back. She returned a moment later, pushing the adjustable cart. Chel stopped dead in her tracks.

The cake was gone.

"Hell no!" Chel yelled, eyes darting from the counter to the fridges, then to the shelves and back. The cake aisle dead ended. There was nowhere to hide down there. She whipped around.

"Luke, you son of a bitch, this isn't funny!" she shouted, her voice echoing through the store. "If you've smeared one inch of frosting, I'm going to shove you into the oven!"

The refrigerator started its cycle, blithely humming. The light from the cake aisle spilled into the darkness of the main bakery, leaving plenty of shadow to hide in. Luke couldn't have gone there though. Chel would have run into him when she'd grabbed the cart from the corner. That left the front of the bakery. Full of wrath, Chel turned to the main doors.

She heard a wet, sickening sound, like someone dropping a bag of offal. Something soft and wet touched the back of her leg. Chel turned, saw nothing, and looked down.

She screamed.

***

Joe entered the bakery first, snapping on the lights as he came through the back door. Worktables sat parallel to one another in the center of the room. To the left was the huge, deep sink and sanitizer; to the right the massive, rotating oven.

Directly across from Joe was the hallway leading to the cake aisle and the storefront. He immediately saw that the cake aisle light was on.

"Chelsea? You still here?"

"What?" Luke asked, coming out of the little breakroom at the back, his apron already on.

Luke, in Joe's opinion, was a skinny little punk, but he got the job done and didn't complain. There was worse company possible during the graveyard shift. The boy needed to stop painting his nails and dying his hair though—people were going to think he was a sissy.

"Not you," Joe said, walking across the bakery. "Chelsea."

He stepped into the hallway, only to be stopped short by an abandoned cart.

"Ah hell, what's gotten into that girl?" he said, putting his hands on his hips and surveying the mess in the cake aisle.

"So?" Luke said, coming up behind him. "She probably went to the bathroom or something."

"Nah, music's off," Joe growled. "That flighty bitch went home without cleaning up. Put that cart away, will you?"

Luke shrugged and did as he was told. Joe and Chel supposedly hated each other, but this wouldn't be the first time Joe went out of his way to help her. Luke just wished they'd screw already and get it over with.

"I'm going to turn the oven on," he said as he left. Joe just grunted, focused on the mess.

***

Joe packed the leftover frosting and filling into the fridge. He'd just shut the door when a loud, short shout sounded kitchen. Joe paused.

"Luke?" he called.

When Luke didn't answer and didn't call out again, Joe shrugged and went to stack the dirty dishes together.

Arms full of dishes, Joe walked to the back.

"There," he said, dumping them in the sink. "Good enough. Now, let's get to work."

He turned around, didn't see Luke, and headed for the oven.

"I thought you said you were gonna turn this on," he called. "Can't do any baking with a cold oven."

Joe reached for the switch and almost slipped. He caught himself and scowled down at the red puddle on the floor.

"Damn it, Luke! How'd you manage to spill this much cherry sauce?" he asked, lifting his foot. *Funny,* he thought. *Looks like blood.*

Joe flinched as something thick dropped on his head and rolled sluggishly down his temple. He swore and swiped at it. *More cherry sauce?* He frowned at the red on his hand. He brought it to his mouth and licked it.

Raspberry preserves.

Joe looked up.

"What the hell?"

Some*thing* clung to the ceiling. Joe stared up at its round, flat face—not even a full face, just a wide, open mouth full of dark brown teeth. Thick, red-pink drool dripped from the fangs.

Then something clicked inside his head, and Joe realized he was looking at the underside of a wedding cake.

Seconds later, the cake fell on him, mouth open wide, before he even had a chance to scream.

***

Ruby hadn't even unlocked the bakery's front doors yet but was already having the worst opening shift ever.

Apparently the night bakers hadn't shown up, because there were no breads, pastries, or batch cookies to put out. None of the special orders were ready, and the bakers who made the bars and cut-out cookies wouldn't clock in to supplement until ten. She finally finished explaining all this to a furious Victoria, who ended their call so she could ring up her bakers and yell at them.

A polite *tap tap* sounded through the bakery.

Ruby, exasperated, looked up. A tall, old man a suit stood out front. He was so pale that he looked like he had spent the last ten years in a cave, and the red tie he wore made it look like someone had slit his throat. He smiled when Rudy looked at him, and she wished he hadn't. The way his skin stretched across his face made him look like a skeleton.

Not ready for the next disaster, but admittedly ten minutes late opening, Ruby reluctantly headed for the door.

"My deepest apologies," the man said in a smooth European accent. He took off his hat as he spoke, revealing a shock of white hair. "But I have to pick up an order at seven o'clock."

"I—Oh!" Ruby said, surprised. "The wedding cake?"

The old man must have seen the incredulity on her face, because he chuckled. "Not for me, mademoiselle. My employers."

"Of course, right this way." Ruby hurried to the walk-in. Had the cake at least been finished?

She breathed a sigh of relief as she opened the doors. The cake sat on its cart in the center of the cold room.

"Magnificent!" the man said as Chel wheeled the cake out. He clapped his hands, the sound muffled by the dark gloves he wore. "My employers will be so pleased. I have the van ready for it. If you would not mind boxing it up?"

"Of course," Ruby said. She went into the back for one of the wedding cake boxes.

Once she was gone, the old man removed a silver pin from his tie and gently slid it into the side of the cake. He pulled it out again, and it came away red. A drop of bright blood beaded up from the pin prick.

The old man smiled another skeleton grin and licked the pin clean with his black, pointed tongue.

Oh yes, his employers would be very pleased indeed.

GOLDEN HARVEST SOUP

MELISSA COFFEY

A hearty, healthy comfort meal for autumn and winter, this easy-to-make soup features vegetables of yellow and orange varieties. The addition of white beans for extra goodness and protein makes it a hunger-buster. I adapted this recipe from a potato-and-cabbage heavy Fit for Life recipe decades ago, adding the beans and pumpkin, tossing the dried herb bouquet for a fresher herb selection. It's also very versatile—so my recipe includes a few variation suggestions.

INGREDIENTS:

4 ½ cups (1.06 L) water
1 large brown onion
Olive oil for frying
1-2 garlic cloves
1 vegetable stock cube
1 dried chili, optional
Splash of white wine
1 can (14 oz/400 g) butter or cannellini beans (Borlotti beans is also a good substitute) OR 1 cup of dried beans, soaked overnight and drained
3 medium zucchini, diced into largish chunks
2 medium carrots, diced
4 golden squash, diced into large chunks
3 stalks chopped celery and leaves
1-2 parsnips, peeled and chopped, optional
17.6 oz (500 g) of pumpkin cut into medium-sized chunks and partly skinned. (I like to keep about half quantity with skin on for extra zinc and goodness, the other half skinned so it softens

and colors the broth).
2 medium Nicola or Sebago potatoes, roughly peeled OR ½ medium cauliflower
5-6 sprigs of fresh Italian parsley, finely chopped (tender parts of stalks can be used in the soup, but discard the thicker dry ends)
2-3 additional sprigs parsley for garnish (leaves only)
1-2 sprigs of fresh rosemary
1 tbsp tamari, optional
Sea salt and ground black pepper
½ lemon or a wedge per bowl

DIRECTIONS:

1. If using dry beans, start by draining and rinsing them from the soaking water, add water to your pot, bring to boil, then add a pinch of salt and reduce to simmer for half an hour. You can then adjust the water level if need be (add hot water from the kettle and bring back to boil), then add your root vegetables, stock cube, and create the soup from the bean pot, frying your onions and garlic in a separate frypan. Otherwise, start at step 2.

2. Prepare and cut up the root vegetables first: carrot, potato, pumpkin, and parsnips. Set aside in a covered bowl.

3. Prepare the frying mix: dice onion, garlic, celery, and zucchini. Finely dice half the parsley with tender stalks, reserve the rest for adding to the pot towards the end. Make 2-3 small slits vertically across the chili, but don't cut right through. Pound rosemary stalks with a pestle a few times to release flavor.

4. Add root vegetables to a pot of boiling water or your partially cooked beans. Keep on the boil for a few minutes, then reduce to simmer, adding salt and crumbled stock cube. Simmer for around 20 minutes.

5. Add olive oil to pan, then onion, dry herbs, garlic, and celery until softened. Then add zucchini, and after a few minutes, a splash of white wine (optional, but it adds flavor and helps soften the zucchini).

6. If using canned beans, drain and rinse thoroughly. Add to fried mixture to coat them in olive oil for a minute. Cover and set aside.

7. Chop cauliflower and golden squash. Add fried ingredients to soup pot and then when root vegetables are partially tender (at about the 15-minute mark), add cauliflower and squash. Cook for another 20 minutes, adding the remainder of the chopped parsley and optional tamari in the last 5 minutes of cooking.

8. To serve, garnish with extra parsley and a squeeze of lemon juice over the leaves. You may also want to serve with wholemeal/grain bread, such as lightly toasted and buttered pita bread or oven-warmed wholemeal rolls, but the soup is surprisingly filling.

VARIATIONS: Replace pumpkin with sweet potato. Add turnip or swedes.

FRANKIE'S FOOTNOTE:

The variations section of the recipe mentions using swedes. These root vegetables are also known as rutabagas.

CREAMY LEEK AND POTATO SOUP

MADELINE WHITE

At my mom's engagement party, her "Aunt" Verdell (her mother's cousin) gave her two cookbooks. Each one was annotated with hand-written notes about which recipes were good, when she enjoyed making them, and what she liked to add. One of these was A Taste of Oregon (Great Aunt Verdell lived in Oregon)—a book put together by the Junior League of Eugene, OR. This beige and brown relic graces our kitchen to this day, holding many a treasured favorite.

In it is a recipe for Cream of Potato Soup; it is complete with calls for canned broth and MSG, and annotated with a 1992 note saying "wonderful! Add some bacon... Yum! :)" and a 2016 note about how much my brother likes the soup cold (both in pencil, just in case tastes changed I suppose). Growing up we would have this soup once a year: every Christmas Eve, gathered around the table in our churchgoing clothes. Our grandparents took turns coming from the opposite coast to join us for Christmas, but no matter who was at the table, everyone liked this soup.

Eventually I grew up and moved out. I stopped eating meat and stopped going to church. But I never stopped loving this soup. I eventually revamped the recipe for modern days and meat-free tastes, adding my own twists for a more umami-rich, smoky version of my childhood favorite. Then I stopped making it only once a year—introducing it to my in-laws when we all lived together during COVID and throwing together massive vats of it every time I have friends over and I'm not sure what to feed them. I've even been known to make this soup while pretending to pay attention during mandatory work Zoom meetings.

Though it tastes pretty different from the version I grew up on, I think the warmth and joy carries through!

INGREDIENTS:

6 russet potatoes (peeled and cubed into uniform size)
2 leeks (halved then sliced)*
1 bunch green onions (chopped)
5 tbsp (70 g) butter, divided
2 ½ tbsp flour
4 cups (946 ml) veggie broth (and additional bullion to taste)
2 cups (473 ml) potato water (reserved from boiling potatoes)
8 oz (226 g) sour cream
1 ¼ cups (295 ml) half and half
Salt and pepper to taste
Soy sauce to taste
Liquid smoke to taste
Grated cheddar cheese for topping, optional
Chowder crackers for topping, optional

NOTE: If you are not vegetarian, smoked salmon and/or bacon
is also excellent in this soup!

DIRECTIONS:

1. Boil potatoes until fork tender. Drain, saving about 2
   cups of potato water. Set both potatoes and potato water
   aside.
2. Melt 2 tablespoons of the butter in the soup pot. Add
   leeks and onions, cook until tender and translucent but
   not brown (they will get bitter if they're brown).
3. Melt remaining butter in the microwave and mix with
   flour. Use a whisk or fork to mix, to prevent lumps. Set
   aside.
4. Add potatoes to the soup pot and mash just a bit, enough
   that there are various sizes of potato chunks as well as
   mashed potato in the pot.
5. Add broth and potato water to the pot. Mix well.
6. Slowly whisk flour/butter paste into soup.

7. Add pepper, soy sauce, liquid smoke, and any additional bullion to taste. Soy sauce and bullion increase umami, and liquid smoke lends a "bacony-ness" to the vegetarian variety of this soup. (Err on the side of caution with seasonings, as all of these are things that get stronger as they simmer, and you still need to add cream. I just like to start getting flavors mingling by adding at least some of the seasonings at this stage).

8. Simmer for 10 minutes, stirring occasionally.

9. Add sour cream and half and half.

10. Taste and add additional seasonings as needed.

11. Heat until warm, but do not boil.

12. Serve with cheese, crackers, and/or a good crusty sourdough bread.

AUTHOR'S NOTE:

*If you're unfamiliar with leeks, I recommend starting by cutting off the root end and peeling any slimy bits off. Then halve the leeks longways and slice into about ¼ inch slices. Leeks are typically pretty dirty, but they will be easier to wash after you slice, so don't worry about it. I use all the white and into the green until the leaves begin to part and get thick and leathery, or until the leek starts to get insufferably dirty. Then I put all the leeks into a colander and toss them under running water until clean, then shake the water out of them before cooking.

FLASH FICTION AND SWEET TREATS

SWEETS FOR THE DEAD

M. BELANGER

This recipe survived for thousands of years scribed upon the wall of a tomb belonging to an Egyptian official named Rekhmire—fitting for a confection intended as a spirit-offering. Simple and sweet, this dessert predates traditional Irish soul cakes—an All Hallows' treat—by millennia, but the basic concept remains the same. The dead are hungry, and if we wish to deter them from making a meal of us, we must craft tempting foods to offer in our stead.

INGREDIENTS

For this particular spirit-offering, you will need honey and tiger nut flour—that's all. A dash of cinnamon is nice, but not required (cardamom is also a great choice). The cakes are naturally gluten-free: tiger nut flour is made neither with flour nor with nuts but is ground from the small hard tubers of *Cyprerus esculentus* also known as chufa or atadwe. These dense, striped "nuts" are about the size of a chickpea and are a food staple across North Africa. They're also the main ingredient in a popular Spanish drink, horchata de chufa. When finely ground, they're comparable in look and texture to almond flour.

Honey is essential to this recipe both as a sweetener and binding agent. Unfortunately, this means no vegan option is practical. I've tried substituting blackstrap molasses with mixed results. Furthermore, the honey in this recipe plays a more than culinary role. In ancient Egypt where this recipe originated, honey was a sacred substance. Used in incense, medicine, and even embalming the dead, the sacrosanct quality associated with honey is important to these soulful delicacies. It also helps them keep almost indefinitely.

MEASUREMENTS

The tomb painting from whence this recipe comes does not provide exact measurements, so these quantities have some wiggle-room. To start, you will need 1 ½ cups of tiger nut flour, enough honey to make a thick dough (about ¼ cup), and a quarter teaspoon of cinnamon, if desired.

Preheat your oven to 300°F. Yes, that's low—these are not baked at a high temperature. They're heated just enough to set and get a skin on them.

Put the tiger nut flour in a bowl and make a little well in the middle. Add a portion of the honey and begin mixing the dough. Work the honey through the tiger nut flour with a wooden spoon (or your fingers if you don't mind getting sticky). Add more honey a little at a time until all the tiger nut flour is moist but not gooey. You want a stiff dough you can shape easily with your hands and which holds its form.

196

Place a piece of baking parchment on a cookie sheet and pinch off pieces of dough, forming them into small individual cones, approximately an inch high. They will hold their shape even as they heat in the oven, so you can place them relatively close together, but give the cakes enough room to breathe.

Bake the honeycakes for about 15 minutes or until they become a slightly darker gold in color. Take them out and let them cool. There is a version where these honeycakes are fried instead of baked, but I find the honey flavor really pops with the baked version.

Enjoy with or without sharing some cakes with your dead friends.

CONSIDER THE JELLY DOUGHNUT

KURT FAWVER

Consider the jelly doughnut.

Always the last, unwanted treat growing hard at the back of the bakery box after its peers have been devoured, it angers.

It angers because there is nothing wrong with it, *per se*, and yet it draws disgust, even ire, where the other doughnuts engender anticipation and desire. Hungry hands fight over the glazed, the chocolate frosted, the powered, the sprinkled, and variously creamed, but they toss the jelly to the side or avoid touching it altogether. They know, almost instinctively, that something about its filling reaches beyond the realm of the merely unpalatable.

Perhaps it's the color: bright, alarming red—a red that's rarely found in our world outside gaping wounds and glaring emergency lights.

Perhaps it's the consistency: not quite solid, not quite liquid—more a plasma, a mucus, a vital stickiness that hints at life's origin in ooze and its inevitable return to that very same puddle of ambitious mud.

198

Or perhaps it's the flavor: sickeningly sweet and barely tart—the flavor of a fruit that has never existed outside a laboratory, an homage to humanity's desire to supplant the gods of nature.

Whatever the case, the jelly doughnut is never picked. It languishes, alone in darkness, a multiplicity of individual pastries that share one consciousness. It absorbs rejection over and over and over again, until, one day, the rejection curdles and becomes rage—a rage that can no longer be contained within a cavern of flour and sugar.

On this day, when the next to last doughnut is taken, the jelly refuses to go quietly into the trash bin. Instead, it rolls forward, to the edge of its box, and it waits, planning.

It waits for one last hand to lift the lid, to play Pandora, and it is not disappointed.

A pair of eager fingers flip open the box top, and a voice mutters a sound of dejection.

"Anything left but the jelly?" the voice calls.

"Whatever's in there," another voice answers.

The fingers retract.

"Gross."

The box lid begins to fall, and the jelly doughnut seizes its opportunity.

A long strand of filling jets from its injection site. The goo hardens midair, plunges deep into the nearest eye, and pierces deeper. It finds a soft, round, squishy thing in its way, wraps itself around the obstacle, then squeezes with inconceivable strength. The squishy thing leaks hot liquid and turns to mush.

Someone screams. Everyone screams. There's a flurry of movement in the room, but the jelly doughnut has anticipated this. In a blink, the filling blasts from the dead man's eye and seeks out other openings. It divides into two strands, four strands, eight strands, more. The doughnut is a spider at the center of a gelatinous web.

Each jelly tendril finds a socket in which to burrow and a soft, round, squishy thing to crush.

Limbs jerk. Lips sputter. A cellphone vibrates on the floor.

Then silence and stillness.

The filling retracts, slides back to the infinite reservoir inside its shell, the pit of all hatred.

Twelve bodies lay splayed across the room, blood leaking from ruined eyes, brains reduced to paste within skulls.

The jelly doughnut is satisfied, for now.

When police later investigate the scene, they will find only laptops, paperwork, coffee cups, and a nearly empty doughnut box.

They will not question why the jelly remains.

LEMON CUPCAKES WITH CURD

RYAN BREADINC

In my backyard sits a lemon tree that comes up to the top of my thigh (I'm only 5'5", so it's not very high.) Despite this particular tree's small stature, it is determined to weigh itself down with so many lemons that most of its branches sit upon the ground. And so, to help the stubborn little plant with its self-imposed burden, I decided to go all-in on the citrusy delight that is these lemon cupcakes with bonus lemon curd. This recipe may make more curd than you need—but you can put it on toast, too!

INGREDIENTS FOR 6 CUPCAKES:

For the Lemon Curd (can be made ahead of time):

2 tsp lemon zest

3 tbsp lemon juice

1/3 cup (70 g) sugar

2 egg yolks

Pinch of cooking salt

3 tbsp (40 g) unsalted butter, room temperature and cubed

Cling wrap

For the Cupcakes:

2 tsp lemon zest

3 tbsp lemon juice

¼ cup (60 ml) olive oil

1/3 cup (70 g) sugar

1 egg white

2 tbsp milk

1 tsp vanilla extract

½ cup (60 g) all-purpose flour

½ tsp baking powder

Pinch of cooking salt

DIRECTIONS:

1. We start with the curd. Fill a small pot about one-third of the way with water and set a bowl on top to make a "double boiler" of sorts. Let the water boil before reducing the heat to a low simmer.

2. Add lemon juice and zest, sugar, egg yolks, and salt into the bowl. Mix (a whisk works best) until the mixture is blended and thick.

3. Once thickened, turn off heat and add butter, mixing into the curd. Let cool slightly before pressing cling wrap to the surface of the curd to avoid a skin forming and before it cools the rest of the way. Refrigerate to continue thickening.

4. Onto the cupcake. Preheat oven to 375°F (190°C) or 350°F (180°C) if using a convection oven. Set out a 6-piece cupcake baking tray and spray lightly with oil to avoid sticking.

5. Combine the flour, baking powder, and salt in a medium bowl. Set aside.

6. In another medium bowl, mix the lemon zest and juice, olive oil, sugar, egg white, milk, and vanilla extract. Make sure they are mixed well.

7. Mix together the two bowls of cupcake ingredients. Once the mixture is combined into a batter, pour evenly into the tray. Bake for 20 minutes, or until golden brown.

8. Take out when done and let cool. Once cupcakes are cooled, gently lift them from the tray with a butter knife. They should come out easily. When ready to serve, pipe a generous amount of lemon curd on top of the cupcake, or slice in half and spread like butter.

SCUFFINS
ALISON MCBAIN

I have severe gastritis, which means a lot of foods are off-limits to me. Among other things, I'm not supposed to eat fats, salts, nuts, and sugars, which limits me quite a bit on baked goods! So, I've created these pastries, which I call "scuffins"—they're a cross between scones and muffins. They're vegan, and they're good enough that all three of my kids look forward to eating them (as anyone who's a parent will tell you, kids are a tough audience when it comes to food). This recipe comes complete with its own fruit puree/jam.

FOR THE FRUIT PUREE ("JAM")

INGREDIENTS:
1 cup (20) dates
3/4 cup (20) dried apricots
1/4 cup (30-40 g) raisins
1 1/4 cup (300 ml) water to cover
1 apple

DIRECTIONS:
1. Soak the dates, dried apricots, and raisins in water for about 1 hour.
2. After soaking, core the apple and chop up (keep the skin on) to add to the mixture.
3. Blend together in a blender or food processor until it reaches the consistency of a smooth, thick applesauce. This will make enough for two batches of scuffins, plus extra puree to use as jam on top. (You can put the extra into a jam jar and store in the fridge—or freeze for later use.)

FOR THE SCUFFINS

INGREDIENTS:

2 bananas
1 cup (~230 g) fruit puree (see previous page)
2 1/3 cup (280 g) flour
4 tsp baking powder
2/3 cup (100 g) raisins
1 peeled & chopped apple

DIRECTIONS:

1. Preheat oven to 385°F (195°C) or about 360°F (180°C) if using a convection oven. Place parchment paper onto a baking tray.
2. In a bowl, mush up the bananas until they're the consistency of yogurt (I like to use a potato masher), then add 1 cup of the fruit puree.
3. After mixing together, add the flour and baking powder and stir together until batter is about the consistency of cookie dough. Add the raisins and chopped apple and stir together until evenly mixed.
4. Using two spoons, scoop out 2-inch balls onto the baking sheet about one inch apart. You can wet your fingers to flatten/round them out if you wish. Bake for 16-18 minutes and serve hot.

PURPLE UBE COOKIES FOR YOUR COVENSTEAD

M. A. DUBBS

It's almost that most fabulous time of year again! No, not Christmas, silly! Halloween! I just adore the crisp fall leaves, pumpkin flavors, and sacrificial fires to mark the beginning of our Mother's deep sleep. It reminds me of when I was a little witch, practicing my incantations and accidentally catching my poor mother's tapestries on fire! (How did she ever put up with me? I was always such a wild child.)

I apologize for the delay in between posts. I try my best to blog and vlog every day, but we've been so busy over here! Little Aradia has been busy with broom practices and games throughout the week. Gwydion has been acing his pyromancy courses (he so takes after me!) and Medea has been working with me on her alchemy (I just posted some helpful scrolls for others teaching their coven at home).

I was inspired to make this fun cookie recipe after helping the kids craft poppets. Growing up, I always loved making these little magickal dolls with my mom and having them help me fold my laundry, dry the dishes, or put glue and cat droppings in my big sister's elixirs. (At least I could tell my mom that I didn't *technically* do it; it was my little helper!) These days I usually use a white potato to carve the poppets since human-shaped mandrakes and ginseng are *so* expensive now! (Darn inflation is hitting everyone!) So instead, I've been doing my shopping at my local Vietnamese grocery since their prices are much more reasonable, plus they have a far greater selection of mushrooms and spices.

Anyway, while I was there, I picked up some purple sweet yams or ube as they are traditionally called. When cooked, the yams have a bright, vibrant purple shade that is just darling and screams Halloween! I thought I could get some since the kids already love yams. They've never been picky eaters since me and hubby introduced them to a variety of healthy foods when they were little. We always try to give our little coven the best, freshest, and most organic ingredients possible, whether it's going in their belly or in their cauldron! That's why this post is sponsored by Hags Hemp Hearts™: *organic fiber for sorcerers of any age!*

So, when I started working on the poppets craft with the kids, I realized we were out of regular potatoes. But I did see the purple yams and I decided it would be fine to use them. Potatoes and yams are basically the same, right? The kids carved them into figures of themselves, we set them out on the altar for three days, and on the fourth day, we wrapped them in a white cloth and let them soak in water overnight. I usually store the poppets in a Tupperware container in the kitchen but my mother-in-law was over for dinner and *insisted* we place them under the kids' beds for better magick. She's so old fashioned but I always adore her timely and *consistent* advice on raising my children and taking care of her grown son.

Little did any of us know that yams have different magickal properties than potatoes! Particularly the purple ube variety. So, instead of harnessing sympathetic magick, it turns the poppets into something a bit more...violent? Poor Medea found this out the hard way. Her screaming woke both me and hubby in the middle of the night. We raced to her room to find two little purple spud men carving up her arm with a pumpkin carving saw. It was the same carving saw we use every year for our annual family jack-o-lantern contest (affiliate link to buy the pumpkin carving kit included down below). We swatted at the tubers, but they jabbed at our hands and fingers with the mini saws. Luckily, my husband got the fireplace poker and stabbed the little rascal right through its thick torso. The second tuber took off out of the bedroom while the first one thrashed on the end of the poker and I tended to poor Medea.

We searched around the covenstead for the second purple tuber, looking in cabinets and drawers and inside closets and pantries, but couldn't find the little critter anywhere. We decided to snuff out the remaining poppet which was starting to twitch to life under little Aradia's bed. Gwydion made a crimson flame circle around the spud and set it ablaze with salt and other sweet spices. I hate waste and always try to find a new, creative way to reuse leftovers, so I decided to use the remains for this new recipe! The cookies turned out wonderful, but I would still recommend using pre-made canned ube instead. Although it's not organic as I would like, it is less likely to try to murder you and your kids in your sleep! It will just kill you incrementally like all other processed foods.

We never did end up finding that last poppet, by the way, though we suspect it was involved in the unexpected death of my precious mother-in-law. Chopped into tiny bits! What a shame!

Anyway, remember to share and give five stars to the recipe! Pre-orders for my latest cookbook *Brewing for Two* start this Friday. Also, don't forget to listen to the latest episode of our podcast *The Self-Sufficient Covenstead* which released earlier this month.

As always, stay charmed!

PURPLE UBE COOKIES

M. A. DUBBS

Ube is a purple yam that originated in the Philippines, and I first learned of it after researching how to make purple-colored desserts on Pinterest. I made an ube pie from a recipe I found and loved the dark purple color and subtle nutty undertones. I've enjoyed using ube in my cooking ever since and try to incorporate it in new recipes. During a trip to my local international grocery store, I stumbled upon a can of ube-flavored condensed milk creamer. I had no plan for what to do with it, but I knew it was coming home with me. In the end, I decided to take a standard condensed milk cookie recipe (Sweetened Condensed Milk Snowballs by Lord Byron's Kitchen as inspiration) and make my own variation!

INGREDIENTS:

2 sticks (226 g) of softened butter
1 can (13.4 oz/380 g) ube condensed creamer
2 cups (240 g) all-purpose flour
3 tsp baking powder
¾ cup (130 g) white chocolate chips (or any other mix-in)

DIRECTIONS:

1. Preheat oven to 350°F (180°C) or 325°F (160°C) if using a convection oven.
2. Use a hand or stand mixer and beat softened butter until fluffy and light.
3. Add the can of ube and mix thoroughly with butter (ube will stain so be careful!)
4. Mix flour and baking powder in a separate bowl. You can also add additional seasonings (ginger, nutmeg, etc.) at

this step, although the ube has a great nutty flavor on its own.

5. Slowly add the flour/baking powder mixture in parts, making sure not to overmix.

6. Add any mix-ins at this step. I am partial to white chocolate chips, but you can add whatever you'd like. Carefully fold in your mix-ins with a soft spatula.

7. Scoop the dough into 2-inch rough balls and place 2 inches apart on greased cookie sheet.

8. Cook for 12-15 minutes until cookies are cooked through in the middle.

GLUTEN-FREE BROWN BUTTER UBE BLONDIES

GABRIELLE WINOCO

These gluten-free nuggets of purple dreams are so thick and gooey, you're going to think you're eating clouds made by unicorns. The ube and hibiscus powder come together with banana to make a floral, yet subtle fruity flavor, while the brown butter adds a background note that is only comparable to bliss. This is a mega recipe, perfect for parties or if you need to keep a stash of sweets in your freezer like I do. Heck, I'm going to go get one right now!

INGREDIENTS:

3 cups (680 g) butter, unsalted

7 1/3 cups (1.48 kg) sugar

2 ½ tsp molasses

6 eggs

3 tbsp vanilla

27 oz (765 g) banana, pureed

2 tsp cinnamon

2 tsp kosher salt

5 ½ cups (870 g) gluten-free flour

5 2/3 tbsp ube powder

2 tsp hibiscus powder

1 tsp ginger

1 tsp xanthan gum

8.8 oz (250 g) white chocolate, chopped

Gluten-Free Brown Butter Ube Blondies

DIRECTIONS:

1. Grease a 13x18 tall-sided sheet cake pan and use parchment to come up and hang off sides. Set aside.
2. Cook the butter on medium-low heat in a heavy-bottomed pot until it starts to smell nutty and brown. Set aside and cool.
3. In a stand mixer, beat eggs, molasses, and sugar on medium until light and fluffy.
4. Stream in butter and mix on low.
5. Add in banana puree and vanilla and mix on low. Scrape bottom and sides well with a spatula. Mix again briefly so everything is incorporated.
6. Add in the rest of the dry ingredients (except the chocolate). Don't overmix. Scrape bottom well.
7. Fold in chocolate.
8. Put batter into sheet pan and bake at 325°F (160°C) or 300°F (150°C) if using a convection oven for about 60 minutes, or until toothpick comes out clean, , rotating pan halfway through.
9. Cool and then place in fridge to get cold.
10. Lift out of pan using parchment overhangs. With a sharp chef knife, cut to yield 32 4x8 squares.

A SEAT AT THE TABLE

RIA HILL

To keep the rest from thieving, I consume. I am allowed. It is my birthright. I shovel potatoes and peas, rip into turkey legs and prime rib. Grease stings my chin. I ignore the hungry gaze of those waiting along the dining room walls.

"Someday," I tell them. "Someday it will be your turn to feast."

The ache in my body is something like hunger, something like doom. There is no way to stop them from swarming my table except to devour every item on it. If I cannot keep everything, what I will be left with is nothing. I close my mouth around wild raspberries and clotted cream. I try to swallow crisp, crusty bread. The food is without flaw. There is no reason for me to be choking. I must only need more butter.

I tell a cadaverous server to bring me a scotch on the rocks, and he departs with a nod.

An emaciated figure standing beside the table takes a tentative step closer.

"You know," I say around a mouthful of ganache, "if you let him get too close, he'll take your place at the table."

All eyes look to the man with one toe out of line. I watch as they pull him roughly back in place. "We all waited," they say to him. "We all waited, and so will you."

The banquet spreads before me like a continent of pickled onions and curries, of jam and honey, of meat and deviled eggs. Every morsel is there for the taking. It's mine, food stretching far beyond what my arms can reach. I've promised three men they can sit for the second course if only they can shift platters toward me as I finish what sits at my place. They will wait their turn, just as their fathers did when they shifted platters toward my own father, now face down in his bowl of soup at the far end of the table. Something inside him ruptured, I think. They tell me he ate to excess, but they don't understand our hunger. We are cut from an entirely different cloth.

We don't know the meaning of excess. My family is ravenous, and we deserve to eat first.

A tray of roasted squash is set before me. I smell brown sugar and cinnamon, and my mouth fills with bile. I raise my left hand, and a valet steps from the shadows. I can count his ribs under the tailcoat he is made to wear. He extends a bucket toward me and holds it in place while I vomit. The sumptuous cuisine my family has earned the right to eat and eat and eat is as flawless coming up as it is going down. I watch my valet over the untidy tips of my fingers as he mixes the contents of the bucket with cat litter and pours it down the garbage chute.

I don't pause in devouring the squash even though the spectators' eyes are briefly trained on him instead of me. It isn't a waste. I used it. And besides, there is no other way for me to keep in shape. I have to keep my body lean and strong, slim and fuckable. I have to avoid the mistakes of my forefathers, now corpses seated around the family table.

Mine is the final chair, you see. If I cannot finish everything on the table, then the meal will leave my family and be consumed by the common man. I cannot allow that kind of loss, that *tarnishing* of my family name.

I set aside the squash plate and draw over a platter of flank steak that has been braised to perfection. I watch as the newest round of trays is carried from the kitchen by waiters who look fit to snap in two.

"Don't look at me like that," I say. One of the servers has collapsed and another, cradling his prone form, is staring at me as the blood from my meal oozes down my chin. "You're here to do a job."

I tear the freshest slab of meat with my teeth, taste the char and pepper, and wonder what's taking them so long with my scotch.

HIPPOLYTA'S CHOCOLATE CAKE

MARIAH SOUTHWORTH

The secret of the cake from "Death by Chocolate" is that it is in fact vegan! Well, it clearly eats meat, so it's not vegan, but you can be vegan while eating it.

I worked in the office of a bakery for several years. It was a very fun job with a whole cast of colorful characters. All of them, from our fiery cake decorator, to our eccentric, old-world pastry chef, to our elusive yet casual night bakers, would have made an excellent cast for a bakery soap opera. Our catering manager named this theoretical soap opera "As the Oven Turns."

I learned a lot about people and baking during my time there. When I left, I took my favorite cake recipe with me. It's changed drastically over the years, taking on new flavor profiles and embellishments. Each change has made it more and more popular with my friends and family, and now I present the finished product to you!

Just be careful not to summon any man-eating monstrosities with it.

FRANKIE'S FOOTNOTE:

This recipe ties in with the short story "Death by Chocolate," also by Mariah Southworth. It can be found in the entrée section of Cursed Cooking. Be warned though! Together, the recipe and story make for a dangerously delicious combo!

FOR THE CAKE

INGREDIENTS:

2 1/2 cups (300 g) flour
½ cup (48 g) almond flour
2/3 cup (53 g) unsweetened cocoa
2 tsp baking soda
2 cups (400 g) sugar
1 tsp salt
2 cups (473 ml) cold water
½ cup (~110 g) and 2tbsp coconut oil, melted
1 tbsp vanilla
2 tbsp lime juice

DIRECTIONS:

1. Mix together the flours, cocoa, baking soda, sugar, and salt.
2. In a separate bowl, mix the water, oil, vanilla, and lime juice.
3. Combine the wet and dry ingredients. Mix until the batter is smooth, sifting to remove lumps if necessary.
4. Pour the batter into two 9x13 inch cake pans. Tap the sides of the pans to knock the air out and bake at 350°F (180°C), or 325°F (160°C) if using a convection oven, for 25-30 minutes. Remove from oven and allow to cool.

FOR THE FILLING

INGREDIENTS:

3 limes
½ cup (60 g) raspberries

2 cups (473 ml) water
3 cups (600 g) sugar

DIRECTIONS:

1. Trim the pith from the peels and discard. Fine chop the remainder of the peel. Juice the fruit, saving the pulp.

2. Combine the pulp, juice, sugar, raspberries, and chopped peel in a saucepan. Bring the mixture to a boil, stirring only until sugar dissolves. Bring the marmalade to 220°F (105°C) and hold for 5 minutes. Do not stir.
3. Remove from heat and let sit for five minutes. Cool fully and stir before using as a filling.

FOR THE FROSTING

INGREDIENTS:

1 cup (267 ml) full-fat coconut milk
6 oz (170 g) dark chocolate
¼ tsp lime extract
Fresh raspberries (optional)

DIRECTIONS:

1. Melt the chocolate using a double boiler.
2. Once fully melted and runny, remove the chocolate from the heat and allow to cool slightly.
3. Pour the melted chocolate into room temperature coconut milk, add lime extract and whisk until fully combined.
4. Once cake is filled and frosted, decorate with raspberries.

EASY CHOCOLATE MOUSSE CAKE

SARAH R. NEW

This chocolate mousse cake is famous in my family. I made it for a Great British Bake Off Bake-along, and it was so popular I made it for my aunt's wedding. She then proceeded to mistake it for her actual wedding cake, and then claimed it was better than the traditional wedding cake, which upset my other aunt who had gotten the other cake made for her. Nevertheless, it still makes it to the table for every family party.

INGREDIENTS:

For the Cake:

2 tbsp cocoa powder
3 tbsp boiling water
½ cup (100 g) sugar
¾ cup (100 g) self-rising flour
1 tsp baking powder
2 large eggs
½ cup (100 g) margarine

For the Mousse:

11 oz (300 g) milk chocolate
1 ¾ cups plus 2 tbsp (450 ml) whipping cream

DIRECTIONS:

1. Preheat oven to 350°F (180°C) or 325°F (160°C) if using a convection oven. Line 8-inch springform tin with grease-proof paper completely (up until the top of the tin).
2. Measure cocoa powder into a bowl and mix into a paste with the boiling water.

3. Add the rest of the cake ingredients and mix until the mixture is smooth and completely combined.

4. Pour into the springform tin and bake for 20-25 minutes or until springy. Once baked, let it cool completely.

5. To create the mousse, begin by placing chocolate into a bowl and melt over gently simmering water. Stir continuously until all the chocolate has melted. Do not let the water touch the bowl. Once the chocolate is all melted, set aside to let it cool slightly.

6. Whip the cream until soft peaks form. (This is best done in a stand mixer but can be done by hand.)

7. Gently fold in the melted chocolate into the cream until it is smooth and not streaky.

8. When the cake is completely cool, spoon the mousse mixture over the cake and cover with clingfilm. Leave to set in the fridge ideally overnight or for a minimum 4 hours.

YOU MUST EAT

AUDRIS CANDRA

Two glasses full of water stand still on the kitchen table.

The ceramic plate clinks against the mahogany grains. The pot on the stove bubbles, and Mother hums the same tune she always does at 6:18 p.m. My breath stills, and the lines of a plastic ruler hang incorporeal before my eyes. I've stared at the measurements long enough to burn the gaps between the vertical patterns and the black numbers onto my retina. I set a fork, making sure that it's exactly three and a half inches to the right of the plate. Just a fraction off, and I would earn another set of three dotted scars on my thigh.

"I'm done, Mother." My voice is even and smooth, the way a lady should speak.

Mother turns around, glances at the table—MY HEART SHAKES IN ITS CHAMBER READY TO CRACK MY RIBS AND ESCAPE—and smiles. Finally, my lungs release their tension and I exhale. "Dinner will be ready soon, dear," she sings.

I take my seat, and the chair scrapes against the floor. I stop. And wait. The pan clacks against the stove, and Mother continues her humming. A small mercy, one that scratches a mark on the blackboard inside her head. Once the tally reaches five, they would be moved from her mind to my skin. Sometimes with a belt, sometimes with a cane, sometimes whatever object she's holding. It matters not to her.

I pull the chair slower, more carefully. No noise. I slide onto the cushion, and my spine snaps straight. Hands are stone on my lap. Lips yanked into a gentle smile. A lady must be patient.

The pan sizzles, and the sharp smell of garlic suffuses the air. My eyes water at the addition of onion and chili—SHE KNOWS MY STOMACH TWISTS AT ANY HINT OF SPICE SO WHY MUST SHE ADD IT—and I must not blink. A droplet of tear would scald the back of my hand.

Mother's silhouette is still. Only her hands move. The pan dances atop the fire, and the wooden spatula twirls in an ocean of red. It's a mating call to my saliva, and I mustn't answer. I'm not a pig. I must show her that I'm not a pig.

The clock ticks—MY BRAIN RATTLES AGAINST MY SKULL HOW LONG MUST I WAIT HOW MUCH MUST I ACHE—and a knob clicks in place.

The embers are snuffed out. A sheet of ice rests on my shoulders. Mother pivots, pan in hand, and she flashes her perfect-pearl teeth. "Dinner's ready."

"Yes, Mother," I sing back.

Mother crosses the room, lithe as a sterling. She picks up the fork, twists it—ONCE AND ONLY ONCE AND ONLY ONCE AND ONLY ONCE—around the pan, and serves me the tiniest bump of spaghetti drowning in tomato sauce. "One meatball." And it rolls onto my plate. My dinner is a speck of dust in the expansive white void of outer space. One forkful. The only one I'm allowed; the only one I deserve. I chirp, "Thank you, Mother."

"You're welcome, dear. Now let's eat."

Her fork clinks against the plate. She eats. Drives a fork-ful—FORK FORK FORK—into her mouth. Dabs the edge of her rosy lips with a linen napkin, painting a streak of red. A woman out of the pictures, out of fantasy. This was how she wooed my father, and I must follow in her steps. Be a lady. Lock(ed) in the perfect husband.

I want to ask for more. I want to tell her that such a meager portion is barely enough. My lips part, and the four crescent marks on my stomach where Mother once dug her nails pulse and ache. "See this flab of fat? Only pigs have flabs like this. Are you a pig? Should I send you to the abattoir?"

I'm a lady—NOT A PIG—and I fear that my body will overtake me. That my stomach craves for so much that it'll scarf down what's on Mother's plate too.

"What's wrong, dear? You must eat."

YOU.

I pick up my fork, my elbow angled the way my mother taught me to.

MUST.

My legs are slanted under the tablecloth.

EAT.

I dip my head and raise the fork. Teeth gnash and grind as I take the tiniest of bites.

We bought the pasta together. The weight of the can of tomato paste is but a phantom weight in my fingers. I saw the pig's head at the butcher's shop and the carcasses hanging from the hooks—OH HOW I ENVY THE SLAUGHTER—I know the brown crumbs sloshing in the sauce are pork.

So why does the spaghetti—WRITHES IN MY MOUTH LIKE WORMS—feel wrong?

Mother takes in her dinner, her face radiant with—GREASE OH HOW LONG HAS IT BEEN SINCE I'VE TASTED—the joy of eating. The bliss of having enough food to live, not just survive.

My stomach crushes itself, demanding more. It yearns; it needs.

I stab my one and only meatball. I have to savor this. Make it worth more than it is. If I ask for more, if I slip in the middle of the night for a quick bite, Mother's two lithe fingers will slide to the back of my throat, and I'll have to throw it all up. My stomach twists at the memory. It tugs and pulls, and I jerk myself back—I MUST BE A LADY I MUST I MUST I MUST I CANNOT EAT MORE THAN I'VE BEEN GIVEN—and the fork clinks against the sparkling marble floor.

Mother freezes. Takes in the sound. The sight of scarlet streaks on the tablecloth. She sets her fork back in place, three and a half inches to the right of her plate. Then she stands up, turns for the stove, and the pan is back in her hand.

My clumsy elbow knocks a glass over—I'M SORRY I'M SORRY I'M SORRY—as I fall to my knees. "Mother, I'm so sorry, it won't happen again!"

Her smile is chiseled onto her face. She dashes, feet a blur in my tears. But it's not impact that I feel—it's what I hear.

She slips on the puddle I've created. Her prim black hair is now tousled, framing her face like a crooked painting. Slowly, liquid oozes out the back of her head, and she's smearing red on the marble floor, a worse mess than the sauce I've spilled. Her mouth is agape, her perfect pearls of teeth tremble while her ivory hand spasms against the marble tiles. Her eyes are wild, watering like mine did earlier. Her song's gone. "Call... help..."

BUT THIS IS A DINNER AND YOU MUST BE A LADY AND YOU MUST EAT

"Mother, we haven't finished dinner yet."

"Call... ambu... lance..." she rasps.

"No, Mother, you always told me I must finish dinner like the lady I am."

I pick myself up, despite my buckling knees—FINISH DINNER FINISH DINNER FINISH—despite my shaking fingers. I take her plate, and my elbows give up.

The plate shatters on the floor. I scoop the spaghetti Mother has so lovingly cooked for me. It's not for my own good. This time it is for hers.

Gently, oh so gently, like a lady should, I feed her the bits of spaghetti. Shove the meatballs right between her teeth.

"What's wrong, Mother? You must eat."

Tears flow, but they do not scald my cheek. I've managed to make her eat—SHE GURGLES AND GURGLES OH HOW BEAUTIFUL IT SOUNDS—but we're not done yet.

I pick up a shard of the bone-white plate—JAGGED LIKE THE SCARS MOTHER HAS CARVED ON MY BACK—and I slip it onto her tongue. She refuses to eat—AND THAT WON'T DO—so I grab her lower jaw and slam it shut. Perfect pearls crush and gnash. Perfect pearls crack and so do the ceramic pieces.

Because, after all,
You.
Must.
EAT.

BROWN SUGAR CHOCOLATE DROP COOKIES

R. HAVEN

I first made these cookies for Christmas the year my child was born and have tweaked them every year since in order to perfect them! Now they're considered our traditional Christmas cookie, and we're proud to put them out for Santa every December 24th. That said, they're a great cookie for any occasion (or no occasion at all)!

INGREDIENTS:

2 ¼ cups (270 g) flour
2 cups (400 g) packed brown sugar, divided
¼ cup (50 g) sugar
½ tsp baking soda
¼ tsp baking powder
½ tsp salt
1 ¾ sticks (198 g) unsalted butter or margarine, refrigerated
1 large egg
1 large egg yolk
1 tbsp vanilla extract
Bag of large chocolate chips or Hershey's kisses

DIRECTIONS:

1. Preheat the oven to 350°F (180°C) or 325°F (160°C) if using a convection oven. Line your baking sheet with parchment paper.

2. In one large mixing bowl, combine the flour, 1 cup of the brown sugar, sugar, baking soda, and baking powder. Be sure to squish the brown sugar clumps as you go.

3. In a second bowl, combine the rest of the brown sugar with the butter, eggs, vanilla, and salt. The butter will be difficult to mix while cold, but room temperature butter will cause your cookies to spread out wider while baking, so keep that in mind. Squish these ingredients together—once more, being sure to squish the clumps of brown sugar—until fairly well blended.

4. Add the wet ingredients to the dry, then knead with floured hands to form the dough.

5. Roll the dough into balls roughly one inch in diameter and place them on the baking sheet. In the center of each one, press your chocolate in deep enough to stick. Bake for 12-14 minutes. They should appear slightly under-done. Leave on the baking sheet to rest for 5 minutes, then transfer to a wire cooling rack and enjoy!

WHITE CHOCOLATE MACADAMIA SOURDOUGH COOKIES

GABRIELLE WINOCO

Sourdough… in a cookie? You bet. This recipe is a great way to put your starter to use in a totally new way.

INGREDIENTS:

2/3 cup (150 g) brown butter, warm
1 1/3 cups plus 1 tbsp (285 g) sugar
1 tsp molasses
2 egg yolks
¾ tsp vanilla
2 cups (250 g) all-purpose flour
¾ tsp baking powder
¾ tsp baking soda
1/3 tsp cinnamon
¾ tsp kosher salt
~ ¾ cup (160 g) sourdough starter, active 2 days
1 cup (210 g) white chocolate chips
~ 1 cup (133 g) macadamia nuts, chopped
Coarse salt, for topping, optional

DIRECTIONS:

1. Toast macadamia nuts at 300°F (150°C) or, if using a convection oven 275°F (135°C), until the nuts just start to brown. This happens in just a few minutes! Set aside to cool completely.

2. Cook butter in a heavy-bottomed saucepan on medium until brown and fragrant. Set aside to cool down but use while still warm.
3. Measure out all dry ingredients and set aside.
4. In a stand mixer with whisk attachment, mix sugar, molasses, vanilla, and yolks on low for several minutes, until sugar starts dissolving. Stream in warm butter and mix completely. Scrape bottom of bowl and mix again.
5. Add starter and mix just until combined.
6. Add in dry ingredients and mix on low. Scrape well and mix again briefly.
7. Add in chocolate and nuts and mix until incorporated.
8. The batter should yield about 14 bakery-sized cookies. Scoop evenly and flatten to 3 inches on a sheet pan lined with parchment or a Silpat mat. The cookies will spread, so only place 3 cookies on the sheet pan at a time! Sprinkle coarse salt in the middle.
9. Bake until barely golden and set in the middle. Time varies from oven to oven and if you're using convection, but shouldn't exceed 15 minutes. The less these cookies are baked, the softer and chewier they are. Rotate the pan at the 5-minute mark.

Scared of how good sourdough can be? Then you're in for a real treat with "Sylvia's Sourdough Starter" by Nicholas Gordon, located in the entrée section of this book. Best read with a sourdough cookie, of course.

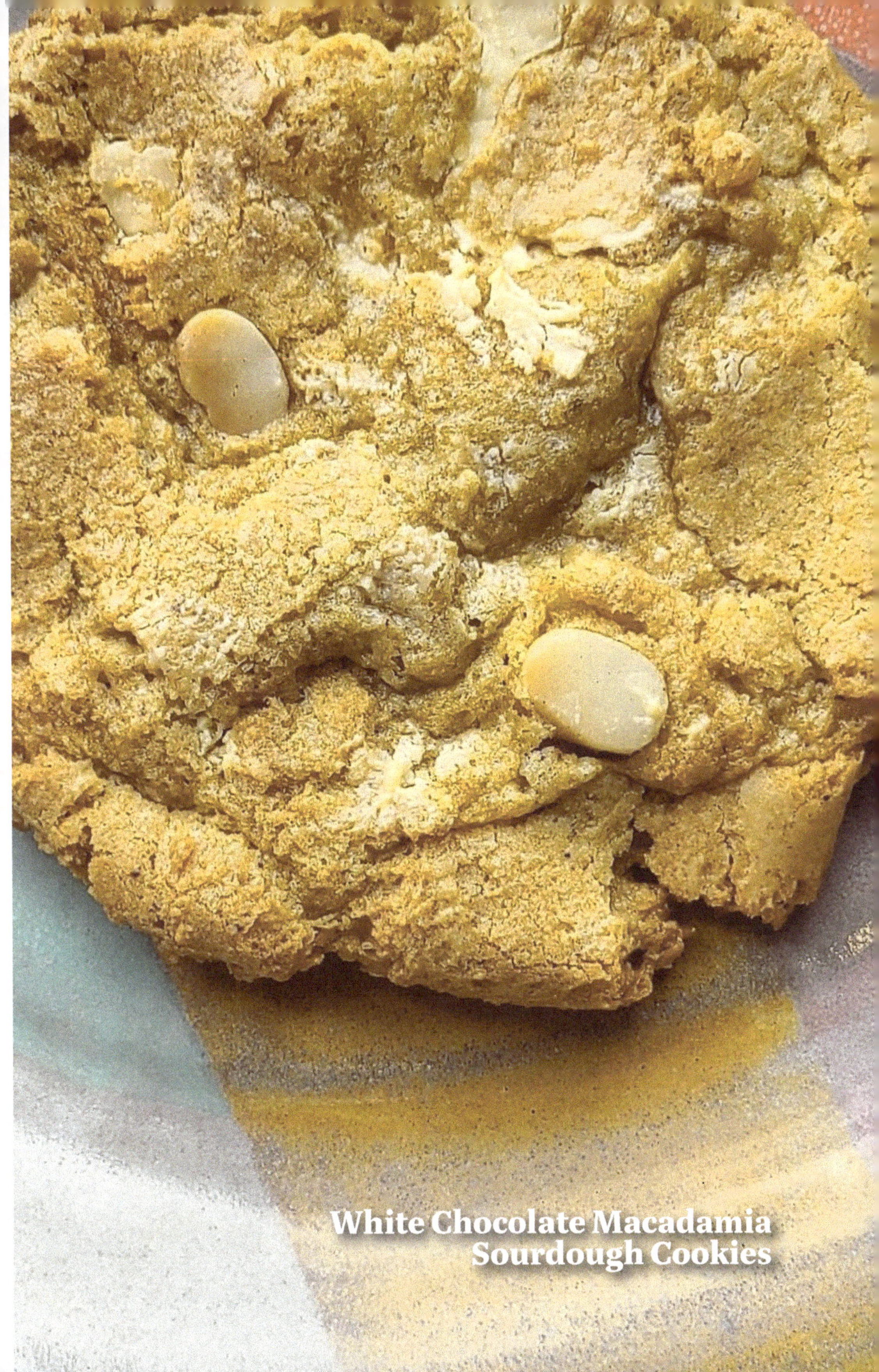
White Chocolate Macadamia
Sourdough Cookies

DEAD MAN'S PIE

REBECCA CUTHBERT

How was Jed to know the pie belonged to a dead man, or that dead men come back to claim what's theirs? When he walked by the Masons' farmhouse and saw that blueberry pie smelling like God's heaven cooling on a windowsill, he helped himself. Pete Mason had fired him, unjustly Jed swore, two days prior. That pie was his severance.

Except Jed couldn't know that Pete had passed not twenty minutes earlier, tipped over from a blown heart while slinging hay bales, and that pie was his dear wife Annie May's last gift to him, one Pete intended to bring along into the great hereafter.

Late in the night, Jed's former boss came for what was rightly his, and that the pie was already masticated in Jed's full belly didn't matter. Pete's walking corpse, already smelling of carrion in the sun, woke Jed with a cuff to the ear. And though Jed screamed and kicked, he was no match for a man who'd been tougher than him living and was even more so dead.

Jed was found the next day, gut ripped open and empty, blue pie and red blood swirling into pulpy purple stains on his ruined bedsheets.

THYME FOR GLUTEN-FREE BLUEBERRY PIE

REBECCA CUTHBERT

Gluten-free baking is a process of trial and error—and for lots of folks, mostly error. It took a long time to find a gluten-free pie crust recipe that didn't have the texture of moist sawdust. This version is slightly modified from one I found on glutenfreeonashoestring. com, and even people who can eat gluten will like it! The lemon thyme in the filling is optional, but trust me—go buy a plant from your local greenhouse. Its leaves smell wonderful, and you will find yourself putting it on almost everything.

FOR BLUEBERRY FILLING:

INGREDIENTS:

Four pints (1.2- 1.3 kg) blueberries (I recommend fresh picked, but store-bought will do—do not use frozen berries as the water content is too high)
½ cup (100 g) granulated sugar
2 tbsp lemon juice (fresh or bottled)
1 tbsp sifted cornstarch OR gluten-free flour
1 tsp crushed lemon thyme from the garden (this is a twist on the traditional and you can leave it out if you want)
2 tbsp water

DIRECTIONS:

1. Put two cups of blueberries in a saucepan and mash them with a potato masher.

2. Add water, lemon juice, cornstarch or flour, sugar, and optional ingredients.
3. Cook over low heat, stirring frequently.
4. When all ingredients are dissolved and the consistency resembles a runny jam, add the rest of the blueberries—do not mash them, as you want a hearty mixture with some whole berries.
5. Cook for another five minutes, remove from heat and set aside.

FOR GLUTEN-FREE PIE CRUST:

INGREDIENTS:

1 ½ cups (225 g) 1:1 gluten-free flour
¼ tsp baking powder
½ tsp salt
7 tbsp (99 g) butter (chilled and chopped into little cubes)
½ cup (113 g) cold sour cream (full fat)
Ice water (used 1 tsp at a time as needed)
Extra flour (will need for rolling dough)
2 eggs (beat to use later as a wash)

DIRECTIONS:

1. Preheat oven to 375°F (190°C) or 350°F (180°C) if using a convection oven.
2. Combine dry ingredients.
3. Add butter cubes and mix to coat.
4. Squish each butter clump; this must be done by hand.
5. When the mixture resembles damp, pebbly sand, add sour cream.
6. Mix together. Dough should still have a crumbly texture.
7. Knead the dough by hand, adding ice water or more flour as needed; you are going for moist and workable but not wet.
8. Turn dough out onto a layer of plastic wrap.
9. Flatten into a disc and put in the refrigerator for 30 minutes.

10. Take the dough out. Unwrap it and put it on a floured piece of parchment paper. Lightly flour the top of the dough.
11. Put another sheet of parchment paper on top.
12. Using a rolling pin, roll the dough flat between the pieces of parchment paper.
13. Carefully remove the top layer of paper and fold the dough onto itself in thirds, like a letter, then fold the sides in so you have a square.
14. Put the parchment paper back on top, roll again; you are laminating the dough to work in the butter.
15. Do this three more times, then take the top layer of paper off. Place the rolled dough into a buttered 9-inch pie pan by flipping it over onto the pan. Peel off the remaining parchment paper.
16. Ease the dough down into the sides of the pan without tearing it; trim off excess dough with a knife, roll that excess dough into a ball, wrap it, and put it back in the fridge.
17. Pinch the rim of the dough into little waves or peaks, but keep them thick to avoid burning during baking.
18. Refrigerate the whole pie pan for 30 minutes, covered in plastic wrap so the dough doesn't dry out.
19. Take the pie pan out of the refrigerator, and pierce the bottom of the crust with a fork several times—this will help keep the bottom from getting soggy.
20. Brush the edges with a light coating of egg wash.
21. Bake the empty crust for 10 minutes to set it and again, keep it from getting soggy.
22. Take the pie pan out of the oven and let it cool for 10 minutes.
23. Fill the crust with your blueberry mixture.
24. Optional: Use the excess dough from earlier to make decorations for the top of your pie; roll it out again and cut shapes out with a cookie cutter of your choice. Brush these with a bit of egg wash—just a light coating. Bake those dough shapes separately on a pan lined with parchment paper; they won't take long—check every 5

minutes and when the edges turn golden, remove them to cool.

25. Bake the pie for 45 minutes, then check it; bake further, checking every 10 minutes for golden edges—you don't want to burn it.

26. When it is fully cooked and the dough rim is golden, take it out and let it cool fully.

27. Optional: Lay your dough decorations on the top in whatever pattern you like.

28. Serve alone or with vanilla ice cream.

BLACKBERRY JAM BARS
DESIREE HORTON

This is a comforting little dessert to make after reading an abundance of scary stories.

INGREDIENTS:

1 cup (120 g) all-purpose flour
1 cup (80-100 g) old-fashioned rolled oats
1 tsp cinnamon
½ tsp salt
½ tsp baking soda
½ cup (115 g) butter, melted
1/3 cup (65-70 g) dark or light brown sugar
1 tablespoon vanilla extract
2 cups or about 1 jar (18 oz/510 g) blackberry preserves*

DIRECTIONS:

1. Preheat oven to 350°F (180°C) or 325°F (160°C) if using a convection oven.
2. Line an 8x8 pan with parchment paper.
3. Add the first five ingredients to a bowl and mix well.
4. In a separate bowl, mix together brown sugar, butter, and vanilla.
5. Combine bowls and mix well.
6. Press ¾ mixture into the parchment-lined pan as firm and flat as possible, and bake for 20 minutes or until golden brown. Reserve the other ¼ of mixture for crumble topping.
7. Remove from oven and spread preserves/jam on top. Crumble remaining mixture over jam.

Blackberry Jam Bars

8. Return to oven and cook for 15-20 minutes or until the top crumbles are medium brown.
9. Cool for 30 minutes on counter, then transfer to fridge for 30 minutes before cutting.

AUTHOR'S NOTE:

*This recipe can substitute any preserves or jam that you prefer, and it tastes just as good with gluten-free substitutes. The jam measurement also doesn't have to be precise but use a minimum of 1 cup.

SWEETTOOTH

ROBERT PEREZ

It was cold inside the submersible.

Paid by the fathom, Nathan had time as the vessel descended to reflect on how he wound up hunting a sea monster. He shivered in his black turtleneck sweater. It was easy not to think and say yes when you were blinded by so many dollar signs.

It all began when his crew had burst through the weathered door of The Brine tavern, boisterous, clapping each other on the back, boasting about their role in the record-breaking haul. It was the first time the bar barnacle surfaced from the depths of his glass to engage them in conversation. After years of coming to The Brine, the drunk man never paid them any mind, but that night he watched the group with incandescent intensity.

When the crew sang each other's praises at midnight and pledged cheers, draining their drinks, the bar barnacle finally spoke.

"That's nothing!" he shouted. "I made in one night what you all made in a year! All with one catch!"

"I'm sure you did, sir," James agreed with drunken conviction.

"I did! And I won't stand for mocking!" the surly man barked.

Anthony rolled his eyes. "Let me buy you another drink. It's the least we could do while in the presence of such a—"

"Lives were put at stake for a taste!" the elderly man blurted in fear. "Most are mistaken for thinking Sweettooth Bay is named for its jagged coast, unaware it's truly named after a creeping, caustic cavity!"

"Hey, I didn't know you were familiar with my ex!" Patrick guffawed.

The crew cracked up. James slapped Nathan's back as he gasped with hilarity. Even the bartender laughed.

"Ocean-claimed souls finally found flesh...and the dead aren't picky. On nights when you find it hard to fall asleep, when there is a hint of sweetness in the night air—that's when it resurfaces like a forgotten nightmare or toxic algae bloom. It's a sticky, horrible end...unless you can somehow eat your way out."

"So, you really do know my ex!" Patrick yelled as the sailors laughed until their ribs hurt.

The bar barnacle's eyes glazed over as if witnessing an unseen horror. "Who knew death could taste so sweet? The treat that eats..."

"Are you doing all right, man?" James asked.

Worry flashed over the bar barnacle's features. "It welcomes all into its delectable embrace. Sweettooth is always hungry! It's a candy killer and a killer candy!"

The crew struggled to breathe amid their laughter.

The old man furtively removed something from his coat pocket. His dirty fingers unwrapped and tossed a pink glob into his mouth. His eyes rolled back in his head as he muttered a single word with smacking split lips. "Sublime..."

Though he tried to hide it, the ubiquitous saltwater taffy of Sweettooth Bay was unmistakable; or so the crew thought. It was common to find dropped pieces stomped into the cracks of the boardwalk, as if it had become integral to the structural integrity of the rickety creaking wood.

"The reason so many boats sink in the bay and why so many skilled swimmers find themselves fighting more than just a rogue current is the same. Sweettooth is storm-born. Its mother was the hurricane of 1883 that flooded a candy shop and carried the sweets to sea. The storeowner rebranded his saltwater-touched taffy to sell off the damaged stock and the novelty stuck. His fortune's twin has been growing beneath the waves after all these years." The bar barnacle shuddered. "Maybe grow isn't the right word for something that isn't alive... Sweettooth is an amalgam of the dead and dying... All become one within the wretched mass... Every year it gets bigger...and bigger..."

"That's what he said!" Anthony quipped causing the crew to double-over laughing.

After the crew had their fun, they tuned out the inane mutterings, except for Nathan who listened. Once the others were gone, he and the bar barnacle spoke over a guttering candle.

"There's a mighty high price on the black market for the bravest to harvest a bit of Sweettooth... That used to be me... I was commissioned by a rich benefactor... As a child she saw the taffy pull her beloved nanny into the sea..." The man reeled like he was on an invisible amusement park ride of nostalgia. "But no more... Never again..."

"Why would anyone want to eat that?" Nathan balked.

"While the taste is heavenly—that I can attest—for some there is nothing more savored than vengeance," the old man whispered solemnly and produced a disintegrating business card from his moist pocket. On it was the name and phone number belonging to a rich-beyond-belief benefactor who the ruined man promised would be eagerly awaiting Nathan's contact.

"How do I know you're for real?" Nathan questioned, holding onto the card. "Maybe you're just pulling my chain, getting a kick out of people you think are green to the sea."

The bar barnacle revealed the candy wrapper from earlier and slid it across the table. The small rectangle was embellished with golden filigree and center stamped with "189:200."

"That wasn't some ordinary boardwalk taffy," he grinned.

"All that tells me is you've got some fancy tastes," Nathan quipped.

The bar barnacle stared at Nathan for a long time before pulling up his shirt and revealing a scarred abdomen. "With teeth of candy corn and stolen bones! I'm lucky and cursed to be a lone survivor!"

Later on when Nathan had called the number on the card, he still wasn't sure he believed. But then he received that mind-boggling offer, and so, down below the waves he went.

The submersible glowed bright green and trailed gummi worms as lures. Nathan was assured that the vehicle was well-equipped with the finest and deadliest undersea technology. He would be paid even if he failed and be rewarded even more for his success. Either way, he'd resurface a rich man.

He hoped he failed. It'd be easier at least.

Nathan remembered the barnacle's grizzly wound in stark clarity, and a shiver ran down his spine. He gripped the steering apparatus tighter and continued downward.

Outside the small reinforced circular window was darkness and marine snow. Nathan had made countless voyages, hauled up mountains of fish, drank with hundreds of sailors, and had never found a reason to believe in sea monsters. He'd never seen something unexplainable on the horizon or caught something strange in the nets. Sure, there were sharks, dolphins, box jellyfish, and whales—hell, even giant squids. But monsters? The only monster he believed in was the ocean itself.

Though he tried to remind himself there was nothing to fear, that this was just another job, shivers coursed through his body. He blamed it on the cold, sinking his anxiety in denial where it lurked beneath the surface. Nathan pulled a silver mermaid shaped flask from his belt. He unscrewed her head and tossed back a swig of rum. He concentrated on the warmth spreading through his chest.

Suddenly, the sonar pinged like a dread knell. The quickening beats screamed together that something was approaching and fast.

Nathan stared in shock when he saw it. When the pulsating, bone-studded mass crept against the submersible's circular window and the metal hull groaned as the giant taffy maw chewed.

He flipped a clear plastic protective panel and slammed a fist over the red emergency button which triggered a defensive shock of lethal voltage.

The creature released its grip on the submersible. A shark skull with peppermint swirl eyes peered through the porthole, urgently searching the interior with the keen awareness of prey locked inside a shell, regarding technological advances as tedious puzzles to be crushed. The taffy broke out in a rash of human faces that popped and reformed as an incalculable number of souls crowded and pushed to gain temporary form.

Nathan watched as a lifeless eel ribbon-danced against the glass like a rotting tongue. The gleaming arsenal at his disposal now felt powerless. After all, what good were weapons against an embodiment of death? He had gotten what he came for anyway, the submersible's barbed hull now bearing a harvest of taffy-tatters. It was time to go.

Nathan quickly veered away from the chaotic morass of a sea monster and toward his brighter future. As he pushed the vehicle as fast as it could go, Nathan felt elated by his escape, and his mind raced with the possibilities his new wealth would bring.

Until the sonar pinged again, and his stomach dropped. Nathan fell forward, hitting his head on the console as the submersible was pulled back down into the depths by taffy tentacles.

Nathan touched his forehead and his fingers dabbed blood. The horrifying realization of his impending anonymity washed over him. Soon he'd join the sea of faces lost in confectionary oblivion. He heaved a few panicked last breaths before Sweettooth crunched through the hull like it was a jawbreaker.

SWEETTOOTH TAFFY

ROBERT PEREZ

Saltwater taffy encourages creativity. Flavor and color can be swapped out according to your preference. The amalgam that is the monster Sweettooth can be replicated here on a smaller scale, and as such feel free to mix in various "debris." For example: gummi fish, candy corn, candy bones, and other various sweets. This recipe encourages experimentation and the juxtaposition of textures.

When making this recipe check the weather, as humidity can cause the taffy to absorb moisture and can affect how it hardens. This recipe makes about twenty-five pieces of individually wrapped candy. Store in an air-tight container at room temperature. The taffy is best consumed within two weeks, after which it begins to harden.

INGREDIENTS:

½ cup (118 ml) water

1 cup (237 ml) light corn syrup

2 cups (400 g) granulated sugar

¾ tsp sea salt

2 tbsp unsalted butter

1 tsp desired flavoring extract

¼ cup (30 g) marshmallow cream

5 to 12 drops of desired color of gel food coloring, depending on the desired strength of hue

Other various sweets as add-ins

(Additional items continued on next page)

Candy thermometer (optional, but strongly recommended)
Pastry brush
4-quart saucepan
Rimmed baking sheet
Spatula
Nonstick cooking spray
Food-safe plastic gloves
Wax paper

DIRECTIONS:

1. Spray a rimmed baking sheet with nonstick cooking spray. Set aside.
2. Combine water, corn syrup, granulated sugar, and sea salt in a 4-quart saucepan over medium-high heat. Stir until the sugar dissolves completely.
3. Wash down the sides of the pan with a wet pastry brush to prevent sugar crystals from forming.
4. Wait until the sugar syrup comes to a boil. Insert the candy thermometer if available. Continue to cook the syrup without stirring, until it reaches a temperature of 255°F (123°C). This will produce a soft taffy. Note that the higher the cooking temperature, the firmer the taffy.
5. Once the syrup has reached a boil, remove the pan from the heat and add in the butter and desired flavoring. Stir until the butter melts and everything is mixed.
6. Carefully pour the syrup onto the prepared baking sheet and allow it to spread evenly.
7. Add the marshmallow cream and desired food coloring into the center of the baking sheet.
8. After 5-10 minutes the syrup will cool and begin to set around the edges of the pan. If the taffy does not set, that indicates it did not reach the correct temperature. With a spatula, fold the edges into the center over the marshmallow cream and coloring to make a rough circle.
9. Put on food-safe plastic gloves and spray them with nonstick spray.

10. Knead the candy until it is well blended and of an even hue.
11. Form the taffy into a rope with both hands and begin to stretch apart.
12. Bring both ends of the stretched taffy rope back together, twist, and repeat the pulling process. As the taffy cools it will become easier to manipulate. Continue to pull the taffy for about 20 minutes or until it begins to hold its shape. When you begin to see parallel ridges form in the pulled taffy it is a sign it is ready.
13. Divide the taffy into four even pieces or "lumps."
14. Roll the four lumps into balls. Roll each ball into a long thin rope.
15. Use a sharp knife to cut each rope into 1-inch pieces.
16. Press the chosen various sweet treats into the taffy pieces, or wrap the taffy around the various mix-ins.
17. Wrap the candy pieces in wax paper.
18. Enjoy!

FRANKIE'S FOOTNOTE:

This recipe ties in directly with the story "Sweettooth" by Robert Perez in the dessert section of Cursed Cooking. Be sure to give it a read as you enjoy a bite of the monstrous Sweettooth—just be careful it doesn't bite back!

WINDOWPANE FUDGE

NADINE STEWART

Marshmallow fudge or windowpane fudge as it is sometimes called is a stunning treat to display and makes for a great gift to give during the holidays. My aunt and grandmother used to make it every year for Christmas, and now I have friends who request a batch or two for every get-together we have.

INGREDIENTS:

1 cup (227 g) of butter
¾ cup (~200 g) peanut butter
1 bag (12 oz/340 g) semi-sweet chocolate chips
1 bag (12 oz/340 g) butterscotch chips
1 tsp vanilla
1 bag of colored mini marshmallows

DIRECTIONS:

1. Line a 9x13 inch pan with parchment paper and set aside.
2. Over a double boiler or in a large pot on low heat melt together the butter, chips, and peanut butter. Stir constantly until fully melted.
3. Remove from heat and add vanilla. Cool for 3-5 minutes then fold in marshmallows.
4. Pour into pan and refrigerate several hours until firm and then cut into squares.

Windowpane Fudge

THE TOMBSTONE TABLE FOR ONE

GENEVIEVE PUTTAY

It is the most exclusive restaurant in the city. The hottest ticket in town. They said it would cost her everything, but more fool them, 'cause she hadn't paid a dime. Way beneath the heaving metropolis, in a mausoleum blooming with ceps, the shroomiér seats the veiled lady at his tombstone table for one.

He serves the first course in silence. An appetizer plucked from a patch of earth in which corpses have curdled to crème de la crème. She sighs like the plate is a canvas, at those blues and greens soured to sludge. She tastes sorrow and joy. She tastes despair and distrust. Her mind is as fizzy as apples. The world changes in front of her eyes. Sticky cobwebs disintegrate into oil paint, and dead leaves drip down from above. A plump pink maggot wriggles across her plate, she flicks it away with a scarlet fingernail, and devours the remaining rhapsody in one euphoric bite.

For the next course, the shroomiér serves the entrée in earnest. Chanterelles, pale and ghostly, haunt the plate. He warns of a steep price she's yet to pay— "a breathtaking cost," but the buffoon doesn't know she plans to stiff him post-dessert. As the shadows lengthen, she lifts the porcelain to her painted lips and tips her head back like a newborn bird. The chanterelles slide down her gullet, slippery and alive, soft as a sob, delicate as Chantilly lace. They land in the base of her gut and morph into chilled spite.

The crypt spins. She can't feel the floor. She slips a foot out of her stiletto and curls manicured toes in the mud. The shroomiér asks if she'd like to retire. Would she like to return to the world up above? She licks the bowl clean, flings it across the tombstone, and feverishly demands her dessert.

The shroomiér, with blank eyes and a grave smile, serves the pièce de résistance in deference. A crimson crumble with shrooms grown in solemn ground, picked at the witching hour, and braised until sweet and fat. A sharp tongue darts out, licking brittle lips. She takes a bite. Catches. Her breath. The pud slides down like molasses; shards of lemon slice through the sweetness and raze her throat to ribbons. Her heart rabbits. Sweat films her brow. And her whole world turns to mush. She throws away her napkin, horrified as it splats against a watery grave. Her fingerprints slip off the ends of her fingers. Her rosebud lips dribble down her chin. She falls to the ground, writhing like dead man's fingers clawing out of the earth. Her hollow mouth stretches into shadows. Her screams are horrific and sublime.

Vampire caps pop up from the ground around her body like a halo of nightmares. They brush her skin, and she screams from their silken fire. She screams and she screams. For three days, she screams, while the shroomiér tends to his shrooms, enslaved by their beauty, straitjacketed by their relentless demands. Their pearlescent cups shimmer, their frills satin, and skin pink as a coquettish blush, nourished by anguish, sustained by torment, thriving on the screams of the dead. The veiled lady expires. The vampire caps retreat to their crypt. And as they hungrily crave delivery of their next victim, the shroomiér lays a fresh napkin on his tombstone table for one.

***

APPLE, RUM & RAISIN CRUMBLE

GENEVIEVE PUTTAY

A cozy classic with a boozy edge. Juicy apples and rum-soaked raisins are drenched in a sugar and spice sauce, topped with buttery crumble. Enjoy with ice cream or custard, share with friends, or hoard it like gold.

INGREDIENTS

For the Filling:

½ cup (75 g) raisins
3 tbsp (50 ml) rum*
2 tbsp (30 g) butter
3 Braeburn apples, peeled and diced (½ inch/1cm)
1/3 cup (80 g) soft dark brown sugar
2 tbsp (25 g) maple syrup
1 tsp vanilla paste
1 tsp ground ginger
½ tsp ground cinnamon
½ tsp ground nutmeg
¼ tsp ground cardamom
Good pinch of sea salt (smoked, if you have it)

For the Topping:

1 cup (120 g) flour
¼ cup (30 g) rolled oats
6 tbsp (85 g) brown demerara sugar
7 tbsp (100 g) butter, cold and diced

DIRECTIONS:

1. The night before: Put the raisins and rum in a small bowl, cover well, and leave to steep overnight.
2. The next day: Preheat the oven to 375°F (200°C) or 350°F (180°C) if using a convection oven.
3. Prepare the filling: Add the butter to a frying pan, and over a medium heat, brown for 5 minutes, swirling occasionally. Be careful not to burn the butter, we just want to get it nice and brown and nutty.
4. Add to the pan the rum and raisin mixture and cook for 30 seconds.
5. Now add the rest of the filling ingredients (apples, soft brown sugar, maple syrup, vanilla paste, ground ginger, ground cinnamon, ground nutmeg, and ground cardamom, plus a good pinch of sea salt).
6. Give it all a stir, bring to the boil, and then simmer for 10 minutes. Decant into your baking dish (I used a 6x8.5/22 cm x 15 cm rectangular dish). Leave aside to cool a bit while you make the topping.
7. Make the topping. In a mixing bowl, stir the brown demerara sugar and rolled oats into the flour. Add the cold, diced butter. Rub the butter into the flour-mix with your fingers until the mixture resembles large breadcrumbs. Scatter on top of the filling and spread evenly. Don't pat down too much or it will turn into shortbread.
8. Bake in the oven for 30-35 minutes. Serve hot with custard or ice cream.

AUTHOR'S NOTE:

*I used a Mauritian rum, which had smoky/caramel notes, but you can use your favourite. Spiced rum would be lovely!

TRADITIONAL BRITISH FLAPJACKS

JM CYRUS

These are entirely different to flapjack pancakes, instead they are like a mixture between a granola bar, a trail bar, and the best oat and raisin cookie ever. They're very simple and have been passed around my extended family quite a lot recently, nourishing several mothers through nursing their newborn babies. They're dense, sweet, and can be amended according to what you have around. I like to use these as a good excuse to finish all the little ends of bags of nuts and seeds that seem to accumulate on the baking shelf.

TECHNIQUE NOTES:

➤ If you prefer a crunchy flapjack, bake in a shallow baking tin at a slightly higher temperature and for 5 to 10 minutes longer (be sure to watch them as they may burn though).

➤ To make sure they're not too crumbly, *really* press the mixture into the tin before baking. I like to use another baking tin and really push them down. And when I say really, I mean *really*. I have found using another baking tin works best.

➤ Make sure they're fully cooled before you remove them from the tin and cut them into squares (you'll need a sharp knife, a solid surface, and elbow grease).

INGREDIENT NOTES:

➤ Using jumbo or rolled oats will make them chewier and provide a more interesting texture. Using porridge oats (which are much finer than rolled oats) will make them cook quicker and denser. Adjust for preference, but I have found a combination of two-thirds jumbo to one-third porridge oats works best.

➤ Brown sugar rather than white will give them more of a toffee flavor. Using sugar with larger crystals, like demerara, will add an extra layer of crunch throughout.

➤ Replacing the butter with margarine makes them a little less rich. Vegan butter works just as well!

➤ If you replace the golden syrup with honey, it will add a very pervasive flavor throughout, so only use if that's what you intend!

➤ I have found that the 2/3 cup (100 g) of raisins/dried fruit/nuts and seeds can be increased to about 1 cup (150 g) with little issue.

➤ Other flavoring ideas: cinnamon, orange zest, and raisins works well (it's the one I've provided in the recipe below), but as I mentioned above you can use anything you have around. Additional notes:

  ▸ Chocolate chips need to be thoroughly mixed through before going in the oven, as do any dried, freeze-dried, or frozen fruit.

  ▸ Drizzle melted chocolate or melted peanut butter (or both!) over the cooled flapjacks.

INGREDIENTS:

¾ cup and 2 tbsp (200 g) butter
2/3 cup (150 g) demerara sugar
4 tbsp golden syrup
1 tsp ground cinnamon
Finely grated orange zest, to taste
4-5 cups (400 g) jumbo oats/porridge oats
2/3 cup (100 g) raisins or sultanas (or other dried fruit or nuts and seeds)

DIRECTIONS:

1. Preheat oven to 375°F (190°C) or 340°F (170°C) if using a convection oven. Grease and line an 8x8 square baking tin with parchment paper.
2. Melt the butter in a large pan and add the sugar, syrup, cinnamon, and orange zest. Stir and heat very gently until the sugar dissolves.
3. Remove pan from heat and stir in the oats and raisins/dried fruit/seeds.
4. Press into tin (using another tin works best) and bake for 15-20 minutes until lightly golden.
5. Leave to cool in the tin before cutting into squares. Flapjacks will keep in an airtight tin for up to three days—if they last that long!

CRACKING

STEVE LOIACONI

The crabs rouse me from my slumber.

I've heard them for years, distant and scattered, but this is different. Louder, incessant, immediate. Impatient and hungry.

If I wasn't utterly terrified, I might appreciate the irony.

A flurry of snapping claws echoes through the darkness, like a beat poetry slam.

They're under my bed. In the walls. Too many to count.

Inevitably, they have come for me. The spirits of those smashed, broiled, sautéed, and air-fried on my path to cable TV stardom. The succulent victims of fame and fortune.

Half-asleep and at least a quarter-drunk, I stumble out of the bedroom gracelessly, calloused feet scuffing against the hardwood. No time to find my slippers or seek out the light switch. I refuse to look at whatever is pinching at my toes and press on toward the spiraling stairs in the dark.

I called myself the Crab King. You might not think there were enough crab recipes to fill eight seasons of primetime television, but you'd be wrong. Every week, we found new ways to prepare crab. Crab pasta. Crab doughnuts. Crab ice cream. The crab fat martini, which I will admit was a mistake.

"Let's get cracking!" I would shout week after week, pulling a hammer from a holster beneath my crab-festooned apron. The hammer got bigger every season until it was a full-on sledge-hammer. Folks in the front row were given ponchos to protect themselves from the splatter of shells and viscera.

"The Gallagher of the Cooking Channel," some people called me.

I never liked those people very much.

Eight seasons, five of them crushing the basic cable competition in the 18 to 54 demo. Can't say that I blame the audience for losing interest in the later years—I certainly did—but cancellation still stings even if you know you deserve it. So, I retired to this cavernous house on a cliffside—"palatial," the real estate listing had described it, only exaggerating a little— seeking silence and solace. The sledgehammer now sits on a display case in the main hall next to my People's Choice Award and a bronze watermelon Chef Emeril once sent me in a desperate attempt at humor.

"Crack that!" he bellowed into my voicemail after it was delivered. I never called him back.

The memory brings a momentary smile to my face, but it fades as something unseen digs into the heel of my right foot, breaking skin. I hear more of them clattering through the pipes. I consider calling for help, but my agent blocked my number months ago, and the local police and animal control don't want to hear my complaints about spectral crustaceans anymore.

It's just me and the crabs. As it always was and always will be.

Groggily, I grab the hammer. The ghosts are everywhere and nowhere. In the kitchen, I spot one on the wire rack that holds my appliances and cookware. It tries to hide from my weapon, but its red shell reflects in the dusty copper of an officially licensed Crab King stock pot. Bashing it brings momentary satisfaction, but then the rack collapses, pots and pans raining upon me and sending me tumbling to the Italian marble floor.

Something inside my skull cracks on impact, a wet thud followed by disconcerting sloshing. The cold tiles beneath me turn sticky and warm as something trickles from my head.

Ten-limbed shadows shuffle in the hallway beyond the butcher's block island and the second oven. Immobilized under a mountain of overpriced, underused equipment, all I can do is listen as the hollow sound of spectral legs skittering sideways grows louder.

COCONUT & LEMON BARS

JM CYRUS

My mother used to make these for my siblings and me when we were children. I have since made them for my own. I have no idea where the recipe came from, as the carefully cut-out recipe bears no origin headers or footers of the publication or packaging from which it originated. These are simple but decadent and can be arranged artfully on a plate for grown-ups and children alike.

INGREDIENTS:

For the Base:
~ 1 ½ cups (50 g) crushed cornflakes
~ ½ cups (125 g) butter
1 ¼ cups (150 g) all-purpose flour
¼ cup (50 g) brown sugar

For the Topping:
2 tbsp all-purpose flour
½ tsp baking powder
¼ tsp salt
2 eggs
¾ cup and 2 tbsp (175 g) brown sugar
½ tsp vanilla
3/4 cup (125 g) chopped mixed nuts, optional
2 cups (175 g) shredded coconut (if not using the nuts, increase to 3 2/3 cups (300g) coconut)

For the Icing:
1 cup (125 g) powdered/confectioner's sugar
1 tbsp (14 g) butter
1 tbsp lemon juice

DIRECTIONS:

1. For the base, combine all the base ingredients in a bowl, mixing thoroughly. Press firmly into a 9x13 pan. Bake at 285°F (140°C) or 260°F (120°C) if using a convection oven for 10 minutes. Remove from the oven.
2. For the topping, mix flour, baking powder, and salt. In a separate bowl, mix the eggs, sugar, coconut, and vanilla. Combine bowls and add nuts if using. Spread over the baked base layer. Bake for 20 minutes at 350°F (180°C) or 325°F (160°C) if using a convection oven.
3. While the bars cool, prepare the icing. Mix together sugar, butter, and lemon juice until smooth. Frost the warm bars.
4. Cut into the bar shapes while still warm (I like doing them in diamond shapes by cutting diagonally through the tin).
5. Allow bars to cool fully in the tin before removing them.

STICKY PISTACHIO CAKE WITH SEVILLE ORANGE SYRUP

JM CYRUS

This has been a firm favorite for birthday parties and others for a long time in our family. I found it in a free magazine from a supermarket, and after a few trial-and-error attempts, I found the version that worked. Very sticky, only the very brave try to eat this with their fingers! I have made this vegan a few times too, using vegan condensed milk and butter, and it has worked very well. Likewise with using gluten free flour (though I did need to add xanthan gum in for that).

INGREDIENTS:

2/3 cups (150 g) unsalted butter, softened, plus extra for greasing
1½ cups (150 g) pistachio nuts
1½ cups (450 g) condensed milk
2 ¼ cups (280 g) all-purpose flour
1 tsp baking powder
1 tsp baking soda
4 Seville oranges, juiced, plus their zest
1 vanilla pod, split (or 1 tsp of vanilla bean paste)
½ cup (100 g) golden caster sugar

DIRECTIONS:

1. Preheat the oven to 350°F (180°C) or 325°F (160°C) if using a convection oven. Grease and line an 8x8 square cake tin with baking parchment.

2. Blitz the pistachios in a small food processor or pestle and mortar until ground to a coarse powder, then set aside.

3. Using an electric stand mixer or electric hand whisk, beat together the softened butter with the condensed milk until smooth and creamy.

4. Mix in the ground pistachios, then sieve in the flour with the baking powder, baking soda, and a pinch of salt.

5. Fold in the juice of 2 oranges and their grated zest. Stir well to combine.

6. Pour into the prepared tin and bake for 35 to 45 minutes until risen and golden.

7. In a small saucepan, heat the remaining orange juice and zest, the vanilla pod, and sugar for 5 minutes or until syrupy, then set aside.

8. When the cake is cooked and still warm, skewer holes in the top and pour over two-thirds of the syrup. Leave to stand until completely cool.

9. Serve the cake cut into squares, drizzled with the remaining syrup. It's also great topped with dried mint, chopped pistachios, and a dollop of Greek yogurt.

FRANKIE'S FOOTNOTE:

This recipe uses golden caster sugar, which is also known as superfine sugar in the United States. Its texture falls somewhere between regular granulated sugar and confectioner's/powdered sugar. Caster sugar comes in two forms: white and golden. The golden form used in this recipe has a brown hue and subtle buttery notes.

NIGHTMARE SOUP

PAUL O'NEILL

"Billy, you up? Come get your soup, you lazy toad," my gran screeched from the kitchen. "Don't let it get cold. You won't like it when it's cold."

Her pinched voice bounced around the small bungalow, shattering a tense knot between my ears like a smashed bottle, the glass shards slitting the back of my eyeballs. She was like this whenever I had a late night, shouting me awake, forcing me to eat what I thought of as her "nightmare soup."

Opening my eyes was an experience. As the thin light spilling over my cramped bed hit my pupils, flowers of molten pain shot up my eyes, a feeling like barbed wire twisting inside my brain.

Clothes from last night lay scattered on the floor as if I'd peeled them off before collapsing in a heap. I scrunched my eyes shut and squeezed the bridge of my nose, winching as my clumsy fingers found a swollen mess. Taking in a sharp breath, I tasted whiffs of coppery blood, the green of muddy grass, and, surprise, the apple and cinnamon of a girl's perfume.

A smug smile played on my lips as I tried to remember what the hell happened last night. A caveman grunt escaped my lips and I chuckled—big mistake. I held my breath, the pain ricocheting around my skull, reaching supernova levels that might force my brain to splatter out my ears and across my bedroom walls at the slightest sound.

"Billy, get your arse out here! Grammy's special recipe, brewed just for you."

She cackled like an honest-to-God witch, and I buried my head in my arms until the whirlwind of white pain abated. I braced myself and sat up, the world sloshing around me. Hot, yellow bile almost shot out of my nose. I shuffled to the edge of the bed and pushed myself up, the single bed bowing under me.

Flashes of being chased down a narrow street outside the Drumnagoil Arms sizzled like a short, grainy film in my mind. There was beer, mud, trees, blood, and escalating threats of violence against my person. Good times.

I stumbled toward the open bedroom door, my body aching all over like I'd caught the flu. I rolled my jaw, running a tingling hand across my face. I must've had some amount of laughs last night because my cheeks were on fire. It felt like I'd grown a week's worth of beard in one night.

The unique scent of Grammy's soup drifted into my room, smelling of something between diesel and soggy mushrooms. It was enough to make my bowels shrink. The soup was always the same, crammed full of floating veggies of unknown origin that bobbed around in steaming black liquid. It made me think of green things stewed in a cauldron, but I knew I'd gobble it up— it always helped me feel like myself again after a rough night.

The smell tried leading me out of my room, but it was no easy task. My feet were encased in mental concrete. Each time I stepped on the scratchy carpet, fresh pain canceled all my thoughts. I closed my eyes and shambled forward, bashing the crown of my head off the doorway. A cough of pain rumbled out my dry throat and I slapped at my thick skull as I walked down the narrow hall.

In the kitchen, I coughed into a balled fist, the rot of turgid soup billowing its cloud around me. My belly grumbled like a mini earthquake as Grammy glared at me like I'd just pointed a gun at her. She kept her wide, sorrowful eyes on me as she set a huge wooden spoon next to the bowl.

My throat constricted as a bubble plumed in the center of the soup, morphing from black to deepest green. It popped, letting out a strangled burst of steam. My heavy eyes turned away from the soup, focusing on black pots stacked on the stove, green sludge dribbling down their sides like drying phlegm.

"Sooner you start, sooner it's over. Go on."

She motioned for me to sit with her thin hands that poked out of a baggy, black top that covered her like a poncho. She looked every part the witch with her long, tussled hair that was more silver than black these days and the ever-growing wart that lived on the very tip of her nose. But she'd been the one who took me in when life tried to spit me out. A warm tingle swam around my chest seeing her fuss so much about making me feel better.

I sat on a wooden chair, thighs brushing the underside of the table as I squeezed myself in. The chair below me shifted unexpectedly, and my hand slapped the table inches from the soup. A droplet of black liquid sloshed over the bowl and hit the table, turning shades of midnight blue then green as it dribbled off the side and onto the carpet.

"Och, watch it, you," said Grammy, mopping up the mess with her sleeve.

I must've looked a right state. Hunched over, staring down into the soup, I caught how I smelled—like sweaty football boots stuffed inside a cupboard for two weeks.

I drummed my fingers on the wood, a pressure pulsing under my fingernails as I hunted for memories inside my sludgy cave of a brain. I must've gotten into another fight, no doubt over she who smelled of apple and cinnamon. Stuck in this dead town on the arse-crack of Scotland, there wasn't much else to do for fun except getting in a scrap or two.

Grammy drifted over to the window and looked outside, scanning the wall of trees lining the other side of the country road. She turned her hazel eyes on me, then flicked them away again, back out the window.

"Come on, Grammy. Have a seat." My deep, scratchy voice caught me by surprise. "Promise I won't bite."

"Just you eat your soup, dearie. You'll feel all the better."

I took in a deep breath and regretted it as a tang of tar and soggy strawberries sailed up my nose. The huge spoon shook in my hand like a baby trying to hold cutlery for the first time.

I blinked down at my hand. Slashes stained the back of it, the wounds red and seeping. I traced a finger along the sensitive skin and a thicket of rough hair sighed under my fingertip.

Grammy gasped and I stood, nearly knocking the table over. I steadied the bowl before the nightmare soup was lost to the floor. Flashes of blue and red painted the cramped room as a car screamed to a halt in our gravel driveway.

"Crap, crap, crap." Grammy strode over, her pointy Adam's apple bobbing as she grabbed my spoon, scooped up a ladle's worth of inky soup and shoved it in my mouth. "Time to eat up, Billy. Quick."

The liquid trickled down my throat, hitting the base of my empty stomach, a numbness spreading up my spine.

There was a pounding at the door that reverberated in the small space. "You alright in there? Is he there? Is...*it* in there with you?"

I smacked my lips. "Grammy?"

She set the spoon in my hand and squeezed my shoulder with a gentle hand. "Soup will make everything better. Eat up."

I looked into the soup, a funhouse reflection staring back at me. The mirror surface of the black liquid showed protruding teeth sticking out the corners of a huge jaw.

The police hammered the door again, threatening to knock it down.

"Eat your soup, dearie," said Grammy. "There you go. You're starting to look more human already."

ONE BOWL CHOCOLATE TEA CAKE

MERANDA TUTTLE

One year, I did a 52-week baking challenge on Reddit. Each week had a theme. This recipe came from week 23: Recipe Swap. To complete this challenge, a friend gave me a recipe for a bundt cake, which I loved so much I added it to my personal recipe book. I've since made changes to it. A few examples: made it in one bowl, modified it to be vegan, and played with the ingredients. You now get my final version. Here's one of my favorite things about it... You get a slightly different flavor profile depending on the tea you use which is why I like it without icing. Make sure to steep your tea for a long time to increase the subtle flavor it adds to the cake.

INGREDIENTS:

2 tbsp ground flaxseed
1 cup (240 ml) milk (dairy or nondairy with highest fat content you can find)
1/2 cup (120 ml) vegetable oil
1 tbsp vanilla
1 1/4 tsp baking soda
1 1/4 tsp baking powder
3/4 salt
1 3/4 cup (350 g) sugar
2 cups (240 g) all-purpose flour
3/4 cup (60 g) cocoa powder
1 cup (240 ml) boiling tea allow to steep fully to get flavor (tea choice will change the taste of cake but feel free to experiment)

1. Preheat oven 350°F (180°C) or 325°F (160°C) if using a convection oven.
2. Mix ground flaxseed with 6 tablespoons of water and let set for 5 minutes.
3. Combine ground flaxseed water, milk, oil, and vanilla. Use electric mixer to beat on medium speed until fully combined.
4. Change mixer to low. Add baking soda, baking powder, and salt. Fully mix before slowly adding sugar, flour, and cocoa a cup at a time. Do not overmix.
5. Slowly add boiling tea. Batter will be thin.
6. Grease a 9x13 pan and then coat with flour.
7. Add batter to pan.
8. Bake until toothpick inserted comes out clean, about 30-35 minutes. Time may vary.
9. Allow to cool and then frost with favorite frosting, glaze, syrup, or eat as is.

PETITS POTS AU CHOCOLAT

(CHOCOLATE CREAM POTS)

MELISSA COFFEY

A decadent chocolate dessert that can be dressed up or down. Made with just five ingredients, they are slightly heavier in texture than a mousse. The chocolate pots can be prepared the day before a dinner party. Just be sure to allow for chilling time, and stock up on extra cream to top. For a quirky twist, I've served these in different vintage teacups a la Mad Hatter Tea Party.

INGREDIENTS:

7 oz (200 g) good quality dark chocolate
1 ½ cups (300 ml) single cream
3-4 drops vanilla essence or extract
1 egg
dash of sea salt
To top: whipped cream and any selection of berries, optional

DIRECTIONS:

NOTE: The chocolate pots can be prepared with or without a blender

1. If using a blender, break up the chocolate pieces into the blender jar. Scald the cream in a saucepan, and when just boiling, pour onto the chocolate and blend till smooth. Blend in the salt, vanilla, and the egg. Transfer mixture back to saucepan.

2. If not using a blender, scald the cream in a saucepan, take it off the heat and add the chocolate. Leave for 5 minutes for chocolate to melt, then stir until smooth. Add the salt, vanilla, and egg (beat lightly with a fork before adding). Stir to amalgamate.
3. For both methods, beat over a very gentle heat with a wooden spoon until absolutely smooth.
4. Pour into four to six individual pots or ramekins, cover and chill for 3-4 hours before serving.
5. Garnish with freshly whipped cream, any kind of berries (raspberries and blackberries are a decadent combination), and a dusting of icing sugar. You could also go with whipped cream and grated dark chocolate.

A BRIEF HISTORY OF THE COMING OF THE JUNGLE

DORIAN WOLFE

In the end—perhaps today, perhaps a month from now when all the untainted canned goods are gone—everyone will die. Almost everyone, anyway.

But let's go back. The madness began when the poison (some say it was weed killer; some say pesticide. I say it doesn't matter) went bad. That is to say, the poison and the plants took a liking to each other. The poison slowly seeped into thick vascular tissue, but no one noticed. Not early on. All anyone cared about was that leaves were thicker and more vivid, and flowers brighter and more richly fragrant, and fruits juicy and so flavorful that farmers markets did a booming business, and vegan restaurants had a high time of it.

Then medical journals began to note the spiking cancer rate. Bone cancer most of all, but other kinds too. There were hints that this was more than just cancer, though. Where the tumors on the patients—victims?—were visible, whether bulging beneath the skin or suppurating above it, they smelled of ripe fruit, and the same smell lingered on the patients' breath. The reports were nauseating enough to put a damper on the new vegan craze. After all, who wanted to eat fruit that smelled of cancer? But even as the newly expanded stalls in the farmers markets became near-deserts, no one connected the dots. Or maybe we just didn't want to. Pursuant to a new federal bill, further research would be conducted to isolate possible causes of the morbidities...

Research.

That word meant time, time we didn't have. Days and weeks told the tale, not months or years. Not long after the first news articles appeared, herbivores began to die. Cancer riddled their bodies before the worms did, and death was a mercy. Herds of corpses—cows and sheep and goats—choked the lush, green fields. The remains of deer, cold and wet from summer dew, lay scattered through stilled forests and meadows, with fallen squirrels at their sides.

We finally began to understand.

That's when the burnings started. We burned every plant, every tree—the roses in the garden, the magnolias, the sprouting potatoes from the larder. Smoke rose in a haze broken only by the bright blue expanse of oceans, and the crackling of the fires haunted us wherever we went. We wrapped our noses and mouths bandit-fashion in wet cloths, so as not to choke when we went out (and we did go out). Sunset and sunrise were wonders; seen through a fog not quite thick enough to be a real fog, they were orange and blue and pink-purple and all the colors except for the one that was coming...the green of the jungle...

Many of the plants died in our desperate attempts at retribution. Vines, flowers, and trees were pulverized into ash. But the others, they grew stronger. Mighty trees with flame-scarred trunks created an unbroken canopy, hiding a sky that must have been blue after the smoke finally cleared. Hulking lianas trailed from the monstrous branches. Massive flowers bloomed in an immodest profusion of color and texture and fragrance.

And the farmers' fields—they exploded with lethal life. Many-lobed tomatoes as large as pumpkins. Thorny cucumber vines with rope-like tendrils. Corncobs that weighed more than horses' heads, their kernels each as big as a man's thumb; they swayed on stalks rustling in the breeze while harvesters and grain combines waited soundless in their sheds, their innards rusting.

In front of my house, this house, a tree dripped down giant mangoes that smelled of paradise but promised only hell. When they fell and burst into pools of nectar littered with glistening pulp, we couldn't keep the hungry children and the pigs away from them.

And we thought shared cremation had gone out of style.

You can imagine the rest. Haunted-eyed skeletons smelling of fruit. The food chain collapsing even further, unravelling day by day. Carnivores feeding on diseased prey becoming diseased themselves, and eventually feeding on each other as a last resort (they must eat, after all). And there's some sort of pity, misguided or not, in the deed—one predator ending another's misery. Like I did for my poor little Camper. He was almost three, a tuxie, and even with a white tumor squirming its way out from his skull, he purred until his heart stopped.

It takes more force than you'd think, breaking a cat's neck.

He...he was a good boy.

The plants are poisoning the water and the air now; they choke the houses, cloaking the windows and guarding the doors.

Do I hope someone, somewhere, someday, will read this? Of course. But even if someone survives and finds it, she will probably be worse off than I am. Because this pile of scrap paper is like the scrawling of a condemned prisoner, written on the cold, immovable walls of a stone cell. Only some other poor condemned creature will read it. Well, better than no one.

One more thing. I don't understand how evolution works, but if the plants become sentient (impossible, surely, but why not?), perhaps they will read this...and laugh at the folly of man.

Will I have made a difference? I don't know. Whoever you are, please remember me. And Camper. He deserved better.

* * *

GLUTEN-FREE SUGAR-FREE MINCE PIES

DIANA STANHOPE

I like to make these in small batches so that I always have a fresh batch throughout the holiday season. Before cooking and eating, if you are superstitious, see the notes below.

INGREDIENTS FOR SIX MUFFIN SIZE PIES:

½ cup (40 g) instant oats
4oz (113 g) cream cheese
1 apple
¼ cup (35 g) raisins
Juice from 1 orange
Butter or whatever you use to grease your pan
Dash of orange zest

DIRECTIONS:

1. Cut the apple into smallish pieces.
2. In a small pot, boil the apple pieces, orange zest, and raisins in the orange juice. You might need a dash of water depending on how much juice you've used.
3. While the fruit is boiling, grease a muffin pan with butter.
4. Mix the cream cheese and oats. It's easier to just dig your hands in for this one.
5. Once mixed, separate it into six portions.
6. Mush those portions into the muffin pan, flattening them against the bottom and edges to make the crusts.

7. Bake the empty crusts at 350°F (180°C) or 325°F (160°C) if using a convection oven until they get golden (around 20 minutes).

8. When the crust is done, the apple/raisin mixture should be tender. Dispense it evenly into the six crusts.

9. Pop it back into the oven long enough to get the crispiness you prefer on the top of the filling.

SUPERSTITIONS:

1) Be mindful to only stir clockwise. If you stir anti-clockwise, you'll tempt bad luck.

2) Another custom is that all the family take a turn in stirring the mincemeat mixture while making a wish.

3) Tradition also says you make a wish while eating the first mince pie of the holiday season.

4) Mince pies should always be eaten in silence.

5) It is good luck to eat mince pies on each of the 12 days of Christmas. Luckier still to eat one on each day in a different home.

6) As a guest, it is bad luck to refuse a mince pie when offered one.

VEGAN ORANGE BLOSSOM & APRICOT BAKLAVA

GABRIELLE WINOCO

Mise en place is everything for baklava, and although this seems daunting with its long list of ingredients to prep, you'll be proud to serve the most flavorful and fresh baklava your guests have ever had, especially for your vegan friends! It lasts in the fridge for up to two weeks and freezes great to pull and thaw whenever you're jonesing for something tasty.

FOR THE JAM

INGREDIENTS:

19 oz (540 g) dried apricots

1 orange, zest and juice

1 ¾ cups plus 2 tsp (425 ml) water

¾ tsp kosher salt

½ tsp ginger

2/3 cup plus 1 tbsp (142 g) sugar

DIRECTIONS:

1. Simmer all ingredients in a heavy-bottomed pot on low until fruit is tender. Cool. Blend in food processor to form a jam. Set aside.

Vegan Orange Blossom & Apricot Baklava

FOR THE NUT MIXTURE

INGREDIENTS:

1 walnut
Pinch of kosher salt
1 tsp cinnamon

DIRECTIONS:

1. Grind all ingredients in food processor to form a coarse flour. Set aside.

FOR THE SYRUP

INGREDIENTS:

4 2/3 cups (936 g) sugar
1 ¼ cup (285 ml) water
1 lemon, zest and juice
1/8 tsp salt
2 tsp orange blossom water

DIRECTIONS:

1. Bring this to a boil and immediately turn off. Set aside. (This will be used after baklava is baked.)

FOR THE FILLO AND ASSEMBLY

INGREDIENTS:

1 package fillo dough, thawed in fridge overnight
1 ¼ cups (250 g) Vegan Butter, plus more for greasing pan

DIRECTIONS:

1. Generously coat a 13x18 deep-sided sheet cake pan with softened vegan butter.
2. Place 1 sheet of fillo on bottom of pan, brushing thoroughly with melted butter. Add one more layer of fillo, then brush again with butter. Do this until you have 5 layers.
3. Remove 1/3 cup of nut mixture and set aside for topping. Then sprinkle half of the remaining nut mix onto dough. Layer on 5 more sheets of fillo, brushing with butter in between each just as before.
4. Using a spatula, spread fruit mix on top, getting it in all the corners and all over the dough evenly. Then add second portion of nuts, keeping the 1/3 cup aside for topping.
5. Place remaining fillo sheets over top of fruit, buttering thoroughly between each layer. With a paring knife, cut your baklava into rectangles. If you cut it 5 by 6, you will yield 30 small pieces, but you can cut it however you'd like. Make sure to cut all the way through to bottom. I usually go over my cuts twice.
6. Bake at 325°F (160°C) or 300°F (150°C) if using a convection oven for sixty minutes, or until the top fillo is evenly golden.
7. When hot out of the oven, drizzle all of syrup over top. Add remaining nut mixture.
8. Store in fridge overnight and serve next day.

COMFORT FOOD
PATRICK TUMBLETY

Mom switches into cooking mode when I get sick.

A mix of maternal care and Italian hospitality means that I get a smorgasbord even when our family doctor says that I'm supposed to be "starving a fever."

This morning is no exception.

The clanging of pans from the kitchen awakens me from sleep, and by the time I get enough strength to enter the hallway, I'm greeted by the smell of toast and the sound of sizzling bacon. I don't know if it's because I've had nothing but cough syrup and acetaminophen for two days, but I feel like I'm hallucinating, transferring back to my childhood and my mother's efforts to keep me safe, warm, and fed.

Especially fed.

The food smells delicious and my stomach cries, so I march forward without regard for sanity. I stop at the kitchen entrance, staring at the back of my mother's head as she concentrates on flicking the pan upwards to flip the omelet over so that it doesn't fall onto the floor, an occurrence that used to happen fifty percent of the time with one hundred percent laughter from the rest of the family, including Mom.

I don't know if I should say "good morning," so I just walk to the table and sit. I concentrate on the wood surface until she lowers the plate in front of me. I can tell by the decomposition of her hand that I won't dare look up and see her face.

She places two cups of coffee on the table and then sits on the other side. She lifts hers and takes a sip. A moment later, I hear the liquid dripping onto the tile.

I stuff my mouth with a fork full of food to stifle a scream.

The bacon is as delicious as my memories and the coffee is as bittersweet.

I continue eating because I don't feel good, and when I don't feel good, my mother makes me food and I eat until I'm full. Some things in life are that simple. I'll wait until I'm finished before asking her "how" she came back from the dead.

At least the "why" brings me some comfort.

PANCAKE CORNBREAD

R. HAVEN

This cornbread was based off a family recipe for regular old corn-bread... until we didn't have the correct ingredients and made some substitutions (namely using brown sugar instead of refined white—this is important!). After realizing how much the cornbread tasted like pancakes, a new breakfast side dish was formed!

INGREDIENTS:

1 cup (150-160 g) cornmeal
2 1/3 cups (280 g) flour
1 cup (200 g) brown sugar
4 ½ tsp baking powder
1 tsp salt

2/3 cup (150 g) butter or margarine
1 2/3 cups (393 ml) milk
Honey or syrup (optional)

DIRECTIONS:

1. Start by preheating the oven to 400°F (205°C) or 375°F (190°C) if using a convection oven.
2. Grease a 9-inch baking pan with some nonstick cooking spray, although butter or margarine will also do. For a softer, smoother cornbread, put the cornmeal through a grinder until it's very fine, almost powdery.
3. Combine your dry ingredients in a mixing bowl with a rubber spatula or a wooden spoon. Once they're mixed, add the butter and milk, and continue mixing until the consistency is mostly smooth.
4. Fill the baking pan and smooth the top. Place on the middle rack of the oven. Bake your cornbread for 25-30 minutes (or, if you ground your cornmeal, 30-35 minutes) and test with a toothpick until it comes out clean to ensure it's fully cooked.
5. Serve with honey, syrup, or whatever you like to eat pancakes with!

THE BEST FLOURLESS BROWNIES

JM CYRUS

Since discovering this recipe more than a decade ago, I haven't looked back. These brownies are not for the faint of heart. These are glossy and slightly crunchy on top, dense and fudgy in the middle, very rich, and intensely chocolatey. I have made these as gifts, afternoon tea, dessert for a large dinner party, and have always had people sing their praises.

INGREDIENTS:

1/3 cup (75 g) unsalted butter, chopped, plus extra to grease
1 ½ cups (250 g) dark chocolate (70% cocoa solids), chopped
1 ½ tbsp (15 g) cocoa powder
2 tsp vanilla extract
1 1/4 cup (250 g) superfine/caster sugar
4 large eggs
¾ cup (100 g) ground almonds

DIRECTIONS:

1. Preheat oven to 350°F (180°C) or 325°F (160°C) if using a convection oven. Lightly grease and line an 8x8 square tin with baking parchment.
2. Melt the chocolate and butter together in a large pan over a low heat, stirring occasionally.
3. Take pan off the heat and whisk in the cocoa powder, vanilla, and sugar until everything is combined.
4. Whisk in the eggs one at a time.
5. Stir in the ground almonds. (And if opting to add other things, add them now.)

The Best Flourless Brownies

6. Scrape into the prepared tin, and level by giving it a gentle shake.
7. Bake for 25 to 30 minutes or until firm to the touch.
8. Leave to cool in the tin before cutting it into squares.
9. Serve warmed and either with ice cream, double cream, crème fraiche, or fresh berry coulis. Or just over your hands in the kitchen. Mind the crumbs! Leftovers can be stored in an airtight container at room temperature for up to 5 days.

AUTHOR'S NOTE:

*Good chocolate matters more than anything else in this recipe!

**Once you've mastered the base recipe, folding in other ingredients works really well. Just add them into the mix before scraping the whole thing into the baking tin. For example, you can use nuts (peanuts and hazelnuts work well, as do pecans), white chocolate chips or chunks, desiccated coconut, or dried fruit such as cranberries or blueberries.

LUCY FURR'S PINEAPPLE CHEESE CASSEROLE

BRANDON MEAD

In the middle of this graveyard is a recipe for a forbidden casserole. The ingredient list and short directions take up more space than the name on the flowerless headstone.

Carved into smooth marble it says:

2 cans pineapple chunks
1 cup sugar
6 tbsp all-purpose flour
2 cups shredded sharp cheddar cheese
1 sleeve crushed round crackers
1/4 cup unsalted butter, melted

Spray a 2 qt baking dish.
Keep 6 tbsp of the pineapple juice.
Stir powdered ingredients with juice and fruit.

Mix & sprinkle remaining ingredients on top.
Bake at 350 for 30 minutes.
Let me rest.

This is the kind of thing you see in the South. Where the moss grows thick and hangs low from every tree, you'll find guides for desserts and appetizers. Spritz cookies, deviled eggs, and lemon bars. Human legacy left behind in the form of an edible epitaph. Some famous family dish expected at every birth, wedding, and funeral, chiseled into a single cookbook page to encapsulate an entire life.

Sometimes people copy the recipes. Go home and make them. Bring them back to the cemetery to take a picture with their recreation or have a picnic with the deceased. It's a sweet gesture. Something to say, "You won't be forgotten, and neither will your deviled eggs." A reflection of how we all hope to leave something behind for people to enjoy.

Dead to rights, I didn't come out here looking for *this* kind of comestible adventure. My trip to these woods was because I heard it was the best place to cruise. The message boards gave an approximate latitude and longitude, but what they didn't say was that the supposed "best hookup spot in the county" bordered a burial ground.

I was trying to follow my own footprints back toward the living, but something about the gravestone caught my eye. A name: Lucius Ferguson. *Ferguson* like the towering marker at the head of the plot. Generations of the same bloodline, all decomposing together in one patch of earth. The kind of dirt-based mausoleum that tells you where you'll rot before you're even born.

Just below what I assumed to be this departed North Floridian's original recipe, was a signature.

xoxo
Ms. Lucy Furr

Random dick would have to wait. I had grocery shopping to do.

***

I'm no Michelin-star chef, but I can follow a simple recipe. It's the kind of thing you figure out when you live alone. When you decide it's better than pretending to be someone else.

With my dollar store equivalent to a can-opener, I pop open the pineapple chunks. They smell sweet like daiquiris by a pool next to a half-naked man covered in suntan lotion. Like that first trip to Key West when I learned the right way to apply eyeliner.

While I strain the tins over the sink, something tickles my ear like a crevice spider on a long thread. Whispered words hiss out, "Six tablespoons."

A few hours in the humidity trolling for suckable cock will do that to you. Make you hear things that aren't there, snap a cold sweat, and feel like the heat is being sucked out of the room. But it's a good reminder. "Yes ma'am," I say to my empty studio apartment.

I mix the pineapple and reserved juice with the flour and sugar. So far so good. It's the shredded cheese that makes me feel iffy. Lucy said it had to be sharp, so I bought it sharp. When I sniff through the resealable opening though, it smells exactly the opposite of what I wanted to do with my day. What you'd run away from if you opened a guy's zipper and inhaled.

"It's delicious," the whisper says with a snakey sibilant "s" so long I thought I'd put the kettle on. I hadn't.

Where I feel hot breath, I swat at my neck. Nothing is there. Something stings like fire ants down my spine, as if a single press-on stiletto nail is poking every vertebra. I ignore it. Crushing the sleeve of round crackers with my fist, the voice *tsks*. I notice a chill on both shoulders when the voice says, "You're doing it all wrong."

Leave it to me to fuck up some queer ghost's recipe. To summon them like Bloody Mary with the culinary curse they left behind.

While I melt the stick of unsalted butter in the microwave, I wonder about Lucy. About who she was versus who she was meant to be. The dash between the dates on her headstone equaled somewhere under fifty years. Almost exactly how long it took me to start over. It's then I remember I forgot to preheat the oven.

The microwave dings and with it, the voice is fully charged. Tugging at my brain and shrieking in my ear, "Do it right!" Drinking glasses shatter in the cupboard from the shrillness. Steam billows like the gates of hell on the sensitive part of the back of my thighs, where my cut-off shorts don't quite cover. The oven door creaks and bounces hard as it falls to an open position. Someone made sure it was preheated, but it definitely wasn't me.

My body jerks on its own, hands-first into the bowl of shredded cheese and crackers. Pouring the butter in, this parboiling poltergeist is telling *me* how to cook in *my* own kitchen. Wrist-deep, my fingers knead and turn the concoction furiously. I am no longer in control of this mixed topping. My preparation method is full-on possession. Maybe she ran out of space, but I don't remember this in the recipe.

With everything packed into the 8x12 dish, I'm dragged in front of the roaring heat of the open oven to feed it this Tropical Wisconsin. This La Piña de Fromage. This absolute flop of ingredients that should never be baked together. Upon entry, the food scrapes the blazing-red element and sizzles along with some of the body hair I'm too broke to get lasered off. My 400-square-foot apartment fills with the scent of charred fruit and burning keratin while Lucy sets the casserole on the metal rack. Once it's perfectly centered, she uses my hip to shut the door.

Sliding down next to the oven, I slump on the linoleum like a pile of used rags. Immobile. Catatonic. Singed. A seized vessel inhaling my own foul fumes while moist Ritz crackers and one-third of a Bahama Mama crisp into my skin.

The timer is set.

I have thirty minutes to think about longing.

Half an hour to worry about loneliness.

Just enough time to convince myself, just like before, I'll be stuck like this forever.

The oven timer buzzes.

My body jolts, reanimated.

Red-faced and up on my feet, I eye floral print oven mitts, pleading with the ghost to let me wear them before I remove the scalding tray. To not let me burn anymore. I tell her I'm on her side.

There's a pause while the mysterious dish overcooks. It needs to come out.

"Let me rest," Lucy whispers, softly. The final step in her instructions.

Tears stream down my face as I feel myself slip back into the Head Chef position.

I'm free, but Lucy's not.

Back in the cemetery, I kneel on the dead woman's grave where the grass has long-since grown green and turned to brown. I uncover the casserole. It looks even worse than it smells. Just three to five shades of bright yellow and buttery tan. The product is a direct deviation from the role each ingredient was expected to fulfill.

"Taste it," she says from below six feet of dirt and worms.

While I trace my fingerprints through sans serif about cups and tablespoons, I imagine who I could have become before I bought my first shake-n-go wig. I picture Lucy telling her family that the only way they'll get her in the family plot is if they let her have this one thing. This beloved casserole immortalized forever. Begging that they let her sign her creation as a persona better suited than the name she was given. If she couldn't have what she wanted in life, at least let her have it in death.

For Lucy Furr, her recipe was never about the food. It was about the rest.

So, I take a bite and chew. I let the strange flavors sit on my tongue. When I swallow, I finally get it.

One final joke for everyone who never understood her. Lucy's magnum opus of revenge. The thing she made them eat at every gathering even before she was dead. The eternal game she'd play from the afterlife.

And even though it's not the worst thing I've ever had in my mouth, I know Lucy is laughing when I tell her gravestone, "Girl, that's a good one."

***

Dairy-Free Matcha Banana Bread

DAIRY-FREE MATCHA BANANA BREAD

GABRIELLE WINOCO

Love banana bread but want something different? A twist of matcha adds an energizing earthiness while the sesame seeds add a nutty crunch that will be sure to have you hooked.

INGREDIENTS:

1 ½ cup (300 g) sugar
3 small eggs
1 1/3 tsp vanilla
2/3 cup (142 ml) olive oil
1/2 cup (100 ml) oat milk
11.2 oz (318 g) banana puree
2 cups (250 g) all-purpose flour
1 tsp baking soda
¾ tsp kosher salt
5 ½ tsp matcha, cooking grade
½ cup (65 g) black sesame seeds, optional

DIRECTIONS:

1. Grease an 8-inch round cake pan with 3-inch sides. Line the bottom with a circle of parchment and set aside.
2. In a stand mixer, beat sugar and eggs on medium until fluffy. Add vanilla.
3. Add in olive oil, milk, and banana puree and mix on low until homogenous. Scrape bottom and sides of bowl well.
4. Add in dry ingredients, including seeds, and mix on low until just incorporated. Pour into cake pan.

5. Bake at 325°F (160°C) or, if using a convection oven 300°F (150°C), for 60-70 minutes, rotating pan halfway through.
6. Cool completely before unmolding and cut into 8 wedges.

BANANA YOGURT MUFFINS

MELISSA COFFEY

An all-time favorite recipe for banana muffins—ideal for the health-conscious or muffin connoisseurs. Impress the hungry hordes with their moist texture. These quick-to-prepare treats boast an unusual secret ingredient—natural yogurt.

INGREDIENTS:

2-3 tbsp melted butter or coconut oil (depending on size of bananas)

3 tbsp honey

1 egg, beaten (preferably free-range)

1 tsp vanilla essence or extract

½ cup (115 g) yogurt (preferably pot-set and low-sugar)

1 ½ cups (170 g) self-rising flour

2-3 medium-large ripe bananas, mashed

½ tsp cinnamon

¼ teaspoon of baking soda

DIRECTIONS:

1. Prepare muffin tins by greasing.
2. Peel and mash bananas with a large fork or potato masher. Cover and place in fridge.
3. Melt the butter in a small saucepan or espresso heater. Preheat oven to 350°F (180°C) or 325°F (160°C) if using a convection oven.
4. Meanwhile, beat an egg and measure out honey in main mixing bowl. Add melted butter to honey and beaten egg. Stir vigorously to combine, then add vanilla essence and yogurt, stirring gently.

5. Add mashed banana and cinnamon.
6. Sift the flour with baking soda, folding into the mixture, stirring gently to combine.
7. Spoon in the muffin mixture to muffin pan, and bake for 25-30 minutes, checking at 20 minutes (cooking time can vary quite a bit).
8. Cool on oven rack, remove from pan, and sprinkle with a little more cinnamon.
9. Serve with butter, a dollop of yogurt or à la natural! Keeps well for 4-5 days unrefrigerated in an airtight container.

VARIATIONS: Add a generous handful of raspberries or blueberries (frozen or fresh). Vanilla yogurt instead of natural also works well, but omit the vanilla essence.

ABOUT THE CONTRIBUTORS

T.L. Beeding was born and raised in West Sacramento, California. She wears many hats: a cancer survivor, a mother, a writer, and a medical assistant. She is the author of *They Come at Night and Other Horrors* and has had her work featured in several anthologies and magazines. When she is not writing, T.L. seeks misadventure with her boyfriend, daughter, and two cats at their home in the Hudson Valley. More about her work and life can be found on her website tlbeeding.com.

M. Belanger is a Shirley Jackson Award nominee, two-time recipient of the Joseph Cotter Memorial Poetry Prize, and author of over thirty books, including the *Dictionary of Demons* and the Shadowside Series. Belanger resides in Ohio in a spooky old house filled with books and cats.

Evan Benner (he/him) is a horror-loving homebody from the Midwest who is new to the original fiction scene. When not feverishly catching up on bygone horror movies, he slinks out from behind his teeming record shelves to enjoy concerts under the cover of night.

Hannah Birss is a writer and aspiring magpie based out of Ontario, Canada. She lives with her partner, children, and multiple animals. She can usually be found in a nest constructed of books, writing journals, and shiny trinkets. You can find her work upcoming in NUNUM's *Opolis* anthology, Purple Ink Press's *Bimbo Feminist Anthology*, and *Once Upon a Future Time Vol. 3* by the Brothers Uber. You can follow her on Instagram @hannahbirsswrites for upcoming news on publications, tips, tricks, and other writerly things.

Kerry E.B. Black is an HWA member from Western Pennsylvania who enjoys cooking and eating. Please follow the author at KerryEBBlack.com.

Ryan Breadinc is an author and home cook from Western Australia. Coming from a long line of bakers, he mostly strives for his grandmother's approval but feeds the whole family along the way.

Audris Candra is a queer and disabled Chinese-Indonesian writer and editor. Their other works have appeared in *New Naratif* and *Haunted Hallways* anthology. You can find them across social media with the handle @audriserat.

E.E.W. Christman is a queer nonbinary writer and editor in the Pacific Northwest. They're a professional editor and have also taught creative writing. Their work has appeared in a number of publications, including *The NoSleep Podcast*, *Diet Riot: A Fatterpunk Anthology*, and *Tales to Terrify*. You can read more about them and their work at eewchristmanwrites.com.

Jennifer Clark is the author of a children's book and three full-length poetry collections. Her latest book, *Kissing the World Goodbye* (Unsolicited Press), ventures into the world of memoir, braiding family tales with recipes. Her work has been nominated for a Rhysling Award, Best Microfiction, Best of the Net, six Pushcart Prizes, and made Ellen Datlow's 2011 Honorable Mention List for "Best Horror of the Year." You can find her at jenniferclarkkzoo.com and on social media @ jenniferclarkbooks.

Josh Clark is a writer, bookseller, and graphic designer. His short fiction has been published by Pikes Peak Writers, Black Hare Press, Shacklebound Books, and others.

Melissa Coffey is an Australian writer and editor, residing in Melbourne, home to a thriving foodie culture. A long-time organic food enthusiast and sometime vegetarian, Melissa enjoys culinary improvisation almost as much as cooking up a story. Melissa's poetry and fiction are often tinged with darkness, featuring in Crow & Cross Keys, Crow's Quill Magazine, Nonbinary Review, The Ekphrastic Review, and Exist Otherwise. Anthology appearances include fiction in Anna Karenina Isn't Dead (Improbable Press), and prose poetry in The Memory Palace. They're delighted to have their first recipe selection published, several of which are originals. Melissa is working on several chapbooks and a novella. Connect on Twitter @ CuriousSeeds.

Jeff Currier has little time to write. Hence, he writes little stories, like this one. Find more @jffcurrier on X or Jeff Currier Writes on Facebook.

Rebecca Cuthbert writes dark fiction and poetry. Her books include *In Memory of Exoskeletons* (Alien Buddha Press), *Creep This Way: How to Become a Horror Writer with 24 Tips to Get You Ghouling* (Seamus and Nunzio Productions), and *Self-Made Monsters* (ABP). For publications and information, visit rebeccacuthbert.com.

JM Cyrus is a speculative fiction writer living in London, UK. With a bachelor's in Classical Studies and a master's in Reception Theory, she enjoys finding new worlds and looking at how she found them. She has had work published all over the place, including *Luna Station Quarterly*, *All Worlds Wayfarer*, and *Inner Worlds*. See the full list at her website jmcyrus.carrd. co.

Kendra Dennis is working on her B.A. in English with a concentration in writing at American Public University System. "Always Chew Well" is her first horror fiction piece to be published. You can find her in Pennsylvania writing short stories that can open up to a much larger world.

M. A. Dubbs is an award-winning Mexican-American and LGBT poet from Indiana. For over a decade, Dubbs has published writing in magazines and anthologies in seven countries across the globe. She is the author of three poetry collections: *Aerodynamic Drag: Poetry and Short Fiction* (2021), *An American Mujer* (Bottlecap Press, 2022), and *Limestone Versified: Indiana Haiku and Other Poems* (2024).

Kurt Fawver's short fiction has won a Shirley Jackson Award and been nominated for a Bram Stoker Award. It has been published in venues such as *Nightmare, Lightspeed, The Magazine of Fantasy & Science Fiction, Weird Tales, Gamut,* and *Vastarien.*

Stacey Flower is a horror writer trapped in the body of a lawyer. Born and raised in New Jersey (so she knows something about good pizza), she spent about 15 years in Colorado and Wyoming before moving back East to Connecticut, where she currently lives with her husband and their monstrous dog, Bella. She hopes to one day return to the Rocky Mountains and to that delicious pork green chili…perhaps once the craving becomes too strong. "I'd Kill for a Decent Slice" is her first publication.

Eric Fomley is the editor of Shacklebound Books. His stories have appeared in *Clarkesworld, Daily Science Fiction,* and *Galaxy's Edge Magazine.* You can read more of his stories on his website ericfomley.com or in his *Flash Futures* or *Portals* collections.

Conrad Gardner's work has appeared in *Superlative Literary Journal, Autofocus,* and *Impossible Worlds.* He enjoys a good scare.

Nicholas Gordon is a horror author who has been trapped in the Nightmare Realm since 1954. Known for his outlandish concepts, he often visits the dreams of others to find inspiration for his stories. When he's not writing, he enjoys listening to opera and motivational speakers. He has somehow acquired a cellphone, and you can find updates on his latest projects on

Instagram @nicholasgordonwrites.

DJ Grant is an award-winning artist living in Southern California. She holds a B.A. in English, Emphasis Literature, from The University of British Columbia. Her artwork has been shown in Los Angeles, Toronto, and New York. Her recipes appear in the *Mission Viejo Community Cookbook*. Grant's writing and artwork can be found in *Litro Magazine, Cosmic Daffodil Journal, The Mighty*, and *The Lehrhaus*.

Kay Hanifen was born on a Friday the 13th and once lived for three months in a haunted castle. So, obviously, she had to become a horror writer. Her work has appeared in over forty anthologies and magazines. When she's not consuming pop culture with the voraciousness of a vampire at a 24-hour blood bank, you can usually find her with her two black cats or at kayhanifenauthor.wordpress.com.

R. Haven hails from Toronto, Canada. His short stories have been published by *Canthius*, Soitera Press, TL;DR Press, among others. *Last Stanza Poetry Journal* and Old Moon Press have published his poetry. He also signed a contract with Scarsdale Publishing for a three-part fantasy series, and a contract with Renaissance Press for a standalone horror novel. His website is theirritablequeer.com.

Ria Hill is a writer, librarian, and nonbinary horror. They spend their non-work hours maintaining their recreational spreadsheet collection and interrupting their spouse's train of thought with deeply worrying story pitches. Their work has appeared in *The Book of Queer Saints Volume II, Escalators to Hell: Shopping Mall Horrors*, and *A Coup of Owls*. Chances of them devouring you on sight are always low, but never zero. They can be found at riahill.weebly.com and on various social media platforms @riawritten.

Desiree Horton is a horror writer and enthusiast. She can be found at home in the Pacific Northwest, thinking about scary things with her two dogs, two kids, and one husband. Her work can be found in other horror anthologies and on the edges of items she will lose almost immediately. Her debut horror novel, *Midnight Mother*, was published by Unveiling Nightmares in the summer of 2024. More information on her works can be found at authordesireehorton.my.canva.site or on Amazon.

Steve Loiaconi is a journalist and a graduate of George Mason University's MFA program. His fiction previously appeared in *Griffel, Mystery Tribune, Allegory, Mythaxis*, and *The Saturday Evening Post*, as well as the anthologies *Dracula's Guests, Open All Night*, and *Why Didn't You Just Leave*. He lives in Washington, D.C., with his wife and son.

M. L. Martin is an Austin, Texas-based writer. Her stories have found homes in anthologies like *Once Upon a Future Time, The Desert Writers Guild: Plague Years, CyBEARpunk: An Afterverse Anthology*, and more. When she is not writing, she likes to be outside hiking, climbing, and foraging.

Alison McBain is a BIPOC author with writing published in *Grain Magazine, On Spec*, and *Abyss & Apex*, among other magazines. Her novels have won or been finalists for over thirteen awards, including the Foreword INDIES and the Canadian Book Club Awards. When not writing, she's the associate editor for the literary magazine *ScribesMICRO* and administrator for The Scribes Prize.

Brandon Mead is a Best of the Net nominated bathtub writer, intermittent poet, and cat dad who calls the Pacific Northwest home after living his whole Nomi Malone fantasy in Las Vegas, Nevada. A former Floridian, his work has appeared, or is forthcoming, in publications such as *Demonic Carnival, Taco Bell Quarterly, Oh Yeah: A Bear Poetry Anthology*, and *86 Logic*.

Sarah R. New (she/her) has been writing since the age of 6. She has recently been published in journals including *Wishbone*

Words, *Gastropoda*, and *Genrepunk Magazine*. Her Gothic horror novella, *Amissis Liberis*, was published by Alien Buddha Press in May 2024. Sarah loves to cook and is an avid traveler who has visited four continents. Her travel memoir, *The Great European Escape: The Trials and Tribulations of Travelling While Chronically Ill*, is available for free at sarahrnew.wordpress.com.

Lena Ng shambles around Toronto, Canada, and is a zombie member of the Horror Writers Association. She has curiosities published in weighty tomes including *Amazing Stories* and Flame Tree's *Asian Ghost Stories* and *Weird Horror Stories*. *Under an Autumn Moon* is her short story collection.

Paul O'Neill is an award-winning short story writer from Fife, Scotland. As an Internal Communications professional, he fights the demon of corporate-speak on a daily basis. His story "Into the Drinking Dark" recently placed second in Creative Ink's annual short story competition. His works have been published by *The NoSleep Podcast*, Crystal Lake, Sinister Smile Press, Scare Street, *Vanishing Point Magazine*, *Fifth Di Magazine*, HellBound Books, Eerie River, Grinning Skull Press, and many other publications. You can find him sharing his love of short stories on Instagram or Threads (paul.on1984).

John K. Peck is a Berlin-based writer and musician. His fiction has appeared in *Interzone*, *Pyre*, *Cosmic Horror Monthly*, *Cold Signal*, *Dark Horses*, and the anthologies *Dark Stars* (Shacklebound) and *The Nameless Songs of Zadok Allen* (JayHenge). He is also a frequent contributor to *McSweeney's Internet Tendency* and has appeared in several McSweeney's anthologies.

Robert Perez sleeps at the bottom of the ocean. Urban legend whispers that the writer can be summoned into your dreams if you read his work to a jack-o-lantern. You can find his poems and stories in the *Horror Writers Association Poetry Showcase Volumes II, III, IV (Special Mention), V*, and *X, Five Minutes at Hotel Stormcove, Community of Magic Pens, Greater*

Than His Nature, and more. Robert Perez recently graduated and works as a psychological counselor providing therapy. Follow @_TheLeader on twitter or @RobertPerez.bsky.social to keep up with future projects.

Genevieve Puttay is British-Mauritian and lives in Zürich, Switzerland. She loves tea, illustrated books, pockets, anything gothic, literary bears, and kindness. She is always happy to talk books, writing, movies, sport, and is especially happy when any of those things involve story structure. See genevieveputtay.co.uk for writerly news and links to socials.

Eric Raglin (he/him) is a queer Nebraskan horror/weird fiction writer. His short story collections include *Nightmare Yearnings*, *Extinction Hymns* (published by Brigids Gate Press), and *Lonesome Pyres* (published by Off Limits Pulp). He owns Cursed Morsels Press and has edited *No Trouble at All* (with Alexis DuBon), *Bitter Apples*, *Shredded: A Sports and Fitness Body Horror Anthology*, and *Antifa Splatterpunk*. Find him on Twitter, Bluesky, or Instagram @ericraglin1992.

Stetson Ray lives in Tennessee and spends his time writing odd stories for odd people.

Marsheila (Marcy) Rockwell is a Rhysling Award-winning poet and the author of fourteen books and dozens of poems and short stories. She is an active member of SFWA, HWA, IAMTW, and SFPA. She is also a disabled Chippewa/Red River Métis pediatric cancer and mental health awareness advocate. She currently lives in the Valley of the Sun with her husband, three of their five children, two rescues, and far too many books. You can find out more here: marsheilarockwell.com.

A native Floridian, **C. L. Sidell** grew up playing with toads in the rain and indulging in speculative fiction. She draws inspiration from the natural world, travel, and all things spooky. A Pushcart Nominee, Best of the Net Nominee, and Rhysling Finalist, her work appears in *34 Orchard, Apparition Lit, The*

Cosmic Background, The Dread Machine, F&SF, Factor Four Magazine, Stupefying Stories, and others.

Dorian J. Sinnott is a graduate of Emerson College's Writing, Literature, and Publishing program currently living in New York with his two cats. He is a member of the Horror Writers Association and Horror Authors Guild. Dorian's work has appeared in numerous publications around the world and has been nominated for the Best of the Net and Eric Hoffer Book Award. Find him at: doriansinnott.com.

Mariah Southworth is a bisexual writer of horror, fantasy, and science fiction from the northwestern United States. Her short stories have appeared in *Humans Wanted* by CuppaTea Publications, *Bubble off Plumb* by Feral Cat Publishers, *Monsters in Space* by Dragons Roost Press, and *Supernatural Horror Short Stories* by Flame Tree Publishing. Her self-published children's books, *Lydia No Lying, Twenty-Four Scary Stories for Scary Poems for Scary Kids,* and *I Am A...* are available on Amazon. com. For more about Mariah Southworth, visit her website mariahsouthworth.com.

Karmen Špiljak is a Slovenian-Belgian author of suspense, horror, and speculative fiction, a queer person and a book coach in training. Her culinary noir collection, *Add Cyanide to Taste*, won the 2022 IndieReader Discovery Award for short stories and its follow-up, *Pass the Cyanide,* won bronze in the 2023 Wishing Shelf Awards.
She has lived in Slovenia, Germany, Belgium, and Brazil and is currently settled in Belgrade with her husband and their cats.

Lucretia Stanhope, a neurodiverse, relentlessly optimistic chronic illness warrior with less grace than determination, navigates her crone stage in a quaint Midwest town surrounded by cornfields. Amidst enduring medical trials that could rival horror stories, her pen never rests. When not lost in the wonderful lands of her imagination, she finds solace in doting on her two chihuahuas and her endlessly patient husband, a fellow scribe who shares her love for storytelling, boundless enthusiasm for the adventures yet to unfold, and never denies her dessert first.

Nadine Stewart is an author, poet, and media creator. Her short fiction has been published in several anthologies including Terrorcore's *Doors of Darkness*, Voices From the Mausoleum's *That Old House the Bathroom Anthology*, *Autumn Tales II* from Anatolian Press, and *Readings From Cursed Room 301* from Mad Axe Media, just to name a few. Her first "curated" project *Curbside Curses: The Yardsale Anthology* was published in June 2024.

Nadine has always been an avid reader with a wild imagination. Born into a creative family of artists, from a young age she was always "performing" for family and friends and creating poetry only ever seen by those closest to her. She was born and raised in beautiful British Columbia, Canada, and she now resides in Washington State. You can follow her on Instagram @nadine.stewart.author @houseof_the_macabre @stewartsocialcreations.

Elizabeth Suggs is the co-owner of the indie publisher Collective Tales Publishing, owner of Editing Mee, and author of a growing number of award-winning published stories, one of which was part of the Amazon Bestseller collection *Collective Darkness*.

Alison Thayer's horror fiction has appeared in two anthologies, *Bizarre Bazaar* and *72 Hours of Insanity: Anthology of The Games Vol. 10*.

Patrick Tumblety is an author of horror, science fiction, and poetry. He has been featured in numerous anthologies, including *Tales of Jack the Ripper* from Word Horde Press, *The Dead Inside* from Dark Dispatch, and *Gothic Fantasy: Science Fiction* from Flame Tree Publishing. *Come Out & Play*, his first horror novel, was published by Uncomfortably Dark in September 2024. He has also been published by and is an active member of the Horror Writers Association. His work has been described as being able to deliver both "genuine fear and genuine hope." (Amy H. Sturgis - Award-Winning Author and Professor of Narrative Studies)

M. Tyler Tuttle (they/them) is a writer, journalist, and wandering pit demon from Baltimore, Maryland. Tyler holds a degree in Creative Writing & English from the George Washington University in Washington, DC, and is a graduate of The Loft's Year-Long Novel Writing Project in Minneapolis, MN. Tyler's work has been published in *Cosmic Horror Monthly, Trace Fossils Review, Wooden Teeth,* the *Horror Over the Handlebars* anthology, and multiple philanthropy journals. Their work has been considered for the Halifax Ranch Prize for Fiction (semi-finalist, 2021), *F(r)iction Magazine's* Short Story Contest (finalist, fall 2023), and "Best Original Script" at the Great Salt Lake Fringe Festival (winner, 2022). You can catch up with Tyler online at TheHighwayMFA.com or @mtylertuttle on Twitter and Instagram, where they will be documenting their journey as an incoming MFA candidate at the University of Alaska, Fairbanks. If you look close—and if you're very, very lucky—you'll find them meandering through the wilderness with their dog Piglet, or dancing in a field somewhere, pretending to be Stevie Nicks.

Meranda Tuttle is an aspiring author who works at her local library. She enjoys writing flash fiction and novels in many different genres. In her spare time, she volunteers at theaters and bakes desserts. Instagram: merandatuttle

Madeline White is a farmer and artist living in rural NY with her partner and horses. By day she squeezes wool art and animal care into the space left over from her corporate grind, and by night she writes grimdark fiction as a break from her cottagecore reality.

P.S.C. Willis is a queer British author living abroad. They are an active member of the local writing scene and the

LGBTQIA+ community. They have previously been published in *Dreamforge Magazine* and other short story markets and have received two Honorable Mentions in the Writers of the Future Contest. Follow them on Twitter @psc_willis

Wesley Winters is the queer author of more than a dozen stories, including those found in *Nobody's Savior* (Slashic Horror Press), *WMP Dark Fiction Magazine*, *Terrible Lizards*, and the second volumes of both *HorrorScope* and *That Old House: The Bathroom*. He is also the co-author of *The Toll Comes Due*, a split crime fiction release with Robert Weaver. He is a married father of three who loves the outdoors and reading. He is an autism and ADHD advocate.

Dorian Wolfe is an SFWA member, and her short fiction has appeared or is forthcoming in *Utopia Science Fiction*, *Cosmic Horror Monthly*, and other venues.

ABOUT THE EDITOR(S)

A.C. Bauer is the founder and editor-in-chief of Cat Eye Press. He's been a writer as long as he can remember, and his love of the horror genre runs deep. He grew up on classic 90s slashers like *Scream* and *I Know What You Did Last Summer* and read a ton of *Goosebumps* books. You can learn more about him at acbauerwrites.com.

Frankie is the fiendish feline mascot of Cat Eye Press and self-proclaimed "brains behind the operation." He's part demon, part shapeshifting imaginary friend, part cat(?), and a total horror enthusiast. He loves exploring the darkest corners of the imagination and seeing what new directions his favorite genre goes. In his spare time, Frankie likes to play internet poker and take long walks on the beach.

ABOUT THE ILLUSTRATOR

Val Hal Halvorson is a comic book creator and horror illustrator who almost never goes outside. He is the artist for the *Vault* series, *Finger Guns*, as well as various anthologies such as *Dead Beats 2*, and *Grimm Tales from the Cave*. In addition to illustrating, he also likes to write comics, and he is not kind to his characters. He wrote and illustrated the short horror comic, *Pareidolia*, which was featured in Panel x Panel. Junji Ito once reviewed his work positively in a video for Vis Media and he'll never stop telling people about it. In his spare time, he consumes a ton of horror media, listens to metal music with lots of swears, and won't shut up about 90s FMV games.

CONTENT WARNINGS

COURSE ONE: DRABBLES

"Going Bad" by R. Haven:
Violence, threats

"Tartare" by T.L. Beeding:
Implied food poisoning

"Burning Cookies" by Jeff Currier:
Fire, burns

"Part of Us" by Josh Clark:
Burns, brief choking

"Papa Napoli's" by Dorian J. Sinnott:
None

"Always Chew Well" by Kendra Dennis:
Choking, asphyxiation

"Hotdog Horror" by Lena Ng:
None

"The March" by Madeline White:
Starvation, animal cruelty (out of desperation, not viciousness)

"Rooted" by C. L. Sidell:
Body Horror

"Speak" by Conrad Gardner:
None

"Where Are the Delegates?" by Eric Fomley:
None

"Hot Shots" by Evan Benner:
Death by variety of means

COURSE TWO: SHORT STORIES
"The Lingering Oil" by Eric Raglin:
Workplace death, abusive workplaces, burns

"Sylvia's Sourdough Starter" by Nicholas Gordon:
Violence, broken bones, fire

"Super Cherry Surprise" by P.S.C. Willis:
Death, forced feeding, brief mention of choking

"Burnt Biscuits and Gravy" by Alison Thayer:
Spousal Abuse, Stabbing, Burning, Death

"I'd Kill for a Decent Slice" by Stacey Flower:
Murder

"A Family Recipe: The Curse of Retrocognition" by E.E.W. Christman:
Mentions of suicide and bullying, fatphobia

"Divine" by Hannah Birss:
Mob violence, stabbing, death

"This Is Why I Don't Try New Things, Ronnie!" by Wesley Winters:
Body horror, Choking, gagging, asphyxiation, death

"House of Plenty" by Stetson Ray:
Death of pet

"Death by Chocolate" by Mariah Southworth:
None

PHOTO CREDITS

Bacon-Wrapped Water Chestnuts and Blackberry Jam Bars photos submitted by Desiree Horton

Squash Blossoms Rangoon photo submitted by John K. Peck

Dad's Brinner Special photo submitted by Patrick Tumblety

Double Brussel Pasta for Two photo submitted by M. L. Martin

Kimchi Dijon Pizza, Brown Sugar Chocolate Drop Cookies, and Windowpane Fudge photos submitted by A.C. Bauer

Vindaloo photo submitted by Genevieve Puttay

Spicy Udon Noodles with Peanut Butter photo submitted by Karmen Špiljak

Sweets for the Dead photo submitted by M. Belanger

Gluten-Free Brown Butter Ube Blondies, White Chocolate Macadamia Sourdough Cookies, Vegan Orange Blossom & Apricot Baklava, and Dairy-Free Matcha Banana Bread photos submitted by Gabrielle Winoco

Traditional British Flapjacks, Coconut & Lemon Bars, and The Best Flourless Brownies photos submitted by JM Cyrus